I'll tell you no lies

Norman Wills

ISBN: 978-1-291-89545-2

Copyright © 2014 Norman Wills

All rights reserved, including the right to reproduce this book, or portions thereof in any form. No part of this text may be reproduced, transmitted, downloaded, decompiled, reverse engineered, or stored, in any form or introduced into any information storage and retrieval system, in any form or by any means, whether electronic or mechanical without the express written permission of the author.

This is a work of fiction. Names and characters are the product of the author's imagination and any resemblance to actual persons, living or dead, is entirely coincidental.

PublishNation, London

www.publishnation.co.uk

For my Mum Sarah, simply for being my mum and keeping her sense of humour.

Foreword

Angels are thought, by some, to be immortal spiritual beings which act as intermediaries between God and humanity. In other words messengers from on high. Some people believe angels exist whilst others believe they are a figment of a weakened mind, an imagination far too easily influenced by what others say to be correct.

There are yet others who have never even considered the possibility that there might well be some 'unknown' force guarding us, something lurking in the shadows guiding us through life's highs and lows. Something we don't yet understand, assisting us to fulfil our final destiny in life, the very reason we were all put on this earth. That is, if in fact there ever was a reason, some pattern amongst all the chaos, some good amongst all the evil.

Have you ever wondered how many people on this little planet of ours believe they can communicate with their very own 'guardian angels'? How many people do you know who are guided through their existence, making fundamental life-changing decisions because of what their guardian angel or angels suggest they do? How many are happy to accept the word of an entity that only they can see and communicate with, advising them on the correct path to follow, answering the most important questions a person can ask?

There are people who put all their trust in something they can't even see, something very personal, known to them alone. Some of these people are household names, celebrities in their own right. I think you'd be surprised at how high the number is. You probably know somebody yourself with a guardian angel, maybe a friend, maybe a relative, maybe the person you stood behind at the checkout today. Maybe you have a guardian angel that you know and trust very well. If not it's unlikely many people will ever tell you about their guardian angel. That is unless they feel totally comfortable in this cynical world we live in. Who knows, maybe they've been advised to keep a secret.

Of those people who believe they can communicate with their guardian angels, how many realise that the Devil is nothing more than a heavenly rebel, in fact, a fallen angel?

Not all of them...

If you are one of those people who don't believe in guardian angels then don't be put off, please read on, you might even enjoy the story I've written. If, however, you are one of those who truly believe they are in touch with their guardian angels and communicate with them on a regular basis then I strongly suggest you read on. You might even be able to relate to the story; but not all of it I hope! I don't believe it's going to change your life, but that's up to you to find out for yourself.

As to whether I believe in Guardian angels? Well that's a very personal question to ask, we hardly know each other...

So, ask me no questions, **I'll tell you no lies.**

Some things are best left unsaid. But if you don't like the book don't shoot me, after all...

I am only the messenger...

One

Yes, yes, yes, thank you God, thought Steve, *this is actually going to happen.*

Steve had let her talk him into being tied to the bed, but the truth of it was that he hadn't taken much persuading; he'd practically offered himself up there and then thinking the lads wouldn't believe him when he told them. The reaction would most likely be, "Lucy Kirkpatrick, you lucky bastard!" or more likely, "Lucy Kirkpatrick, You lying bastard!" He could imagine the lads cheering his exploits over a beer in the bar at the rugby club later, when he'd revel in telling them exactly what he'd got up to with Lucy. Would they ever believe him? Probably not, but at least he'd know the truth.

When he'd agreed to be tied up all he was thinking about was having his kinky little sex fantasy fulfilled, at last, after so many rejections. Not only that, it was with Lucy Kirkpatrick, and she was making all of the running. Okay, so in his fantasy he wasn't the one being tied up, but he'd get his chance too, she'd promised. This must be a dream he thought, it has to be. Lucy suddenly reached under the pillow and brought out a gag. Smiling at him provocatively, she slipped the gag over his head and tightened it around his mouth. Steve was not overly concerned at this, *whatever floats your boat Lucy* he thought. There wasn't much he could do about it now anyway he was in this for the excitement of the journey, he was just hoping as he looked at Lucy that he'd be able to make the journey a long and memorable one and not the quick drunken fumble it usually ends up being.

Ever the optimist, Steve offered up his usual quick prayer of thanks to the God of sex. This was a prayer collectively written over a few beers one night after training. He knew that seven of his mates were still in the habit of offering up the same prayer on a regular basis; the guys who had managed to remain single.

> *For this and every other beautiful liaison thou shall ever grant to me,*
> *My heartfelt thanks and gratitude I offer up for free,*
> *I ask only two things O lord in this my hour of need,*
> *Let it be that all my women are a nice tight fit,*
> *And please ensure my condoms never split,*
> *Amen.*

    She got to work on him then. She quickly brought him to a full and, even Steve would have to admit it, glorious erection. In no time whatsoever he was stood up proud and ready for action so to speak. Steve was as ready as he'd ever been, Lucy was not going to disappoint in any way. After making sure Steve was well tied to the bed, leaning over him and giving him a brief taste of what he thought was to come Lucy reached under the bed and brought out a toolbox. Giving him her most seductive look yet she started taking the tools out of the box, one by one. She showed each one to Steve before lining them up on the end of the bed. These were not the sex toys Steve had imagined they would be when he saw the toolbox. She brought out a hammer first followed by pruning shears, saw, electric drill, heat gun, Stanley knife and chisel.

    Steve was now more than a little concerned at his total lack of control, his inability to influence what was happening. But wasn't that what she'd said being tied up was really all about? Losing control, "you've never felt anything like it until you've tried it", those were her very words. So here he was giving it a go, no control, his life in Lucy's hands. Lucy, the woman he knew well but had met for the first time that day.

    He started to sweat, started to test the strength of the bindings that made him so vulnerable. Not to an extent that made him seem desperate, he hoped, but such that she thought he was playing along with the game. He wasn't playing along with the game. He could take a joke as well as the next man. But this, come on! It just wasn't funny any more. Wait until he found out who had set him up, he'd pay them back for this, with interest. He'd set many of his team members up before now. Not like this though, whoever had thought of this had done a really good job. This one would go down in rugby club history, very funny. He wanted to say "good one, you got me, really, can we stop now?" but he couldn't he was bound and gagged he had no control at all.

The thought then struck him that none of his mates knew he was here, in fact, nobody knew he was here, only Lucy. His heart felt like it was going to give up on him, right there and then. Strangely enough though, even in a crazy situation like this, he was still fully aroused. Even with his total lack of control he was still standing proud, he was definitely still up for it. Lucy had been spot on. Sexually, he'd never felt anything like it. He just needed her to put the tools back in the box, point proven and they could screw each other's brains out. When they finished whatever debauched sexual activity she had planned they could have a good laugh about her scaring the shit out of him and how he never lost his appetite for it. That was what he was hoping, praying for even. He'd forgive her everything for that. *Please Lord let it be that,* he said to himself.

When she picked up the pruning shears with a crazed look in her eyes Steve tried to scream but it was useless, Lucy was in control, screaming was pointless. Steve knew then that he was losing his cock, not yet though, and not because of excessive use. Quite the opposite, he wasn't going to use it at all.

Lucy was in the room with Steve but there was somebody else in there with her as well as Steve. The person with the shears was Lucy Kirkpatrick, but Sally-Anne was guiding her, helping her fulfil what she'd set out to do. Sally-Anne was a different proposition altogether. Sally-Anne was about to float her boat in one of several of her favourite methods. Lucy was there taking advice as the game unfolded.

Before she'd finished with him all the tools had been used and what had been left tied to the bed didn't look very much like Steve any more. His mother would have been hard pressed to recognise anything of the pulpy, slimy, stinking mess Lucy and Sally-Anne had made in that room as once ever having been her son.

Sally-Anne had been thorough in her advice; nobody could ever accuse her of being anything else. But then they wouldn't ever get the chance to accuse her of anything, never mind being anything other than thorough. It was a strange relationship that existed between Lucy and Sally-Anne.

...

Come all you sinners,
Come one come all,
Like lambs to the slaughter,
Come live in my thrall.

...

Two

Most women when they saw Lucy looked at her with envy, they thought she was exceptionally beautiful and in reality she was. Most women are only too aware of what true beauty is. They all strive for it from the moment they reach puberty, no matter what hand they have been dealt regarding looks. But most women looking at Lucy would say it was actually possible to become too beautiful. To have too much of what everyone sought was like a sin in itself. It was like being obese as a prisoner in Auschwitz. She stood out.

At a fraction under six feet tall she was a natural blonde, she had big green eyes and a complexion so totally unblemished women would kill to look like her, but at the same time they just couldn't find it in themselves to forgive her for looking that perfect. Nobody should be that gorgeous.

Admiration would, in a lot of cases, turn to jealousy and hatred but also occasionally into lust. The lust from another woman she could more than accept, even relish, especially when she saw what it did to the men around her. She didn't enjoy the hatred though, but she thought she understood it. She knew people, especially men, were weak around her.

She had learned to live with the hatred since she'd been eleven years old, and let's face it, girls at that age can be just a little less than forgiving and more than a little tactless when it comes to the "pretty" girls feelings. At twenty-two years old she was still coming across the same old prejudices only more subtle in their nature, disguised but never the less still there. She was a master at spotting it though; she'd lived with it for ten years.

Lucy Kirkpatrick had no such problems with the men who wanted to be part of her life, and there were men who would sell their souls to get their hands on Lucy, or more accurately all over her, even for one night of passion. Perhaps if they really knew her they would feel differently; but men didn't care about getting to know her well. The men who wanted to be part of Lucy's life had only one thing on their minds, and a long-term relationship did not figure high on their lists of priorities. When it came to Lucy she was seen as too high maintenance. She was like a Ferrari; most people could never even dream of owning one, they probably couldn't even afford to service it, but just to drive one once would be one of life's ambitions fulfilled, something to tick off their bucket list. Lucy figured high on many men's bucket lists. She was definitely something they wanted to 'do' before they died.

Had they understood her sinister side, the side of her that had had to deal with other people's jealousy and ignorance for the last ten years they would probably have taken a big step back; they would have allowed themselves time to reconsider their position, or just turned around and run like hell.

The testosterone levels that Lucy was capable of producing in the men around her rarely allowed those men to see beyond the exterior beauty into Lucy's soul. A soul which had they been able to see it, they would have realised was a very dark place indeed.

Unlike a lot of women in this world, unless you knew her well and she knew you well, Lucy's beauty rarely went any deeper than skin deep. Unfortunately for a lot of women, most men, when they look at the ladies they encounter in life rarely try to see beyond the twelve square feet of epidermis. The first thing they set eyes upon is the first thing they want to set hands upon. First impressions aren't always right, when it comes to girls like Lucy gut instinct should be to the fore, but rarely is.

Three

Lucy's life had been on the whole good up to the age of eleven. Nothing spectacular, nothing out of the ordinary just a good, solid, and for the most part happy, family life spent in Aldershot with the people she loved most and the friends she'd made during the first eleven years of her life.

Lucy's brother John was seven years older than Lucy. She loved having an older brother. He made her feel safe and special. John spent a lot of time with Lucy; he made a real effort to bridge the age gap where some older brothers wouldn't have had the patience at his age. And he loved her, as an older brother should love and guard his younger sister.

Lucy's life started to change for the worse when John told her he had been accepted on to a photography course in Bristol. It meant, just like many of his friends he would have to leave home that summer, take his first steps on the road to a life less ordinary. Lucy was devastated, she felt like her best friend was leaving. In fact it *was* her best friend who was leaving. She felt real sadness for the first time in her life. Life was changing and she thought it would never be the same again. Had she known what was going to happen over the next two months she would have been happy to accept John leaving home if it meant her world could keep some semblance of how it had been for the first eleven happy years so far.

David, Lucy's father and sole provider within the family had a good job; he worked hard within the pharmaceutical industry and provided more than adequately for his family's needs. Sometimes this isn't enough though and people want more. David wanted more; he wanted to achieve more, earn more, give his wife and kids a better future. Call it what you like, ambition, greed, ego gone mad, but as far as David was concerned he was stuck in a rut and needed to get out of it, move on.

David had felt like this for some time before talking it through with his wife and mother of his children, Marie. After several weeks of lengthy discussions and soul searching on both their parts it was agreed that David should apply for the general manager position at his current employer's Manchester site. He'd been told about the position and 'advised' that he stood a good chance. Aldershot to Manchester would be a big move but both he and Marie felt it was an opportune moment, what with John going to college and Lucy changing school after the summer break anyway. They knew it wouldn't be easy, especially for Lucy, but she would understand eventually that it had all been for the best.

No one took the time to consult Lucy on any of this until the decision was made, the interview taken and the job accepted. When Lucy was told that they were moving to Manchester as well as John moving to Bristol she felt as though she would never smile again, and for a long time she didn't.

The decision for David was easy, he was a Northern lad, born and bred. Getting back to his roots would be a good move. He had no family to speak of in or around Manchester, and in fact he only had one brother and a nephew who had emigrated to New Zealand five years earlier, they very rarely spoke these days. He wasn't tied to a location by family but liked the idea of moving 'back home'.

It was the way people spoke their minds up North that he missed, not having to dance around a conversation to get where he wanted for fear of offending someone, especially where no offence had been intended. He knew Manchester was somewhere he could call a spade a spade without fear of hurting someone's feelings; and if he needed to call it a big mother fucking spade then so much the better for doing it in Manchester.

Starting a new school isn't easy, even when you are surrounded by your friends or at the very least some of the people you'd known from your previous school, some sort of continuation. Lucy would have none of this when she moved to Manchester. David's decision to apply for and accept the new job had been made in quick succession in order that Lucy could start her new school with the least amount of disruption to her education.

Lucy didn't see it that way though. John had left home, she'd lost her big brother, or so it felt, the one person whom she felt she really understood and who really understood her. She'd lost all her friends; some would telephone sometimes to talk about their new school and new friends but this didn't continue for very long. It's hard to continue a friendship at that age from over two hundred miles away. The move was done with the least amount of disruption to her education, maybe, but what about her life?

Well thanks for the consideration, dad, Oh yeah, that's right you didn't give a shit about me did you? You didn't find out how I might feel about a move to Manchester did you! You only cared about yourself, you didn't feel let down. Your life wasn't ruined was it?

Lucy's parents thought things would settle down for her when she started high school, and with David working all hours God sends, or so it seemed, there was only really Marie who had the time or patience to see that underneath the façade Lucy was a different girl. Unfortunately Marie wasn't the most perceptive woman in the world and if the truth was told she was having her own problems.

Forty-eight years old, Marie hadn't worked for fully eighteen years. She'd wanted to provide her kids with the best start in life and felt she could do this best by being a full-time mother. David thought she was being over indulgent with the kids but with his job, and the money it brought in, they could easily afford for Marie to be full-time mother and housewife.

While John had still been in short trousers Marie had thought the best time to return to work would be when he reached high school. They had tried for a bigger family within a year of John being born but nothing happened. They'd resigned themselves to the fact that John was going to be an only child when seven years after he was born along came Lucy, unplanned but never the less a most welcome addition to the Kirkpatrick family household. Marie wasn't going to give John her undivided attention and not do the same for Lucy, so Marie's plans for a return to work were put on hold for at least another eleven years.

Now Lucy was beginning high school and Marie could think again about returning to work. Eighteen years bringing up kids doesn't fill you with confidence when it comes to throwing yourself back into the job market. Marie's confidence was at an all time low, she didn't even know what she was capable of doing, how she would cope, things had moved on in the eighteen years since she'd last worked. She felt useless, and she had little self-respect. She was a woman with a crisis going on in her head but not one she could discuss with her husband; he was too busy, he'd thrown himself into his new role with total commitment, he wasn't going to fail. Marie felt like her life was on a collision course with failure.

She didn't need to work, the move meant David was earning more than enough for them to live comfortably, much more than they needed, but she also wanted to feel as though she could contribute something other than being housewife and mother. She wanted a life outside the house. The trouble was she felt useless, suffocated and very much alone. In her head she was a mess; she was a great looking woman but her head was definitely a mess.

Lucy needed her mum. Her mum wasn't there for her. Lucy had to toughen up quickly if she was going to survive.

Lucy tried to toughen up but it wasn't easy, she managed to ignore a lot of what was happening but she was becoming a bitter young girl. It was clear she needed help…

Four

Lucy met Sally-Anne when she was thirteen years old. To say met is not entirely the truth, and she wasn't exactly introduced by a mutual friend. They didn't shake hands or kiss cheeks or anything so formal.

Sally-Anne introduced herself to Lucy when Lucy was in a spot of bother, repeatedly being punched and then kicked in the head by Gemma, one of her so-called new friends. Lucy didn't know exactly why this was happening but later thought it was probably because she'd been seen talking to Dave, Gemma's boyfriend. Dave was now cooling off with Gemma. At times like this Lucy could become detached, turn in on herself.

Gemma knew that Lucy was much prettier than she was and that most of the boys, given half a chance, would drop their girlfriends just for a faint hope of a chance with Lucy. This wasn't Lucy's intention; she didn't even like Dave, thought he was a bit of a spotty bore with bad breath and bad teeth. Dave had been the one pestering Lucy but Gemma would never see it that way.

Sally-Anne, who had been waiting patiently deep in Lucy's subconscious for exactly a moment like this came rushing into Lucy's mind with a blinding flash, and at that moment Lucy's fear of Gemma disappeared. She managed to stand up and punched Gemma once in the face so hard she was unconscious before she hit the floor. Unable to stop herself, she then squatted over Gemma's face, lifted her skirt, and pulled her knickers to one side and started to empty her bladder directly onto Gemma's face.

Lucy picked up her bag and left Gemma there on the ground, slowly coming to, trying to remember what had just happened and wondering why she was wet and stinking of piss. Lucy couldn't believe what she'd just done, but in reality Lucy had nothing to do with it, the deed was totally down to Sally-Anne, Lucy's protector, alive in her head. Sally-Anne was no Superman to Lucy's Clark Kent; she was more Mr. Hyde to Lucy's Dr. Jekyll.

After she had fought off Gemma, and then some, Lucy felt calm. She realised that she no longer had to face up to what had been in the last two years, a tough existence for a 13 year old girl, seemingly always coming off second best in a two horse race. She felt a new inner strength and knew she now had the strength to get her through the hard times. It was as fundamental as suddenly finding God and knowing that something good existed in a world full of badness, just outside a school in wet and rainy Manchester.

She ran all the way home. When she got there she said a quick hello to her mum then rushed to her room, locking the door behind her. She was physically shaking and breathing heavily she didn't know what to think, she'd just pissed all over Gemma, her so-called friend, it must have been a dream. Surely she couldn't do something like that. It wasn't in her nature to.

No dream, Lucy...

I said no dream, Lucy. Hello, knock knock, it wasn't a dream!

Great, she'd just hit a girl so hard it knocked her out, she'd never hit anyone before, and now she was hearing voices in her head. This was turning into a day she wouldn't forget too quickly.

Lucy, come on speak to me, I know you can hear me, I can feel it.

Fantastic, I am going mad. I can still hear the voices. I must have got kicked in the head too hard.

Yes you can still hear the voice, only one of me, and no you're not going mad, like I said before that wasn't a dream. Say hello Lucy, I'm Sally-Anne.

This is crazy, whatever you are just GO AWAY!

Some thanks that was, but hey, at least we're speaking now, you have to admit that. You did just talk to me. NO DREAM, LUCY!

Oh MY God, I didn't really think it was a dream. But who...

We pissed her off didn't we? Literally. The little bitch won't do that again in a hurry.

But...

No buts Lucy, I'm here to help; you could look upon me like your guardian angel if you like. It looked like I came along just in the nick of time; she was really going for it, she could have killed you, the ugly little bitch.

No way, she wouldn't have done that…We're friends, or we were. But I pissed on her or was that bit a dream, please say that was a dream. I didn't do that really, I couldn't have.

Some friend! No dream and strictly speaking 'I' pissed on her. It was your bladder though; I just borrowed it for a second or two.

But it did feel good…I can't believe I just said that. I feel like life's been pissing on me for the last two years. I must be going crazy.

Not crazy and yes it did feel good, didn't it? Just what the doctor ordered. You didn't just say that either, you thought it, we don't need to actually speak, we just think to each other. Anyway, you needed help; I came to help, simple as that.

But... how…

Don't worry. If I explained it to you, you wouldn't understand, just accept the fact that you're not on your own now. We'll make a good team, your beauty, my brains and power, we can't fail.

Okay, it feels good to finally have someone on my side for once…But I'm really not sure about what we just did or what you just did. I couldn't stand it if someone pissed on me.

Lucy, you've got a lot to learn sweetheart, if you don't piss on the people that hurt you you'll be stinking of piss all your life while everyone else smells of roses. You've been pissed on long enough now. Are you happy with your life, Lucy?

It's okay…

Okay. Is that what you really think? Be honest now.

…No not really, I feel lonely, I have no friends and I hate this place.

I thought so. Do you want to start enjoying yourself, break free from your life as it stands, have some fun, and start to take control?

Yes I do, of course I do, but won't I be carted off to the nearest asylum any time now kicking and screaming.

Why would you? Nobody else knows about me do they? You aren't going to suddenly rush out and pronounce it in the street are you? It's all a matter of trust. Do you trust yourself and more importantly do you trust me?

Do I trust a voice in my head? Why not...yes...yes, I don't suppose I have a lot of choice really, what else can I do?

Good. First things first then. I think it's about time we became intimate friends with ourselves. You're thirteen but you've led a very sheltered life.

With that Lucy stripped off, got in bed, and with a little help from Sally-Anne had her very first orgasm, and her second, and her third. Bang, bang, bang multiple orgasms at thirteen. Sally-Anne was a good teacher. Lucy hadn't felt such intense pleasure before; she was a good pupil. She smiled a real smile for the first time in almost two years, she felt great.

She felt so good she'd completely forgotten about the poem she had to read out in front of class the next day. That was a real surprise because she hadn't been able to think of much else for the past week.

Lucy started to take control of her life that day, or more accurately, Sally-Anne started to take control of Lucy's life that day.

The next day in English she approached the front of the class with a self-confidence she had never felt before. Before today she had hated standing up in front of class, she was sure she would make a fool of herself. It wasn't that she couldn't write poetry, she thought she was quite good actually, she just knew that her classmates weren't looking at her for her poetry. They either loathed her for her looks and wanted her to look stupid in front of the class or were intent on looking at her because she raised their pulse rates. They weren't going to listen to the poem, none of them were.

Sally-Anne came rushing forward in a flash.

Watch this, Lucy. But carry on as normal, okay?

Okay, if you say so, but please don't get me into any trouble while I'm up here. You must be able to feel how I feel. I'm nervous enough as it is.

Trust me, Lucy. I won't get you in any more trouble than you are now in front of class. Relax and just let it happen. You'll be fine.

Okay, Sally-Anne. Here goes nothing. Wish me luck.

You won't need it.

At that moment it seemed to Lucy that part of Sally-Anne broke out of Lucy's head and planted herself in the head of everyone in the room including Mr. Williams the English teacher, only Lucy and Sally-Anne had the slightest inkling of what was happening. As soon as Lucy began reading, every boy, girl and even Mr. Williams were receiving a replay of Lucy's first orgasm, directly into their brains. It was as if they were right there in bed with her, running their hands over her body feeling the dampness between her legs.

Lucy carried on with the poem with a big smile on her face. No one was really listening to her, not even Mr. Williams. She could have been singing the American National Anthem in Arabic. Georgie Dunston had been twitching so much she felt sure he was going to fall off his seat; it took Lucy all her strength not to burst out laughing. By the time the poem was finished five boys had embarrassingly sticky, uncomfortable wet patches in their pants, including Georgie Dunston. The others would finish the job off at first break, including Mr. Williams.

As Sally-Anne later told Lucy, she also thought there were at least three of the girls who would bring themselves to orgasm before the day was through. Lucy did well in English from then on; in fact she ended up as a favourite of Mr. Williams. She became a favourite of the maths teacher, science teacher, and the music teacher. More pleasing though for Sally-Anne, she also became a favourite of the new history teacher, she was just out of college and totally innocent. And one or two of the other female members of staff were also beginning to notice Lucy for something other than her academic abilities.

That's my girl!

Unfortunately for Lucy, she also became the favourite of most boys in school too. Fantasies would regularly be played out in the minds of these boys. Well into adulthood these same fantasies, like a XXX rated movie, would be brought out when they felt the need. All played out in their lonely frustrated minds.

Some boys, like Georgie Dunston would want more than the fantasy; they wanted the real thing. They were fighting a losing battle though with Sally-Anne as Lucy's protector, but that wouldn't stop them trying. Some took the hint after two or three attempts and gave up the chase; others weren't as perceptive and set Lucy on a pedestal, held her up as a challenge that had to be worth a hundred rejections just for one success.

Lucy wasn't one to be rushed into anything she didn't want; she didn't need to be rushed into anything with Sally-Anne watching out for her. A lot of boys would never have their dirty little fantasies fulfilled by Lucy Kirkpatrick, but that wasn't going to stop them having dirty little fantasies.

Five

Lucy's brother John had taken to photography like a cat takes to ignoring its owner if they don't have food; he was a complete natural at it. He loved the world of photography and it loved him back an equal amount.

John didn't get home as much as he probably should have done, like Lucy he still thought of home as being in Aldershot, not Manchester. When he did get to stay with the family he noticed how they had all changed. Dad was hardly ever there and when he was he seemed pre-occupied with what was happening at work, he seemed to have aged so much in such a short time, grey hair was taking over his head with wild abandonment.

Mum was always pleased when he came to visit but he noticed she was drinking much more than when they were living in Aldershot. Lucy was growing up, she was changing, still his little sister but with an edge he had never seen before. Lucy was probably no different than any girl of her age, just a normal girl. He put it down to difficult teenage years. When it was just Lucy and John though it was still the big brother little sister relationship they had always had. He knew nothing would change that.

Sally-Anne liked John too but he didn't know that, he didn't know Sally-Anne existed, even if Sally-Anne was only in his little sisters head she wasn't telling anybody. John was good for Lucy; as far as Sally-Anne was concerned John could rest easy in his bed at night.

John's nice, cute even, for a man, in a tight jeans and nice arse sort of way, and you won't hear that from me very often Lucy, I promise.

Sally-Anne, that's my brother you're talking about. You couldn't get your hands on him even if you wanted to. He's also my best friend, always will be. Anyway I thought you preferred girls to boys.

I don't want to get my hands on him, Lucy. He's not my type. There are lots of things you still don't know about me, I may be in your head but I still feel what you feel, when you fall over I'm still there feeling the pain too, when you play with yourself at night I feel your enjoyment.

I know you're there then, you taught me, remember? By the way did I ever thank you for that?

Oh yeah, but seriously, I've got so much more to teach you, you've got so much more to learn. Do you still trust me?

Should I have a reason not to?

I'm like your Guardian angel, Lucy. If you can't trust me who can you trust? John's your big brother; I can be like your big sister if you want. Okay?

Okay.

If Sally-Anne felt John could rest easy in his bed at night it was a different story regarding David, Lucy's dad. Sally-Anne had never taken to David; she knew that deep down Lucy felt that her family should have stayed in Aldershot and blamed David completely for forcing the family to uproot and move north. Lucy was finding her dad harder to communicate with these days; he was either too busy or too tired. Sally-Anne felt something needed to be done; she was going to put things right, turn the tables in Lucy's favour.

Do you trust me, Lucy?

Of course you do I'm your guardian angel.

Lucy's fourteenth birthday was when Sally-Anne finally decided enough was enough.

December 10, 2004

Lucy wasn't the kind of girl who craved lots of birthday presents or a big party, maybe a sleepover with her few friends and a trip to the cinema or bowling like all the other girls did. She was also quite happy spending her birthday quietly at home; she considered the girls from school more as acquaintances rather than friends and wouldn't want to spend any more time with them out of school than was absolutely necessary. One thing she did look forward to every birthday since John had left home though was his phone call on her birthday; he never forgot that. If he couldn't make it home since he'd left he would always make the effort to ring her and make her feel special.

When the phone did ring she was in her bedroom, she rushed to pick it up but someone beat her to it on the downstairs phone. She decided to pick it up anyway as it was probably John on the other end of the phone and they could have a three-way conversation. She heard her father talking to a man who obviously wasn't John so she began to put the phone down.

Let's listen in, Lucy. We weren't doing anything else, and John can't call while your dad's on the phone so you won't miss his call.

Lucy listened.

"Yes this is David Kirkpatrick speaking"
"Good morning, Mr. Kirkpatrick. I hope you don't mind me calling you at home at the weekend but I didn't feel it appropriate to call you at work. My name is Paul Stevens and I work for Gemini Recruiting Consultants"
"Go on, I'm listening." He'd heard this sort of opening line many times before.
"One of my current clients, in the pharmaceutical business, is looking to recruit someone to oversee several sites. They suggested I should approach yourself on their behalf, you've got a good name within the industry and my clients have put together what I believe is an exceptional package for the position. They are keen to attract the

right man, someone who they see as a rising star. They want someone who's got a good track record within the industry and who they see as having the right skill set. Would you be interested in talking face to face so I can give you more details?"

"Of course, can you tell me who the client is?"

"I'm afraid I can't at this stage, you must understand they would rather it didn't become common knowledge within the industry. But I can tell you that they have big expansion plans and are looking at Scotland as a good development area for future expansion. The position they are looking to fill will eventually take over the Scotland sites when they're up and in production. Three sites in total with a management team on each site. The person recruited would have overall control of the Scottish leg of the company. The successful person would have to spend twelve to eighteen months based at the company's headquarters to become familiar with their procedures and have an input into the build phase of the project. Are you still interested?"

"Of course I'm interested, that's an impressive sales pitch, when can we meet?"

Lucy couldn't believe what she was hearing; her father was considering another move, no, two moves, first to wherever the company headquarters are then on to Scotland. Scotland for God's sake, where in Scotland? It could be the Outer Hebrides for all she knew.

She didn't have many friends, two or three since she'd moved to Manchester but two or three more than she'd had when she moved. Her friends weren't the vain types of fourteen-year-old, if you saw them in the street you would have to say they'd taken a severe beating with the "ugly" stick at birth. These were the girls who later in life when they tried a dating agency, which they inevitably would, would have to describe themselves as having a lovely personality and a good sense of humour. Everyone else would just describe them as plain ugly. They may be beautiful on the inside but that couldn't be said for the outside. This didn't bother Lucy, they were friends and that was all that mattered. Lucy knew friends were, for some people, hard to come by.

Lucy felt numb, what a birthday present, she didn't catch the end of the conversation, when she put the phone back to her ear the line was dead, the purpose of the call being only to sound her father out about the position and check if he was interested. She had actually been holding the phone for ten minutes looking into space but hadn't realised how long it had been. What Lucy also didn't realise was that lots of jobs at her dads position in the pharmaceutical industry were filled using head-hunters. David had had two similar, if not as exciting, conversations over the last twelve months with other recruiting consultants. He played the game, listened to them all. Nobody so far had come up with an offer that would make him want to move from his current position, and it would have to be a sensational offer for him to uproot himself and his family again and move to Scotland. He would play the game though, stroke his ego a little bit more, what harm could it do?

Lucy convinced herself that another move was on the cards, she would be even further from John, when would he get the chance to come to Scotland. A new school and starting from scratch again, no friends. Lucy felt empty inside; she didn't think she could handle that all over again.

Sally-Anne was feeling all of Lucy's emotions, all her hurt, all her insecurities. Sally-Anne hadn't liked David before, now she hated him, this was the straw that really did break the camel's back. Sally-Anne couldn't let it happen. She began to plot without Lucy's knowledge. She knew she would have to work alone at times in the future but she also knew this wouldn't be a problem.

Do you trust me, Lucy?

You really don't have much choice now.

Six

The day after Lucy's birthday was what could only be described as a typical winter day in Manchester, grey clouds, rain, cold, pretty miserable and no sign of it easing up. Some would say the weather was like this all year round in Manchester and they wouldn't be very far from the truth. Manchester in July without an umbrella was a risky business. Lucy thought the weather in Manchester was like her mood, mostly shitty, with the occasional sunny day, but these were few and far between.

Sunday in Manchester in December for a fourteen-year-old girl with few friends can be a miserable time. She'd done all of her homework and was bored to distraction. It could be argued that some fourteen-year-olds feel like this all the time. Being fourteen isn't easy, no longer a child but, in reality, far from being an adult, a lonely existence even when surrounded by the people you love most, which Lucy wasn't. Usually at times like this Sally-Anne would have something to say, something to discuss with Lucy to cheer her up, keep her company, but today she was quiet, Sally-Anne hadn't said anything since the phone call the previous day which had upset Lucy so much. Lucy was beginning to think that even her guardian angel had deserted her; this did nothing to lift her mood.

Talk to me, Sally-Anne. Come on cheer me up; give me something to laugh about. Please.

There was no reply, only silence.

Lucy needn't have worried, Sally-Anne was still there, she wasn't talking to Lucy because she didn't want Lucy's mood to improve. She didn't want her to have anything to laugh about. She was doing it so that Lucy would build up some more rage toward her father. It seemed to be working well, she was truly pissed off, she would soon look for someone to blame for this mood and David was top of the list of people who were pissing her off at the moment. Oh yes, she could feel the resentment building nicely.

She was at the "why me" stage; the feelings that most teenagers get but are able to cope with, eventually, and move on. That was usually when something happens to distract them enough, all part of growing up. Lucy was channelling the anger nicely, soon she'd be at the "I hate him" stage and when she was there Sally-Anne had a plan.

Sometime later, Lucy decided to listen to some music in her bedroom to pass an hour or two before the habitual Sunday roast her mum was currently slaving over in the kitchen. John had sent her the latest Kelly Clarkson CD, Breakaway, for her birthday so she slipped it into the CD player, lay back on her bed and pressed play on the remote control.

Five minutes into the CD, when Lucy was chilled out, Sally-Anne took possession of Lucy's body, Lucy felt nothing, she was completely unaware of what was happening, she'd effectively been temporarily switched off, Sally-Anne was borrowing Lucy's body, a necessary part of her plan. Sally-Anne hit the pause button on the CD player, got up and left the bedroom.

Any one who knew Lucy would be hard pressed to see any difference between Lucy and Sally-Anne borrowing Lucy's body. She still looked like Lucy but was maybe a little more measured with her words, but who could see that in a fourteen-year-old girl whose moods seemed to change as regularly as the direction of the wind in January.

She thought she'd find David in his study. He spent a lot of time in there these days since the installation of the company computer allowed him to stay on-line and monitor how his precious little pill producing factory was performing, twenty four hours a day seven days a week if he wanted to. And David seemed to have an ever increasing obsession with being a twenty four-seven company man as time went on.

"Dad, can you do me a favour when you've got some time?" said Sally-Anne "I need some help with my psychology homework."

David stopped hitting the keyboard in his very own style, a style which could only have been described as somewhere between very amateurish and ham-fisted. What are they thinking of giving the crumblies computers? Sally-Anne thought. He looked up at his daughter surprised at the question.

"Psychology homework, what happened to maths and English and things like that, proper subjects. Psychology, since when was that an O- level subject?"

"Dad, we don't do O-levels any more, we do GCSE's, time has moved on since you went to school" Sally-Anne said, "We use pens and paper now, not little blackboards and chalk. We also do other things as well as maths and English you know. We're introduced to things like psychology to give us a broader view of life, or at least that's the line they feed us, we don't all feel the need to be sat in front of a computer for the rest of our lives you know. Boring! That is unless you're a total nerd with nothing better to do of course."

"Okay, point taken," said David, "but I'm not sure I'll be able to help you with that homework, like I said, they didn't have fancy things like psychology in my days at school."

"That's not a problem, I'm not asking you to psychoanalyse me, I only need to get a handwriting sample from both you and mum so that I can do some basic psychological profiling, see if I can tell anything about you just from your handwriting. I have to do it as well to see if there are any similarities between us." Sally-Anne thought the probability of similarities between Lucy and her parents, especially David, were slim at best

"Doesn't sound too difficult, but what if you find out I'm some sort of crazed mad man who's going to kill you in your sleep." David said laughing.

"I very much doubt that, dad." Said Sally-Anne, "Anyway if anyone's crazy in this house it's me, don't forget I'm the one who has to live with you and mum."

"Yeah you're probably right there, can't be easy for you living in a big house with everything you could ever need." David said looking at his daughter "What do I need to write then?" Sally-

Anne thought David was so out of touch with his daughter it was laughable...she wasn't laughing though.

"So that all three of us write the same thing I've had to come up with two short passages. The teacher suggested we write a note from someone feeling quite depressed and then an up-lifting reply. That way we can see if people write differently when writing in two different mood types."

"It all sounds very technical," replied David, "you must be right though, things have certainly moved on since I was your age. I just need to finish off here then I'll be right on to it, I shouldn't be more than five minutes. Leave the two passages with me and I'll bring the chalk and blackboards in to you when I've finished it."

Sally-Anne turned to leave, at the door she turned back and said.

"Funny dad, very funny, by the way each passage on a separate piece of paper and sign your name underneath both passages, apparently the signature tells you most about the personality. I'll be in my bedroom when you've finished it."

"No problem, sweetheart."

That had been the most they'd spoken in a long time, David thought maybe Lucy was finally improving; he was fed up of tip toeing around his daughter so as not to hurt her feelings. When was her 'delicate' stage ever going to stop? He thought.

Fifteen minutes later David brought the homework to Lucy, she asked him to put it on her desk and thanked him, she knew that within ten minutes he would have forgotten all about it, after all, it had nothing to do with making drugs.

When he was gone Sally-Anne jumped off the bed and hid the so-called "homework" in Lucy's world atlas. Some people say the bible is the biggest ever best seller but the least read book in the world, they're probably right about that, but Sally-Anne thought world atlases must come a close second, no one would come across the work until she needed it.

Sally-Anne lay back down on the bed then hit the play button on the CD player and let Lucy have her body back at the same time. The effect was seamless, as far as Lucy was concerned nothing had happened, twenty-seven minutes of her life hadn't just been lost and she was still enjoying the Kelly Clarkson CD. Only Sally-Anne knew differently.

Sally-Anne had a plan. She was on a roll.

I like the music, not bad. John has good taste. I wouldn't mind getting to know Kelly Clarkson a bit better too. She's very much my type.

You're back. Where have you been for the last two days? I don't like being ignored.
I know, sorry, but you were so upset by the phone call you overheard yesterday I thought you'd want some time by yourself, time to see if you could come to terms with it on your own.
Not likely. Some guardian angel you are, go on holiday when I'm really pissed off. I've been lonely Sally-Anne, you just disappeared, and on my birthday too.
Sorry Lucy, it was a misjudgement on my part. I can feel that you're not happy with your dad.
What should I do Sally-Anne, he isn't going to listen to anything I say, he never has done up to now, why should he change? He's either at work doing work or at home doing work.
But it may all come to nothing. You might not even have to move, he might just turn it down, you never know.
Oh yeah, you heard him, it didn't sound like it was going to come to nothing.   Bonnie Scotland here we come, yippee. That includes you as well… Doesn't it?
Wherever you go I'm there, Scotland or not, your big sister isn't just going to jump ship. What would I be without you? I need you, without you I don't exist, so we'll get through this, together. You never know what's around the corner.

Lucy felt much better, maybe nothing would happen. Scotland was a nice place…For a holiday… It would have to be the only place wetter than Manchester. Her dad would see sense, they'd hardly ever see John in Scotland and her mum wouldn't be happy with that and he couldn't just make the decision without her mum's agreement. Lucy felt happy that Sally-Anne was back, Sally-Anne was good for her, she was, after all, her guardian angel; she wouldn't let it happen. Surely that's what guardian angels are for…Isn't it?

> Just trust me, Lucy. That's why I'm here.
> You do still trust me don't you, Lucy?
>
> .
> .
> .
>
> Of course you do.

Seven

Lucy's mum Marie had decided that the only way for her to get back into any sort of work was to re-train, build some confidence before taking the leap. She was doing a computer course at the local college, and surprisingly enough she was having a lot of fun. She'd actually thought she may just continue doing courses during the day and the odd night school course to fill in her time, the list of possible courses she could enrol on seemed endless.

She'd finally found something to do which she felt happy about; it gave her something to look forward to. Going back to work had suddenly lost its appeal, money had never been less of a problem and David was happy for her to 'continue her education', as he put it. He drew the line at more than one night school class a week though; he was a busy man and didn't like having to be back home by seven o'clock to 'baby-sit' Lucy.

Marie's current evening class was interior design, each Wednesday. She'd been doing it for three months and loved it; she'd had all sorts of ideas to improve the décor of the house, which hadn't been touched since they'd moved in over two years ago. She had finally decided that she was going to put her mark on the house and so had decided she should take some time to learn about different styles, colours and fabrics.

She saw much less of David since the move and if the truth were to be told she didn't mind. David was immersed in his work and she was finally enjoying herself for what seemed like the first time in many years, she felt liberated at fifty. If it weren't for David she could see herself becoming very friendly with her tutor on the interior design course, a man at least ten years her junior and still in very good shape. The hints had been there from him that they should go for a drink or a meal after class. She felt flattered but hadn't taken him up on the invitation.

Who knows what the future may hold though? Maybe a little fling was what she was missing in her life, after all Lucy didn't get her looks from David's side of the family, and even at fifty she still looked good, yes nifty for fifty, she liked that.

Little did she know that plans were being thought through which would change her life significantly, and had she known about the plans she probably would have smiled, kept quiet and hoped that nothing went wrong.

Ironically, just as Marie was reaching the age when the menopause was about to kick in, Lucy's body had decided to embark upon the one true journey into womanhood, the journey that will always separate the two genders. No matter what any plastic surgeon can do to make a man look like a woman he will never be able to allow them to experience the pain some women go through each month in order to allow the human race to continue its existence.

Lucy's periods had started a couple of months before and she wasn't dealing at all well with the physical pain. Some girls can fly through life without batting an eyelid during their period, it's seen as just a minor inconvenience every month, whilst others feel like they must be taking on all of womanhood's suffering alone. Lucy unfortunately fell into the latter category.

Marie had been similarly afflicted until she gave birth to John, and although she knew what her daughter was going through every month she could only offer words of wisdom such as "it will improve over time", and ensure that they had a plentiful stock of paracetemol handy for the really bad days. Sally-Anne didn't like Lucy's suffering either, but she was glad of the paracetemol, it would allow her to put a halt to any move to Scotland, either now or in the future, that is unless it was ever Lucy's, and Lucy's decision alone, to go.

Sally-Anne seized her chance the Wednesday after Lucy's fourteenth birthday. Marie had her final interior design night school class before the Christmas break and, as was usual when you get a group of adults together for an evening class so close to Christmas, it had been decided to have a celebratory drink in the Black Swan afterwards. Marie had jumped at the chance and told David he would have to fend for himself for one evening. Marie would make his evening meal as usual but he wouldn't have her company until much later in the evening. Marie had caught Simon, her tutor, looking intently at her while he had suggested it to the whole class. That got her thinking that under different circumstances she probably wouldn't make it home until well into the following day, if at all.

Sally-Anne swung into action the day before the last Wednesday of term. After everybody had gone to bed and she was sure they were all sound asleep, including Lucy, she 'borrowed' Lucy's body for the second time. She crept down stairs, like someone carrying out an SAS blackout mission, to the kitchen where she could begin to put her plan into action. With deliberately slow, stealthy movements making sure the silence was only broken when absolutely necessary, she took a saucepan out of the rack and poured about half a pint of water from the filter jug into it and placed it on the hob to boil.

Whilst the water was heating up she began popping paracetamol tablets from their packaging into the water. Fortunately the stocks of paracetamol in the kitchen cupboard, which doubled as the medicine cabinet had been more than plentiful. She had counted nine full boxes in all, Marie was obviously the sort of person who bought painkillers every time she shopped and had lost track of exactly how many there were in the cupboard. Most were hidden at the back so wouldn't be missed. She took eight of the boxes, leaving one box so nobody would complain. Marie would soon rebuild the stock back up.

When Sally-Anne had started to drop the eighty tablets she had decided to use into the water they began to dissolve quickly. She added some more water to the now boiling saucepan and within twenty minutes of leaving Lucy's bedroom she had a clear, deadly liquid which contained eighty dissolved paracetamol tablets. This liquid was poured with great care into a small flask and the saucepan quickly washed and replaced. Taking the empty paracetamol packaging and boxes she placed these and the flask in a plastic carrier bag. After checking the kitchen to make sure there was no sign that any one had been in there during the night brewing up a deadly liquid, she left as quietly as she had arrived.

When she got back to Lucy's bedroom she hid the carrier bag at the back of a wardrobe under a pile of discarded clothes and climbed into bed. During the night she gave Lucy her body back. When Lucy woke the next morning she knew nothing of her night-time adventure and neither did her parents.

Sally-Anne was good, no she was better than good, she was very good and she knew it.

The following morning was fairly typical, Marie had seemed pre-occupied with something at the breakfast table then reminded both Lucy and David that tonight was the night she would be out with her friends from evening class. Lucy thought she might just spend the evening in her room doing her history assignment. At the moment having her teeth extracted without any anaesthetic would be better than having to spend all evening with her dad. Nothing had been mentioned about the possibility of another move but she couldn't get the feeling of bitterness out of her head, an evening with David was the last thing she wanted.

Her day at school had been uneventful to the point of boredom and when the bell had finally rung at four o'clock she had practically fallen off her chair, the bell having only just stopped her from being sucked into a very deep, very long lasting coma. At least that was what it felt like. Yippee home time, she just couldn't wait to be home… an evening with her dad to look forward to. Bring on the coma, please!

Come on, Lucy. It's only an evening with your dad. What's the problem? He'll probably be in his office and we'll be in your room as far away from him as possible.

I know but don't tell me you don't know. If you can feel what I feel you must be feeling how totally pissed off I am at the moment with him.

Of course I can, I was being ironic, trying to get a reaction. I guess I succeeded. Don't worry. You know you don't have to spend any part of the evening with him alone. I'll be there too, all the time.

Oh yeah, I know that but can you stop us having to move to Scotland if he decides we're going, little guardian angel of mine?

Lucy, you don't know what's going to happen in the future, and I never said I could perform miracles. Any way I think there's something eating at your Dad at the minute, he looks pissed off too, maybe his decision about the future is fucking up his brain as well as yours. Now that would be ironic.

When she had arrived home her mum was in a very strange mood. She had an air of expectancy about her that she very rarely let others see these days. Lucy thought this was sad, her mother getting so excited about a drink with her classroom 'buddies', as her dad had called them. She felt like telling her to get a life and her dad to piss off, but thought better of it; she hadn't seen her mum this excited in a long time. Lucy knew her mum was menopausal and thought this must be just one of the symptoms. Marie knew better, she felt hot, but not the menopausal hot flush type of hot, she wasn't having a 'senior moment' as she called them, no this was wet between the legs hot she was feeling, and yes she did have an air of expectancy about her. Lucy went upstairs to get changed out of her school uniform.

Marie felt good, she was preparing Lucy's tea and David's evening meal for later, he could reheat it in the microwave when she had gone out for the evening, roast beef and Yorkshire pudding with all the trimmings, his favourite. She had decided to treat him because of the guilt she felt when she'd thought her evening might just have more in store for it than David would want it to have.

Marie was looking good, she should do, she'd spent all morning at the health spa being pampered, she liked to treat herself occasionally, not too often, and some women were there every week. Marie went when she wanted to feel special. She'd had a relaxing massage session, spa bath and her nails were now looking perfect. She felt great.

She may have been a fifty-year-old but she knew she had a body that most thirty-five-year-olds wouldn't mind trading in their own body for. She'd picked out a nice outfit to wear for the evening class but then they were going out afterwards so she wanted to look good. She had also called at a small, very exclusive shop she'd heard about in the next village on her way home and spent well over one hundred pounds on the most delicate lace lingerie imaginable. She'd had fun picking it out and when she arrived home she ran up the stairs like she was going to pee her pants and needed the toilet to try on her new purchases.

She had been very pleased with the results, so pleased she had reached into her bedside cabinet for her 'emergency TOOL kit', switched it on and spent the next ten minutes in a world of her own with only a low buzzing sound and Simon's imagined body for company.

When Lucy came downstairs again it wasn't Lucy at all but Sally-Anne, borrowing Lucy's body. She carried with her the flask she had prepared the previous evening, putting it into the fridge before Marie could see what she was doing; Sally-Anne turned round with a carton of milk in her hand.

"So you won't be eating in tonight, mum?"

"No, I might just have a sandwich later before I go out, like I normally do on Wednesday. We're supposed to be going to the pub after class and I might get a bite to eat while I'm there if they serve food. It's just you and dad tonight."

"Is that roast beef? I'm starving. Don't we usually have a casserole on Wednesday night?" Lucy said.

"Yes dear, normally but tonight I'm going to be out until late so I thought I'd do your dad's favourite" said Marie, "another hour and you can eat. Your dad can warm his up later."

"Anything I can do to help while you get yourself ready, make the gravy perhaps? It's about time you let me do something in the kitchen without watching me like a hawk, I won't burn the house down you know?"

"I do not watch you like a hawk," Marie said, "but that's very thoughtful, Lucy, yes you can do the gravy, tonight I need to spend a bit more time getting ready since we're going out after class, the older you get the longer it takes, you'll find out yourself one day."

Sally-Anne had taken a gamble on this and had even been prepared to remake the gravy after Marie had left if she had needed to. When Marie left the kitchen Sally-Anne made the gravy using the paracetemol solution, gravy granules and some of the juices from the meat. She made only enough to use up the solution and boiled it up to reduce it, after all she wouldn't be pouring it on her own plate and she knew David couldn't resist finishing off the gravy if there was any left, he was a sucker for gravy.

When the gravy was finished she tried a small amount to taste, it tasted just fine. With this done she poured the gravy into a gravy boat, washed out the flask put it back in the cupboard and went back up stairs, sat on the bed, put the headphones on, hit play on the CD, lay back and returned Lucy's body to its rightful owner.

Lucy thought she must have been daydreaming for a little while but wasn't surprised after the day she'd had at school, she carried on listening to the CD as if nothing had happened. When the CD finished she went downstairs just as her mum was serving her tea. She skipped the gravy, didn't feel like it tonight for some reason, but like most fourteen-year-olds she made short work of the rest of it, eating like she didn't know where the next meal was coming from.

Sally-Anne had thought about letting Lucy in on her plan, she wanted her to know that she was looking after her but she wasn't sure that Lucy would fully understand. Fourteen was still young to fully take on board what was happening. She would be old enough one day and when that day came she would look back on this and laugh, Lucy would be so grateful.

When David arrived home Marie was ready to leave, she pecked him on the cheek telling him not to wait up, she hadn't been out on a Christmas party for a long time and didn't know what to expect.

"Enjoy yourself, dear. But don't drink too much you know what you're like when you've had a few. You can tell me all about it tomorrow if I don't see you later. I'm knackered I'll probably have an early night, enjoy yourself. By the way what's for supper I'm famished."

She was gone before she heard the comment about supper, her mind was elsewhere.

Lucy was in her bedroom working on her homework so he popped his head round the door to say hello, told her he was going to have a shower then eat. This was about as good as conversation got these days with Lucy, but it seemed after speaking to his colleagues at work that this was the norm for a fourteen-year-old girl and her father so why should he and Lucy be any different.

While Lucy worked on her history assignment David tucked into his supper, he relished it, even wiping a roast potato around the gravy boat to make sure he hadn't missed any. Yes indeed Marie was a fine cook, always had been. It was a wonder he wasn't built like a twenty stone sumo wrestler.

After supper he did the dishes just like any other Wednesday then settled down to watch television for an hour then an early night. After a short while he decided he would feel more comfortable in bed and if he dozed off he would be in the right place. England were playing Sweden tonight on the box and he wanted to watch it if he could keep his eyes open. He popped into Lucy's room to say goodnight, got a grunt back for his efforts and went to his and Marie's bedroom, got undressed, turned on the TV and got in bed.

Marie had forgotten just what a good night out felt like, she realised her life had become humdrum. She had made a decision within five minutes of entering the Black Swan, when she had found herself separated from the main group with only Simon for company. Should the opportunity come her way to leave the pub with just Simon she was going to take it. Life was too short to carry on worrying, she knew what she wanted and she wanted it now, she wouldn't be denied.

As soon as Simon suggested that the group was getting along fine without them and would she like to go somewhere where they could be a little more intimate she surprised him by how quick she said yes, with no hesitation, and no second thoughts. Simon knew his luck was in tonight and he lived only five minutes away by taxi.

When the taxi came they slipped away quietly; they couldn't keep their hands off each other all the way to Simon's flat. She could feel Simon's erect penis straining through the cotton of his trousers and couldn't believe what she was about to do, the anticipation was unbelievable, and she had to remind herself to breathe, she felt dizzy.

When they were in his flat they were like two animals, tearing at each other's clothes in a race to see who could undress the other first. Their mouths were devouring everything in sight, Simon's tongue flicking at her nipples gave her her first orgasm of the night; about three minutes after entering his flat, she soon slowed her pace, but not by much, only enough to allow her to savour every moment of their lovemaking. It had been a long time since she'd felt this good sexually. Simon was a good lover and so was Marie. They made love until midnight but could have gone on much longer.

Before she left they'd promised each other that this was not a one-night fling and would happen again, very soon. Shortly afterwards she left, just like Cinderella rushing to be away from there and get home. The taxi ride vanished into oblivion as she hugged herself and caught the smell of Simon's aftershave on her skin.

She felt reborn, why hadn't she done this earlier in life? She had been faithful to David since the day they'd first met. She was sure that this affair would continue behind David's back for as long as she wanted it to, and she wanted it to go on for a long time.

When she got home she crept up the stairs into an en-suite bathroom in one of the spare bedrooms and quickly had a wash to get rid of the scent of their lovemaking. She hid her new lingerie, worth every penny according to Simon, in the bedside cabinet so that David wouldn't question her about it if he saw it. She then crept into the main bedroom, making every effort not to disturb him from his sleep. In doing this she didn't notice the envelope that Sally-Anne had placed on David's bedside cabinet only an hour beforehand.

She was too busy dreamily thinking about Simon's smooth hands and expert lips touching her like she'd never been touched before and the feel of his thick cock deep inside her for her to notice the complete lack of movement from David's side of the bed. She reached down between her legs and felt a satisfying dampness developing, she slipped in a finger and for all she cared David could have been buggering a dead pig in the bed next to her, she wouldn't have noticed that either.

Eight

David was dead before Marie had even reached Simon's flat, overdosed on paracetemol. Severe liver failure was what killed him, Ironic really since he'd had overall charge of the plant where the painkillers that killed him had been manufactured. They found the note while waiting for the doctor to come and certify the body.

Marie and Lucy had been stunned by the discovery of David's cold body when he hadn't made a move to switch off his alarm clock at six thirty that morning, but they were both speechless when the suicide note had been discovered and realised that he had taken his own life.

I can't handle this anymore; it's just too hard to go on, I just want it to stop now, put an end to it all.
I'm very sorry
David Kirkpatrick

Marie had never seen this before; Sally-Anne had never asked her to help with the handwriting task for psychology homework. There had been no handwriting task at school. Lucy didn't even do psychology at school. No one would ever see the other piece she had asked David to write out either, the upbeat piece of writing, full of encouragement. That had been destroyed soon after it had been written.

The police had been very sympathetic; after all, nobody would wish that on the wife and daughter, both looking genuinely shocked. They had said they would speak to David's work colleagues but had tried to reassure Marie that it was not uncommon for a spouse to first find out about their loved ones true state of mind by reading their suicide note. They said she shouldn't feel guilty, but she couldn't help it, David had been at home taking his own life while she had been having the best sex she'd ever had in her life with another man, and she didn't even have an inkling of what David had been about to do to himself.

The police had asked for a specimen of David's handwriting to check against the note, to make sure it was David who had written the note, but they had been pretty sure it was his when they had seen the empty paracetemol packaging by the side of the bed and the glass of water the note had been found under. When they saw David's hand written meeting notes, taken from his briefcase, they were in little doubt that the note had been written by David. They would take it away for comparison but they had little doubt in their own minds that the poor sod had had no outside help in ending his life. They saw it all too regularly these days and put a lot of it down to the pressures of modern society, more and more they were coming across cases of people David's age committing suicide.

Looking at the wife the two policemen had passed a knowing glance at each other; it conveyed the unspoken thought that she was probably playing away from home regularly anyway. She looked much younger than her dead husband and neither of two of them would have passed up the chance had it been on offer, after all, there was a lot to be said about the expert touch of an older, more experienced woman. Couple the experience with a body like Marie's and it was a winning combination in most men's eyes.

Marie felt guilty but only for a short time, she soon realised there could be no way that David had known about Simon, she only knew it was going to happen herself shortly before it did. She had been completely faithful to him beforehand, he couldn't have known. He just decided to choose that night to kill himself, selfish bastard! She thought she would have probably left him anyway in the next two years, get Lucy through her exams without the upheaval of a divorce then take him for everything she could get. As it was he had saved her the bother of a messy divorce.

The mortgage wasn't an issue, when they'd moved North they hadn't needed one, they were able to buy their new house with cash and still have a sizeable amount left over. Marie had inherited a large house in Aldershot when her mother died six years ago and David had been good at making investments. Fortunately for Marie most were in her name, so as not to lose the extra tax David would have paid at the highest rate.

The company David had worked for had been very understanding. Because David had committed suicide any insurance policy wouldn't pay out but they hadn't wanted to leave Marie and Lucy with nothing. David had been well thought of within the organisation and so a decision was made, and a payment was eventually made equal to the sum David had been covered for in the event of his natural death. His pension would also be paid to Marie for the rest of her life. Thirty five thousand pounds each year, index linked. Marie wasn't sure whether it had been the fact that they thought they had worked David into a suicide or the bad publicity they might get if it ever came out that someone so high in the organisation had killed himself by overdosing on their own drugs.

The two hundred thousand-pound 'hush money', as she called it, had been most welcome and helped her overcome completely the small amount of guilt she'd been feeling about his death. She didn't ever have to work again, she thought she would definitely continue the interior design course; after all, she didn't want to lose touch with Simon. Guilt free sex, it was as if she had been reborn.

Lucy had also been able to get over her father's death very quickly. She'd never seen a dead body before in her relatively short life and this was what affected her more than anything, that and the fact that he had chosen to take his own life only feet from where she herself had been asleep. When she'd sat down later in the day with only herself and her mother left in the house it dawned on her that any move to Scotland would never now take place. Sally-Anne had wanted Lucy to come to this conclusion without any help so had been quiet all day long. It was only when Lucy saw the upside of her fathers premature death that she heard Sally-Anne's voice in her head.

Oh my God Lucy. I never would have taken your dad for someone who'd just jump ship. I must have misjudged him badly. Still if there is any good side to this at least now the move to Scotland won't happen. That's a good thing isn't it?

Yes it is, I suppose. It's just very hard to take it all in at the minute. I spoke to John earlier he was really shocked about it, he said it would have been much easier to take if he'd just had a heart attack or been killed in a car crash, anything but suicide. I know what he means, you think you know somebody but apparently you don't know them at all, don't know what's going on in their head.

I hope you don't mind me saying, but that's rich coming from you. I know about your call from John, I was there, remember, still it sounds like he'll be home soon for a couple of weeks, support for you and your mum and he'll be here for the funeral. I can't remember when you last saw John for so long without a break in between, you must be looking forward to seeing him again. I know your mum will need yours and John's support.

Yes of course I'm looking forward to seeing him, I always love seeing him. I just wish it wasn't because dad killed himself. It's awful. I don't know what to think at the moment. I think I must be in shock.

Every cloud has a silver lining, Lucy. Just look at it like that. Don't get too upset; he was about to pack you all off to Scotland. Or have you forgotten about that? Everything must happen for a reason and now you don't have to go. Your mum seems to be coping well; she'd cope even better if you could be strong too.

You're right, mum needs me to be strong she must be really hurting just now. She's hiding the pain because of me I'm sure. I'll be strong for her.

That's my girl.

John came home, and the body was released after the autopsy had been carried out to establish the cause of death. Instead of it being assumed that David had killed himself with an overdose, they now knew for certain that he'd killed himself with an overdose. Whichever way you looked at it though the same conclusion was reached, David had committed suicide, pure and simple, and this was the most difficult thing to accept for anybody left to cope with it. What a selfish act to carry out. Once again, Lucy thought, her dad hadn't given a shit about her feelings; he only cared about himself, selfish, selfish man!

The funeral passed off without a hitch. There were very few relatives to make much of a show of grief, both Marie's and David's parents had passed away over the past twenty years and Marie had been an only child. She'd received a letter from David's brother expressing his sorrow and deepest sympathy but explaining how he couldn't make it over for the funeral because of other work commitments. Marie understood, it must have been a family trait, they had never been very close even when they'd lived in the same house, she could hardly expect him to drop everything and fly from New Zealand to attend his funeral.

Of course there was a good turn out of his colleagues, Marie thought this was handy, and otherwise there would have been a very poor show for a man who had lived for fifty-two years. If Marie felt any grief on the day it was that this was all a man amounted to when he died. She thought that must be what came of chasing the glory, trying to get better results than last month, improving production figures, pleasing the corporate wage payers, wanting the next move onwards and upwards. What had it achieved for David? Being lowered into a seven foot by three foot by six-foot hole on a cold, wet and windy day between Christmas and new-year in a miserable, cold, bleak cemetery in Manchester.

The death of his dad had seemingly affected John more than anyone else; he just couldn't believe he'd picked up none of the inner turmoil that must have been going on deep inside his dad's head. He'd been struck down with remorse at how he'd apparently lost touch with the everyday aspects of family life. He thought he might have been able to help, maybe even prevent what had happened, if only he'd kept closer contact.

He felt guilty at the fact that he'd planned to go skiing this Christmas and had only been planning on visiting the family for the new-year. Some Christmas this was turning out to be. He couldn't change what had happened, it had been his dad's choice, but it was no easier to accept than if he'd been innocently caught by a stray bullet from a street shooting. In some ways that option would have been less distressing for him, at least he could have felt no blame for what had happened. Shit just happens sometimes, and sometimes being helpless to stop it happening makes it much easier to accept.

He'd done what he could for his mum and Lucy, tried to comfort them when they needed comforting. In reality it was John who needed the comforting arms around him, mum and Lucy were getting on fine. He spent days trying to make sense of why anyone would decide to take his own life, the one thing a person has the ultimate control over. For a twenty-one year old, just getting into his stride on life's journey, it was impossible to understand.

Problems in the marital bed had been dismissed as a cause for the suicide when he'd found his mums lilac lingerie set in his bedside cabinet, she'd obviously been making an effort to keep the fires burning in that department. She'd blushed so deeply when he mentioned it in an attempt to lighten the atmosphere, he thought her head was going to burst open.

After days of torment he decided to stop beating himself up trying to find an answer and just accepted the fact that he would never learn why it happened, the one person who could have told him was now dead. It was time to move on.

It had been good to spend time with Lucy; he'd noticed straight away how she was changing from little kid sister into something resembling a much younger version of Claudia Schiffer. The tragedy had brought them even closer; he felt much more of a need to protect his sister, be even more the big brother figure, now that she had no dad to look out for her.

His mum was doing okay, she just said she needed to keep busy, not dwell for too long on what had happened. She said she thought the full force of what had happened would hit her later when things had settled down a bit. John suggested she should get right back into college and evening classes after the Christmas break and she quickly agreed.

John had been pleased his mum had taken up his suggestion of an interior design course; he thought everyone needed to satisfy his or her creativity in some way. Little did John realise, however, that his mum's creativity was currently being used on thinking of how many different ways she was going to fuck Simon senseless the next time they were together again. As for learning about fabrics, colours and styles her mind was buzzing, she'd seen how powerful a combination lilac, silk and lace could be now she was thinking about a red basque, maybe some leather or maybe even PVC in pink with the finest silk stockings she could buy. The possibilities were endless.

It was good for John to see his mum coping so well, especially at what must obviously have been a terrible time for her.

Nine

John had stayed in Manchester until 4 January when he'd had to get back to London for a photo shoot. At the age of twenty-one John had landed his dream job at the Stein studio in Soho. He was an assistant to Patrick Stein, one of the top London fashion photographers. The role was going to keep him busy, Stein was often called upon to shoot the covers for the top fashion magazines such as Vogue and Elle, as well as covering the major fashion shows in all the major locations.

Stein was a major player in the world of fashion, the work was plentiful and as with everything at the top end of the fashion industry he could demand a top fee for his art. Stein demanded a lot from his assistants but he ensured that they were well rewarded, both financially as well as educationally. John would learn the latest techniques, use the best equipment available, mix in all the right circles and get all the fringe benefits that go with that lifestyle.

Stein had seen a quality in John's work which he felt he could nurture. The raw talent was most definitely there. When John took a photo shoot he was able to get beyond the mask that most people tend to wear in front of camera, he could get to the very essence of someone's personality by capturing a particular gesture or a certain peculiar look. John could see the allure in every subject and worked well in order to bring it to the wider audience.

The fact that Stein chose John, a relative novice at his trade, was no gamble on his part, Stein was a master. He saw things with a clear eye. He could sense the passion in John's work. It was the same passion he himself had possessed at John's age. He had some rough edges but over time these would be smoothed away. John would learn his trade at the hands of a master; Stein believed that in time John's talent would even outgrow that of his own.

Stein was also looking at John with an eye to the future. Stein had been diagnosed with a brain tumour; it would soon enough be affecting his work. The specialists couldn't tell him how long he had left; all they could tell him was that it was unlikely to be any longer than 3 years. It was inoperable and relatively slow-growing but he didn't know how long he would be able to continue. He might have twelve months, two years, five years he just didn't know. His future was down to an irregularity in his brain and how well it could cope with the consequences of the tumour. Stein was quite the optimist but in this circumstance he felt he should be a realist. Stein wasn't holding his breath. He had led a hedonistic lifestyle; his life may end up being cut short but he'd packed an awful lot into it up to now.

Stein worked with a lot of male models and a far greater than average percentage of these models are so gay it would make most straight girls weep for days at the waste of it all. During the eighties and nineties Stein had photographed some of the gayest amongst them, these men would do anything for the man who had the power to make them look just that little bit better than the next man. The world of the female model can be a bitchy one, but that is nothing compared to the bitchiness in the world of the male model. Competition for contracts is fierce. Stein was a sucker for a nice arse on a man and when that same arse was being offered up as homage to his particular talent he just didn't have the heart to refuse it.

Patrick Stein wanted to leave a legacy when the deadly growth in his head did finally take him; he didn't want people just to look at his past work and see his art, a talent that died when he died. He wanted people to look at John Kirkpatrick and see a Patrick Stein creation; a photographer with Stein's blood running through his veins. He wanted his reputation, his name and his art to live on, and in John he was sure he'd found the right person to allow his art to thrive long after his death.

John met Stephanie Wilkins on 15th January 2005 in the Soho studio. He'd met lots of models since he'd become Stein's assistant six months previously, but none of them had had the same affect on him as she'd had. It wasn't that she was the most beautiful; he'd seen other girls that were considered in his world to be more beautiful. It was her uniqueness. She was just so different. She seemed so much more complete. She had a beauty that went far beyond the normal boundaries. Stephanie Wilkins had an allure that was like a blinding white aura all around her. Every gesture, every expression, the way she spoke, the way she looked at you, John had never met anyone who came remotely close to having what she had, whatever it was seemed to ooze out of every pore.

Steph, as she'd insisted he should call her, was twenty-eight years old but could have been taken for anything between eighteen and thirty-five. She had a face that would keep you guessing her age until she showed you a copy of her birth certificate as proof positive.

Stein would let John set up the studio for the shoot, commissioned by Vogue for a front cover. He would adjust the background lighting, flash lighting and screens to achieve a particular mood for the session. Stein only made minor adjustments where he felt genuine improvements could be made; this was becoming less frequent as John was honing his skill. As with each session, he would have John take the first part of the photo shoot, to get the subject relaxed he'd say, concentrate their mind on the job at hand before he took over. Stein had never worked this way before, he'd always liked total control, but John was on a fast track, and a swimmer would never become Olympic champion without being able to dive in at the deep end.

The session went like a dream, John and Steph seemed to bond into a single entity, and it was as if they could read each other's minds. John was lost in the moment, for him no one else existed, just Steph. He had needed this after the past three weeks, he needed to forget, concentrate his mind on something else other than his dad's death. Stein watched his pupil work and was loath to put an end to it, but it was, after all, his name on the credits that meant he could demand such a huge fee for the shoot.

Looking at the results later in the day with John, Stein had had to admit that John had produced all three images that he believed the final cover shot would be chosen from. His own work had looked tired in comparison. John at twenty-one years old would be the youngest photographer to be credited with a Vogue cover shot; he was about to become a name in the industry.

Any guilt that Marie might have felt over David's suicide was quickly forgotten. She was fifty, looked good and felt like a teenager who'd just discovered the joy of sex for the very first time. She wanted more, and she was now free to have it. With only Lucy to look after and college on Tuesday and Thursday mornings and evening class on Wednesday, she decided to join a gym. If she was going to enjoy herself why shouldn't she look her best? She would test the water; see what reaction she could arouse. After all that's just what some men went to a gym for, the chance to flirt with a pretty lady and maybe a bit more, if they got lucky. That's all some of the ladies were there for too.

Towards the end of January both Lucy and Marie received a large brown envelope through the post with the Patrick Stein studio Logo in the bottom left hand corner. They opened them together over breakfast and discovered a copy in each of the February edition of Vogue. The cover of Lucy's was signed - to my little sis Lucy, love John. Marie's was signed - Thanks for everything mum love John. They both sat there confused as to why John should send them signed copies of Vogue and it was only when they turned the cover and saw the credits that John had highlighted in yellow marker pen that they understood.

Front cover
Model: Stephanie Wilkins
Photographer: Patrick Stein studios.
                         (John Kirkpatrick)

"Wow, mum, look at that, John's got his name in Vogue. He's photographed the front cover."

Wow yourself, Lucy. Just look at that girl, she's a complete goddess; I wonder how well he knows her. Do you think he knows her intimately? Is that big brother of yours having his wicked way with her? Let's face it Lucy, he'd be hard pressed to say no, I certainly wouldn't, given half a chance.

"Let's call him tonight and congratulate him. I was thinking we should visit him soon anyway, let's aim for your next school holiday, Easter I think. We could make a week of it stay in a hotel, see the sights spend some time with your brother without funeral arrangements getting in the way. What do you think?" Marie said.

"That sounds great, mum. Let's call him now...Please, please, please." Lucy looked like a puppy that'd just seen its master reaching for the treat jar. If she'd had a tail it would have been causing havoc by now.

"Have some patience Lucy we'll have longer to speak to him tonight, and anyway he's probably on his way to the studio by now."

John couldn't help sending them the signed copies, he knew Lucy would love it, probably get it framed and hang it in her bedroom, and he was still on a high from the excitement of it all. He knew that if Stein had been credited with the shot it would have just said Patrick Stein instead of Patrick Stein studios with his name in brackets afterwards but he was okay with that, he knew that the kudos lay in the name Patrick Stein. But he was on the ladder, and it was Steph who had helped get him there.

...

Lucy was probably least affected out all the three of them over her dad's suicide. She'd considered him selfish in life so she thought suicide was a well-suited death for him, why would a leopard suddenly change its spots? She wouldn't exactly say she liked her current situation, Manchester wasn't Aldershot, it didn't hold many happy memories for her, she saw it more as a temporary necessity in life's journey, but at least she hadn't had to move again to Scotland.

Sally-Anne was glad too; after all, she'd only been acting on Lucy's innermost feelings. If Lucy had wanted to go to Scotland, if she'd been happy and didn't blame her dad for her misery, he'd still be alive today. Sally-Anne had only been doing Lucy's bidding after all. As Sally-Anne saw it, she was Lucy's only true friend in Manchester and a true friend would do anything to end the pain the other was feeling.

Looking forward to London, Lucy?

I can't wait. When mum said John had got tickets for fashion week and he was photographing at most of the venues I couldn't believe it, it's just going to be so cool. He might even let me assist him on one of the smaller shows.

I know, some of the planet's finest looking ladies all under one roof strutting their stuff and I'll be there to see them all…we'll be there to see them all.

Yeah, you can look but you can't touch big sister.

There could be a way. I think it's about time we both felt the pleasure of another person's flesh. First hand so to speak.

You already get the pleasure of another person's flesh, remember? Mine, first hand, usually my right hand. Anyway what do you mean, there could be a way?

You could let me borrow your pretty little body. Then I'd have something to trade with. And let's face it Lucy, you're walking around in a body that deserves to be shared for the pleasure of others, let it realise its full potential. It would be just like your mum lending someone her car; your body is only a vehicle for your mind and soul anyway. It just so happens that you drive a Ferrari while most people get lumbered with a Ford.

Hang on, you're saying I could let you take over my body while you play out your sordid little sexual fantasies for real, then you'd just hand it back.

I think we could make it work. I know you're only fourteen years old but there are a lot of sexually active fourteen year olds in the world Lucy and I can't wait much longer. You're good at pleasuring yourself but I need to feel the flesh of another.

Cool… But your fantasies are always about other women. Wouldn't that be a bit gross? For me I mean.

Don't knock it 'til you've tried it, anyway if you don't like it you can just switch yourself off from the outside world while I enjoy myself. You don't think I'm going to be watching you while you get your tight little pussy pummelled by some sweaty member of the lower order do you?

Don't knock it 'til you've tried it, that's what you just said.

Yeah, but the word bastard, even though it was meant to describe a child born out of wedlock, must have been re-used with men in mind. It captures them perfectly, everything they stand for and everything they do. I think I'll just give them a miss if it's all right with you. So do I get your body then?

I'll think about it, maybe... but only if you treat it with care. This is scary. My first sexual experience and I'll be a passenger.

But your body is my temple, Lucy. I'm not going to damage it in any way. Trust me...

You do trust me don't you Lucy?

I think so.

Easter couldn't come quickly enough for Lucy, but when it did come Marie decided they should travel in style. No four-hour road trip journey down the M6 and M1 motorways, struggling past Birmingham like everyone else packed into their cars. No stuffy train rides either, sat opposite Mr and Mrs sweat-stain. Marie had decided they would fly from Manchester to Heathrow. Although the British Airways shuttle wasn't cheap for what was, in reality, only a thirty-minute flight, money was never going to be an issue.

Marie enjoyed the freedom to do something different; she liked to try things she wouldn't have dreamed of doing had David been alive. And, in David's mind, to have flown to London for anything other than a major business meeting would have been seen as far too extravagant. So Lucy and her mum flew British Airways Manchester to Heathrow then took a taxi to the Grosvenor hotel where they were staying for the week.

John had been so pleased to see them. He'd lived in London for only eight months so he was looking forward to seeing some of the sites for the first time himself. The highlight for him, however, was definitely going to be taking Lucy and his mum to the fashion shows. He was really looking for an excuse to show them how far he'd come in such a short time. The fact that he would be one of the photographers working the catwalk on one of the top fashion shows was something he'd kept secret from them, even though he'd been bursting to say something sooner. He wanted to see the look on Lucy's face.

The look when it came had definitely been worth the wait. Lucy was asking questions quicker than he could answer them and the fact that Stein had been able to swing a couple of really good seats with one short phone call meant that, as far as Lucy was concerned, he was the best big brother a girl could ever wish for. Marie was also enjoying the glow of satisfaction that a mother feels when she believes she can stop worrying about one of her children because it's no longer an appropriate emotion.

It made the handing over of the two building society accounts, one to John and one to Lucy, so much more enjoyable on their first night at dinner in London. Marie had decided that her children should be given a leg up in life and she was more than able to do that financially. John was given an account, which contained fifty thousand pounds in his name, and Lucy had the same in Marie's name that she would gain sole control of on her sixteenth birthday.

Her children were stunned, neither of them quite believing what their mum had just done. For John it would be a massive help to establish his career or get on the property ladder, and for Lucy a tidy nest egg, which would carry on growing until the time came that she needed it. Both knew that this was only possible because of the recent death in the family. Both would need to come to terms with the fact that they were benefiting from their father's death.

Fifty thousand pounds, Lucy! Well maybe your dad wasn't such a selfish bastard after all.

It wasn't him who opened the account, it was mum. You don't think I would have seen anything like this if he'd still been alive do you, maybe a couple of hundred pounds on my birthday, if I was lucky.

Lucy came to terms with it very quickly.

In reality it had been David who had mentioned something like this, but to a lesser extent, only the previous year to Marie. The tax benefits would be well worthwhile and he knew the money would only go to the kids eventually anyway. Why not do it while they could both rejoice in the happiness it would bring, instead of them being six foot under and their kids too well set up to appreciate it fully.

John had hoped that his dad would have been proud of what he was achieving with his life, but was saddened by the fact the he would never get the chance to see it. And he would never forget how hard his dad had worked to allow his mum to be able to do such a wonderful thing in his dad's memory.

Marie had hoped that the money she gave to John and Lucy would help her to get over any remaining guilt she felt over her distinct lack of heartfelt grief following David's death. And the sex she'd been having while he had killed himself, she didn't want to forget that either, she felt no guilt at all at this. She just didn't want to forget it.

On Sunday, Monday and Tuesday Lucy and Marie did many of the usual tourist sites while they were there. They visited Madame Tussaurd's, a particular favourite of Lucy's, The Tower of London, The Tate Gallery, Buckingham Palace, the Houses of Parliament and the Natural History Museum where John was doing a shoot later in the week in the grounds. John joined them when he could afford the time, which wasn't enough for any of them.

Marie and Lucy hit Knightsbridge with vigour and spent the best part of Wednesday in some of the most upmarket fashion house shops in London. If John could get them such good seats at the fashion shows they wouldn't let him down by looking like a couple of girls down from Manchester. Girls who were down from the North of England for a day in the capital city to watch United in the football league cup final at Wembley with their boyfriends. Eighteen hundred pounds later, twelve pounds of which went on a bar of soap so Lucy would have a Harrods carrier bag to carry around London, they could have dressed for afternoon tea with Coco Chanel, Lady Diana and Gianni Versace and not looked out of place.

Ten

As far as Lucy was concerned, Thursday and Friday were purely for John. Lucy was going to spend Thursday at the studio and the Topshop venue in Cardinal Place with John, while Marie pampered herself in the hotel's health spa facilities. She felt that she generally needed to recharge her batteries, which were pretty low after the best part of a week in London trying to keep up with her youngest child. Lucy would be helping John carry his equipment, generally soaking up the pre-show atmosphere of rehearsals and feeling in complete awe of her big brother.

Lucy had been waiting at the front of the hotel for John at 8.30 am on Thursday as agreed. She was dressed in jeans and a skimpy T-shirt; she wore no bra beneath the T-shirt with which to conceal her upwardly pointing, upwardly mobile nipples.

If the models can do it why not you, I bet you look just as good under that flimsy layer of cotton as any of them. Go on show them what you've got to trade with, I'm sure they won't mind, John might be a bit embarrassed but that's only because he's a man and you're his little sister.

John arrived to pick up Lucy just as Marie was waking up. She'd booked herself in the previous evening for an appointment with the hotel manicurist at eleven and then a relaxing massage at twelve. She had plenty of time to shower and saunter down for a late breakfast, taking her time to enjoy the peace and quiet compared to the hustle and bustle of the previous three days. She was spending some time by herself and she felt she deserved it. Lucy's enthusiasm was great to see but a hard act to keep up with.

After breakfast she lazily glanced over the newspapers in the hotels lounge area then made her way to the manicurist at eleven. She spoke with pride at how she was going to be at the fashion show the following day at the invitation of her son John Kirkpatrick the up and coming photographer, personal assistant to Stein. It had made her day to talk to a complete stranger about her son who was taking his first steps on the road to wealth and fame. The manicurist feigned interest at a story, the likes of which she heard every day.

Twelve o'clock arrived and she made her way to the massage rooms for her appointment. She was shown to her room where she showered, dried off and lay on her front with a towel across her buttocks. When the masseuse entered the room a short while later Marie was so relaxed she was already nearly asleep, and the massage hadn't even started.

When the masseuse spoke Marie was a little taken aback to find that the masseuse was actually a masseur, but she hoped she hadn't let herself down by showing any shock at him being a man in this newly discovered liberated world she now lived in. She'd been expecting a woman. The thought never occurred to her that it might be a man. Joe explained that Wendy one of the girls had called in sick and that if she wanted a masseuse one would be free in about ten minutes. Marie took a quick glance at Joe and decided Joe rubbing his hands all over her body and manipulating her at his will for the next hour would be just fine.

Joe was a tall man, probably six feet two; broad, tanned and toned with the softest hands Marie could ever remember having touched her. They talked only sparingly at first; Joe quickly and skilfully putting Marie into a trance-like state using just his trained hands and some scented massage oils. When she'd had enough relaxation Joe started to revive her body by using a greater force to get the blood flowing and the circulation going.

Marie was coming out of the trance and waking up to a body that felt like it was on fire. She felt so good she jokingly told him he should come and massage her where they could be a bit more private. He said it could be arranged with a little laugh and said he finished work at two that afternoon and was thinking just the same thing himself. Marie didn't know if she'd just taken part in some harmless flirting to guarantee Joe a good tip or she'd set herself up for an enjoyable afternoon romp in the sack. Nothing more was said about it until she signed for the massage against her room number, gave Joe a twenty-pound tip, winked at him and said "see you later" with a little giggle as she left.

Lunch was a sandwich and iced tea taken in the hotel restaurant, then back to her room. It might have been only flirting, but if Joe was going to show up at her door shortly after two that afternoon she was going to give him something he would enjoy. She slipped into a see through lacy black basque, pulled up her stockings put her clothes back on and ordered a bottle of champagne on ice. If Joe didn't show then at the very least she could get pissed and enjoy an afternoon of passion all by herself. She'd decided she would wait until half past two to open the champagne anyway. Nothing ventured, nothing gained. At ten past two the knock came on her door and she let Joe into her room.

"Hello Joe. Come in. I hoped that wasn't all just some harmless flirting, so I ordered champagne, just in case."

"Mrs Kirkpatrick, I just couldn't say no to an offer like that, I was enjoying the feel of your body too much to refuse the chance to touch it again."

"Call me Marie, please. Let's not waste time just standing around talking."

With that they were on each other, forcing their tongues into each other's mouths. Marie expertly unfastened Joe's belt with one hand and unzipped his trousers to release his cock so she could work on it, teasing it to its full size in no time at all. While this was going on Joe was marvelling at Marie's prowess, he'd heard from some of his male colleagues that sex at the hands of a woman with experience was something to savour and enjoy, and very rarely if it's offered should it be turned down. But he thought he was going to embarrass himself by emptying both barrels before he was even out of his pants. He was working off Marie's top when she knelt down to take him in her mouth. Joe lasted another fifteen seconds before his sticky juices were filling her throat.

She was hungry for him; she pushed him back on the bed where he finished getting undressed while Marie got down to her stockings. She then invited him to take his pleasure any way that he wished to. This he did, with a fervour Marie had rarely seen, working her into a sweating, panting frenzy using his soft hands, expert tongue and hard cock. By four o'clock both Joe and Marie were happy in the knowledge that it would probably be a long time before either of them experienced anything so pleasurable on an afternoon in London, or even Manchester for that matter. Life was good.

Lucy was also having a lot of fun. Helping John had been the best thing she could remember having done in years. She was still his little sister but there was a real pride in John's voice when he introduced her to other people. Stein had taken to her immediately, even suggesting that John should try and talk her into letting Stein take a photo-shoot with her on her next visit. "Strictly no charge for such a beautiful girl, call it a one hundred percent staff discount." John was shocked, if Stein were to charge for a one to one session with a model agency footing the bill the invoice would have been well over three thousand pounds just for a couple of hours of his time. John had thought of doing a photo session himself, while Lucy was in London, but any portfolio with Stein's work in it was likely to get most girls through any model agency doors.

"John, my dear young chap, where have you been hiding that little sister of yours?" Said Stein, "she's adorable, she has the face of an angel. You must be aware that she has the potential to be better than any model we've had in these studios during your time here. At her age you can spot them instantly, the ones who could really do something in the business. Two, maybe three years time she'll have all the top agencies falling over themselves to take her under their wings, without a doubt."

"It's difficult sometimes for me to see Lucy in that way," replied John, "she's still my little sister. I can't say I've really considered her as anything other than a little sister, I've always known she was pretty but what you're suggesting goes way beyond pretty, it is a little hard to take on board at the moment."

"She'll always be your little sister, John; even when you're my age. Nothing ever changes in that sense, believe me. June is still my little sister and it's her fifty-third birthday next week, ugly as a London Irish prop forward and weighing in at sixteen stones." Said Stein, "Mind you, she was never a beautiful baby and it just got worse from then on I suppose. Lucy though, now you really must promise me that you'll bring her down to the studio regularly. Such beauty must never be denied a wider audience."

"I'd planned on having her visit more often anyway, now that I'm getting more settled in London and things seem to be getting back to normal again in Manchester after dad…"

"Yes, good, splendid, you must tell her the good news at the show tomorrow. You'll be able to see what I mean about her looks there, just watch, I won't be the only one singing her praises, mark my words dear boy, the juices will flow when they see Lucy, just you wait and see if they don't."

In the afternoon John and Lucy went to Cardinal Place. He could have just shown up on the day but that wasn't John's style, or Stein's. He wanted to get the feel of the place, soak up the atmosphere, see the models on the catwalk, and check out the lighting. It was also a special treat for Lucy, Stein had worked his magic yet again and a pre-show pass for Lucy was waiting on the front desk.

Lucy couldn't believe it; here she was with her big brother in a totally foreign world in which he was completely at his ease. She thought her pride in him couldn't get any stronger, that was until Naomi Campbell came over kissed him on his cheek and said Hi. Naomi knew he was going to be a future hot property, she'd heard it from Stein.

My god, Lucy, just take a look at that pretty black ass. And look at those legs, have you ever seen legs so. . . wow they just keep on going. I love it here, and that brother of yours, he's a dark horse and no mistake.

"John. Was that really Naomi Campbell who just kissed you?" asked Lucy.

"Don't tell me you have to ask that. Said John, Any way, it was nothing more than a peck on the cheek, it happens all the time." John replied with a smile on his face. "Handshakes would be so out of place in this business. She'll probably not even recognise me in a week, she only knows me now because Stein introduced us a couple of days ago. He told her I had his full seal of approval, apparently she's very fussy, Stein should know; he's probably photographed her more than anyone else has. But let's face it, Lucy, when you get to be as good as she is you can afford to be fussy."

I bet she could have any of the women here. With a body like that she could take her pick.

Sorry, Sally-Anne, but if you read the gossip columns you'd see her preference is definitely for men not women.

You know you didn't have to say that. Let me have my fantasy at least. That pretty tight black ass and a face to die for.

No point raising your hopes up, She's well off the scale as far as you're concerned.

Hey, I'm only temporarily disappointed; you heard what Stein said to John. If he's right, and let's face it he should know, you, or should I say we, will soon have our own pick of what's on offer, black, white, yellow, female even male if you must.

Shortly after the Naomi Campbell experience Steph Wilkins came looking for John, she was wearing what Lucy would describe later to her mum as a see through knee length body stocking, split down the front to her navel, backless with a red bow at the base of her spine. This time the peck on the cheek was a lingering kiss on the mouth, and when she finished she turned to Lucy and hugged her.

"You must be Lucy. John's told me so much about you. We can have a good chat later after the run through."

Steph turned back to John, "Got to get back, hectic back stage. See you later, John. See you later Lucy." With that Steph turned and walked away, admiring glances following her all the way backstage.

Thank you John I think I love you. Next time she does that Lucy your body is mine and I'm not even asking for permission.

Lucy couldn't believe it. Here she was at the rehearsals with her big brother, who, as far as she was concerned couldn't only walk on water, he could levitate six inches above it, when Steph Wilkins comes over and hugs her.

"Lucy, that was Steph, she was in a bit of a hurry, apparently" Said John.

"I know who that was, John. Show me someone who doesn't. But how come she knows me?" replied Lucy.

"I was saving it as a surprise, I'm still pinching myself actually, I'm moving in with her next week," said John, "we're going to be living together as of Sunday."

"You and Stephanie Wilkins! Living together?" Lucy's mouth was hanging open and John had to put his finger under her chin to help her shut it.

"She prefers to be called Steph, but yes, me and Stephanie Wilkins."

"My God, you're going to be living with her." Lucy could barely hold in her excitement.

"Yeah, scary isn't it, we met in January and really hit it off. Things have been moving really quickly here, we only decided last week about living together, what do you think mum will say?" said John

"Wow, you and Stephanie Wilkins living together. Totally mind-blowing."

"Yeah, but what about mum?"

"No problem she'll love her. After all, didn't she come second in the, 'woman men most want to take home to meet their mother poll', recently?"

"You mean she didn't come first, oh no what's mum going to say." John said laughing and really enjoying the time with his little sister. "Joking aside, Lucy. What do you think of her?" They were now really back in the old routine they played on when they were together.

"She gorgeous, John. Really nice, but you should hope she wears something a bit less revealing when she meets mum for the first time."

"You do see some weird and wonderful creations in the name of fashion at these events," said John, "I'm sure a lot of the designers just set out to shock, but what should I care, I'm just a guy with a camera who takes photographs for a living." But John just couldn't help grinning like a Cheshire cat.

Yeah yeah great, she's straight, just my luck, and spoken for anyway. There must be some models around here that prefer the taste of female flesh. But Lucy, did you see those nipples? What a complete waste.

I don't think her nipples will be wasted on my brother, Sally-Anne. Jealousy is such an ugly emotion in a woman, or a man.

Ha. Ha, Ha, you're just so funny. You crack me up. I'm pleased for him really, they make a great looking couple...And I bet she shags like a bunny on a mission to repopulate the world.

Later, when her days work was done, Steph joined the two of them for a drink. Lucy had excitedly rung her mum and told her she was going to be back a bit late but asked if it was okay if John brought a friend for dinner. Marie was looking forward to it, she was so relaxed he could have invited the Queen mother to dine with them and it wouldn't have bothered her in the slightest.

Dressed in jeans and a baggy sweatshirt with all her make-up removed Steph could just about blend in with the masses with a little bit of effort. This was Steph's preferred code of dress, fashion models get to wear some spectacular clothes but nothing is ever just comfortable. Lucy could see the recognition on the faces of some of the other people in the bar when they looked Steph's way. People couldn't help themselves, nudging the people they were with and whispering in their ears that they were sure that was Stephanie Wilkins sat at the table in the corner. Lucy was in dream-land; any fourteen year old would have been, as far as she was concerned this is what life should be like.

"So what's he like as a big brother, Lucy? Please don't tell me he's fantastic as a brother but a real horror to live with." said Steph

" Well… he's a fantastic brother…" replied Lucy.

"And I'm a real joy to live with I think you were just about to say weren't you, Lucy?" added John

"Only if you insist. But there was that time…" Just then John reached over playfully to cover Lucy's mouth with his hand.

"A sense of humour as well as superstar looks. She'll go far John. Stein wasn't wrong." said Steph.

"What's it like being so famous, Steph?" asked Lucy, "People keep looking over at us and whispering."

"It's great to begin with, but it can get to be a bit much at times, you just learn to ignore it. Men try to chat you up all the time though, if they feel adventurous enough, which usually means they're drunk. It wouldn't be so bad but you should see the state of some of them. The really nice ones don't need to try very hard." Steph said looking over at John.

Ask her about women, Lucy!

"I bet it's not only men though, do you get women chatting you up aswell?" asked Lucy.

John looked over at Lucy with a puzzled expression on his face as if to say, 'did you really ask that then, Lucy?'

"All the time, the fashion industry is like a magnet for weirdoes and all their mates, and most of the male models are gay. There's a lot of jealousy and bitchiness too, which you just have to turn a blind eye to." replied Steph, "Looking at you, Lucy, I'd say you've got a good chance of finding all this out for yourself one day."

Yes!

"But not just yet" Marie said to Lucy. "Plenty time for that, if it's what you want to do."

"Oh I want it, mum. Who wouldn't?"

Correct answer, Lucy. That is exactly what we want.

Dinner that evening was a very pleasant affair. Marie had been very surprised when Stephanie Wilkins had come walking into the hotel, arm in arm with Lucy, and at first she appeared a little flustered. Steph put her at her ease very quickly, demonstrating that she was only a normal human being, just like anyone else; she was not someone to be feared. Steph had mastered this at an early stage of her fame and found it paid dividends not to act like a prima donna.

She was highly respected inside and outside of the fashion world for her attitude and easy going nature, unlike some of the little bitches these days that see themselves above everyone and everything.

John did however nearly choke on a mouthful of food when Lucy blurted out that he and Steph were going to be living together from next week. It ended with all four of them laughing out loud about Lucy's eagerness to say something in her state of excitement.

Marie couldn't have felt much happier than she did that evening. Her son was making a name for himself as a photographer, he'd met Steph Wilkins the famous supermodel and it appeared their relationship was going from strength to strength, and her daughter seemed really happy for the first time in years. Oh, and she couldn't forget the sex, she was more excited about that than she had been when she was an eighteen year old about to lose her virginity on the back seat of an Austin A40, after a day trip to Oxford.

The next day was magical. Lucy got the full on experience of the world of a supermodel. The lights, the music, the tempo of the show; the audience's appreciation for the spectacle totally blew her mind.

At that moment Lucy knew where she wanted her future to be. She was loving every minute of it. Everything was so alive, so vibrant she wanted to be a part of it. She hardly noticed John for the whole of the show, the catwalk captivated her, each time Steph appeared she felt like jumping up and waving to her, but she just stopped herself short and felt a little embarrassed at how foolish she would have looked. Sally-Anne wasn't being any help either, she was just as hyped up by the whole event as Lucy, she'd never seen so much beauty concentrated into one area. She was high on it. Lucy's mind was on overload and within it was another mind, also on overload.

There was no escaping the fact that Lucy liked Steph, liked her a lot, and it was obvious from their body language that John and Steph had become very close in the short time they'd known each other. Steph liked Lucy also; she'd felt a bond developing in the two days she'd known her and she felt good about it. Steph had no brothers or sisters of her own and felt she'd missed out because of it. Looking at how John and Lucy were so comfortable in each other's company made her feel like she wanted to be a part of that whole family thing that was going on between them. She was falling in love with John and she felt it wouldn't take much for her to love his little sister too.

Stein had mentioned the stir that Lucy would cause at the fashion show and he wasn't wrong. The modelling world is always on the look out for the next generation of young talent, the stars of the future; the people with the potential to earn their agencies the top fees available. Where better to spot that talent than at a fashion show, it shows a young person's willingness to be part of their world, to embrace a particular lifestyle from an early age.

Lucy was approached by three agencies on the day, each one telling her and her and her mum that Lucy had great potential within the industry if she was interested in pursuing it further. Because of her age they suggested they keep in touch and wanted to see updated photographs every six months or so in order that they could keep an eye on her physical development and then they could talk further in about eighteen months if both parties were still interested. The modelling industry had attracted some bad press in the past few years regarding under age sex and drug abuse which they were keen to stamp out, so very young models were not being thrust into the adult modelling world too early.

Lucy couldn't believe how her life had suddenly changed. In the space of a week she'd met several of the country's top models, had seen a world which excited her like nothing else ever had and been told that she most probably could be part of that same world herself in the future. She'd had a great time with her mum, seen her brother looking as happy as she'd seen him in a long time and also met his new girlfriend, a famous supermodel in her own right. Not a bad week, all things considered.

Eleven

Seventeen was how old Jayne Parkinson had been when she finally understood her sexuality; it had been a pivotal point in her life. That had been six years earlier. She'd been on so-called dates with lots of boys in the three years previous to that, quite often enjoying herself in their company. But she always felt that there must be something better, as if she was missing out on something she hadn't yet discovered, a missing link. She thought that maybe she'd find it later on in her life, when the boys became men and matured into something that she could appreciate more and would appreciate her more.

She discovered what it was she'd been missing out on during a school skiing trip to France. It was during this trip that one of the young instructors, a French girl, not much older than Jayne had been herself at the time, taught her how to give and receive pleasure from the close physical contact of another woman. She didn't do a half-bad job of teaching her how to ski also; Jayne had been a quick learner.

She'd learnt a lot from Claudine during those two weeks and she still kept in touch with her, always skiing the slopes where Claudine was instructing when she returned each year for her winter skiing holiday in France. Claudine had been a good instructor, both in and out of bed, and they still maintained a close bond of friendship, a bond which only two women who have known each other physically could possibly share together.

The start of a new school term after a two-week holiday was always the hardest, and the start of the summer term for Jayne had been no exception. At twenty-three she was in only her second year out of college and finding life as a PE teacher a demanding but also a very enjoyable challenge.

At only five feet two inches tall Jayne was quite short, but she could hold her own at most sports. Hockey was her first sporting love and the main reason she'd been offered such a good teaching post with her very limited teaching experience. She'd been a very good Lancashire county schools hockey player since the age of fourteen, making captain when she reached under-eighteen level. She was now on the fringes of the full England squad and pushing hard for her chance to represent her country. The school was keen to have a possible future sporting heroine in their midst.

She'd had relationships with girls from the hockey club after she'd discovered her preference for the female form, but none of them could come close to Claudine in that sense, they tended to be too well built for her taste. She preferred the slim, toned form, which was becoming more of a rarity since she finished her sports science degree course. There had been lots of women who could satisfy Jayne' tastes at university.

Being so short had never held Jayne back in life, she was instantly recognisable in a crowded room, and her long flowing red locks instantly drew the eye. Her pretty face, pale complexion and hazel eyes made the eye stay for longer than they would have on any of the plain girls in the same room. She was one of the red heads who had been gifted at birth with the looks that compliment the hair colour, a face unblemished by a single freckle. Only too often, or so it seems, a lot of women blessed with red hair had not been blessed with the good looks and skin to go with it. Jayne was one of those rare exceptions where everything had come together so well you just had to stand and admire.

Easter marked the end of the school hockey calendar and in the summer term the girls would be concentrating mainly on athletics, with some tennis thrown in for good measure. Athletics was her second area of sporting prowess.

Lucy was also a good athlete, her long legs and slim frame meant she was good at the jumping events and many of the longer distance running events. She couldn't throw to save her life, but then she didn't exactly have the physique that was typical of a lady shot-putter. Lucy was just happy to run and jump; the well-built Miss Piggys of the world could keep the throwing events for themselves. Jayne had a soft spot for Lucy; she had good potential as an athlete, and she also fit her idea of what all young women should look like, in an ideal world.

Jayne would often catch herself daydreaming at this time of year; the sexual stimuli that her body responded to so well were so much more in evidence as the weather improved after Easter into summer. Outer layers of clothing would be discarded allowing a clearer view of the potential that lay beneath to those who chose to notice. Lucy had often been the subject of many of Jayne's daydreams of late.

Jayne was aware that Lucy hadn't been the happiest girl in school; she'd seen that last year when she took up the position at the school. Losing her father last Christmas to an apparent suicide couldn't have helped. She'd seemed like she needed a friend and Jayne Parkinson had given her more of her time than she'd given to any other pupil since Christmas, she felt that Lucy's circumstances had warranted the extra effort on her part. Of course she would have felt inclined to feel the same about any of the girls she took for lessons if the same circumstances had befallen them, but she probably wouldn't have found herself daydreaming about many, if any, of the other girls she taught.

Five weeks into the summer term was when it happened. Sally-Anne finally persuaded Lucy to give her free reign of the 'vehicle', as she called it, that was Lucy's body, and Lucy allowed herself to be taken on a journey.

Tuesday was athletics training after school; the track had been marked out at the start of term and the long jump pit filled with fresh sand. The only problem with this particular Tuesday was the weather, it had been raining for the past two days and only five of her girls had turned up for what was meant to be a conditioning session on the track. Having looked at the state of the track Jayne suggested a cross-country run was more appropriate. After a few playful moans about having to run a cross-country the girls set off dutifully, with Jayne bringing up the rear.

There were no stragglers on this run; these girls formed half of the year nine girls' athletics team. Jayne was competitive and she expected her girls to be competitive too, especially with the inter-schools athletic meeting coming up in two weeks time. As was usual on cross-country Sally-Anne in the guise of Lucy ran ahead of the rest, her long legs not having to work as hard as the others did to cover the same ground. When they reached the turning point to head back Sally-Anne tripped over a tree root, falling and seemingly spraining a calf muscle.

It was Jayne's decision that the other four girls should run on and complete the course, showering and changing while she helped Sally-Anne hobble back the rest of the way. She could stand on it so the damage wasn't too bad. With Lucy's arm over Jayne's shoulder for support and Jayne's arm around Lucy's waist they made their way back to school along the public footpaths they'd used for the run.

Thirty minutes later they reached the girls changing rooms just in time to see the last two of the other girls heading for their parents cars or the bus stop. Lucy's leg had apparently improved greatly when they got back to school and she could walk much more freely unaided. Still it was Jayne's decision that she should see if there was any noticeable damage. Physiotherapy had been an enjoyable part of her sports sciences course and she was hardly ever given the opportunity to use it these days.

In Jayne's office, her inner sanctum, where students were very rarely allowed, she sat Lucy down and started to examine her leg.

Sally-Anne, what's happening here? My calf muscle feels fine there's nothing wrong with it is there? It doesn't feel sore. You tripped up on purpose.

I know that, you know that, but Miss Parkinson doesn't know that. And I've had a feeling about her for a while now, she's one of the prettiest teachers in school and I think she's got a very soft spot for us. It's my intention to get my hands on that very soft spot if I can, and if I can get my hands on hers I'll let her get her hands on yours.

Jayne looked into Lucy's eyes, "The sooner this is worked on the sooner it'll get better. Will your mum be waiting for you on the car park?"

"No she goes out on Tuesday evening with some of her girlfriends from college for a drink." replied Lucy. "They meet in town after the others have finished work." The bit about meeting some girls for a drink was a lie that Marie had told Lucy several times, she was actually meeting Simon after he finished work, and having a drink wasn't top of the agenda either. "She leaves me my dinner to warm up in the microwave and I'm mature enough now to look after myself, and legally I'm old enough to be left on my own. I couldn't deny her an evening out after the year she's just had." said Sally-Anne; working hard herself on Jayne's sympathy nerve.

"No of course not, it must be hard for you and your mum after what happened at Christmas." Jayne said.

"We seem to be getting by okay now."

"I think you're very brave, both of you." Jayne could feel her heart going out to this girl who had suffered so much over the past six months and she could also feel other emotions began to stir from deep within. She'd felt her nipples begin to stiffen as soon as she shut her office door, but now a heat was gathering between her legs. She knew it was wrong to feel that way about a pupil, any pupil, but she couldn't help herself. She'd tried to convince herself that Lucy was only fourteen years old; still only a child in the eyes of the law. She just didn't look like a child though, and she didn't act like one either. She had seemed to grow in confidence since the Easter break and Jayne's emotions were now being tested to their limits.

"I could work on your leg then, Lucy," said Jayne, "if you're not in any hurry. Then I could drop you off at home to save you having to catch the bus."

"That sounds great. Thanks Miss," replied Lucy.

"You can call me Jayne if you like when we're alone. I don't let many pupils use my Christian name, in fact you'd be the only one, but I like you Lucy. You can call me Jayne in private. I know all about what you've been through lately and it must have taken a lot of courage to go through all that and come out on the other side relatively unscathed. I admire anyone who can do that. But don't forget though Lucy, when were not alone its Miss Parkinson as normal okay?"

With that a tear fell onto Lucy's cheek, Jayne was mortified, she thought she must have over-stepped some invisible boundary which had been too much for Lucy to handle. She got to her feet apologising for hurting her. When she looked at Lucy's face again she was weeping, the tears were real, Lucy hadn't been treated like this by anyone since she moved to Manchester, and at that point she felt a genuine love for Miss Jayne Parkinson her PE teacher. Sally-Anne may well have been in control of the body but these were Lucy's tears falling from her eyes.

Jayne's emotions were also jumping off the walls. She took Lucy in her arms to comfort her, all thoughts of Lucy's injured leg now gone. It wasn't Lucy's leg that needed her attention anymore. Reaching up she kissed Lucy's cheek gently in a motherly way, to calm her down, but was shocked at the charge that leapt through her whole body. Here she was a twenty three year old teacher in school with her favourite fourteen-year-old pupil and all she wanted to do was take her home to bed, comfort her, love her, and make the world a better place for her. When Sally-Anne responded by kissing Jayne gently on the lips any thoughts of impropriety were vanquished.

They kissed for some time, and they explored each other, taking their time, feeling totally at ease with what was happening. Nothing about it felt wrong, it just seemed like the natural thing to be doing for two people who felt the way they did about each other. There was no animal passion that first time; no tearing clothes off to get at their prey. It was strictly a case of them gently introducing themselves to each other. When they were satisfied that they knew so much more about each other than they strictly should have they showered together, gently dried each other off and got dressed as if they'd been lovers for many years, it felt so right. They left in Jayne's car.

Each of them was aware that something had just happened that shouldn't have happened, not in the eyes of the law anyway, or in the eyes of most God-fearing Christians. But it most certainly had been meant to happen, they were both sure of that. Neither of them would ever forget that first time, it would change both their lives for the better from that point on, both felt sure that was the case, or it should be said, all three of them were sure.

Mmmm, thanks, Lucy. That was just divine. I think I'm in heaven. The red rose of Lancashire, her tight little rose bud was perfect.

Everything about her was perfect, Sally-Anne. She really is beautiful naked. I have to admit it; you've probably converted me to the delights of the female flesh before I've even tasted what a man has to offer. She knew exactly what to do. It was like she could read my mind. She knew exactly where to touch, where I wanted to be touched, where we wanted to be touched.

Oh yes, she's done that lots of times before, Lucy. She was good. And now we've found her we should keep her to ourselves for a while, enjoy ourselves, all three of us. We can have so much fun. I get the feeling she feels the same way about us.

I hope so. I think I could quite easily fall in love with her.

She already loves you; I could feel it in her touch, so gentle, so sincere. You'll never get a man to understand that, they just fumble about as if they're playing with a new toy and haven't bothered reading the rules of the game. All they want is sex, they don't understand how to give pleasure, they just want to receive it. They're all selfish in that sense.

There was no way Lucy was going to be able to argue the point about men with Sally-Anne; she'd had no previous experience of men except her dad and her brother and thankfully neither of those relationships had included having sex in any manner.

She'd thought her dad had been a selfish bastard for some time before he died, and he even died like the selfish bastard that he was. John wasn't like that though; he was thoughtful, kind and considerate. He and Steph were going from strength to strength; the perfect couple; and he loved Lucy too.

Marie and Simon were also becoming closer, not that they could get much closer physically, it felt to Marie that they'd just about rewritten the Karma Sutra several times over. Since returning from London at Easter she'd realised, after seeing John and Steph together, that she craved more than the odd afternoon or evening of stolen passion with Simon. She was growing closer to him.

It had been barely more than six months since David's suicide and she didn't want to upset Lucy and John with the rapidity at which she'd been able to move on, been able to continue her life without David. Lucy was maturing quickly into a beautiful young woman. People were saying she had a great future. John was settling down with Steph and seemingly making a great start to what everyone in the know was saying was going to be a very successful career. She didn't want to throw everything off course, so she kept her secret lover just that, a secret. She would say something when the time was right. No need to rush when life was so good, she didn't want to ruin what they had, what they were having, at every available opportunity. She could live with the cloak and dagger aspect of their relationship just as long as their relationship was allowed to continue, forever if needed.

Twelve

Terence Sandford, Terry to his friends, the few of them that existed, was what some people, the less cruel of our society, would describe as slow. They'd look at him with pity but they'd be wrong to pity him, he was probably happier, more fulfilled than those very same people who were looking at him through such biased, critical eyes.

With an IQ of sixty-seven Terry could just barely be classed as retarded. He was slow, nobody would question that, but at twenty-seven years of age he was more than capable of being of some use within his community. He had a pleasant enough manner and he certainly posed no threat to anyone, he was just slow.

He'd worked at the school for nearly a year now, sweeping the floors from half past four until seven o'clock Monday to Friday. He loved his job; it gave him a real sense of worth, and let's face it, how many people going to work five days each week can say that these days? The government paid his wages out of the care in the community budget so the school governors were happy, and he didn't need any supervision, so the school caretakers and cleaning staff were happy. Everyone was happy and the school was seen as doing its bit for a less fortunate member of society. Something looked upon kindly by those running the country.

Terry had been particularly happy for the past three weeks. Three weeks earlier he'd caught sight of Jayne and Sally-Anne in the gym equipment storeroom, they'd been doing what all naked girls in love do when faced with a three-foot high stack of gym mats in the corner of the room. They were having some fun on them. Terry shouldn't have been there then and he shouldn't be there now.

He'd borrowed the key to the gym because he sometimes liked to see how long he could hang from the wall bars before falling off; his record was four minutes thirteen seconds. So he'd forgotten all about wall bars three weeks earlier and found himself this Wednesday evening furtively peeking through the glass of the fire door into the equipment store. His penis was clutched in his right hand and he was rubbing himself off as if his very existence depended on it.

He'd never done this before, never even seen a woman naked before, but over the past three weeks some dormant emotion, a yearning, had been awakened in him. He certainly wasn't prepared for his first orgasm and when it came he couldn't help himself, the moan of pleasure wasn't loud, but it stopped Jayne, Sally-Anne and Lucy dead in their tracks.

"Did you hear something, Jayne?" said Lucy.

All thoughts of a blissful release had vanished in that instant. Jayne had never considered that someone might some day catch them at their sordid little tryst. The gym was strictly off limits to everyone after five o'clock who didn't have Jayne's permission to be there. The cleaning staff's first priority was the gym and they were usually gone well before five o'clock, leaving the place empty and 'safe'.

"I thought I heard something," was Jayne's reply, "but it could have just been the wind, Oh God, please let it be the wind."

"That didn't sound like the wind to me. I think there must be someone out there."

Lucy got to her feet, slipped on her blouse, and crept to the door just in time to see Terry making his way through the door at the far end of the gym.

Let's say nothing, Lucy. Jayne will just worry and it's only the little retard, he's not going to say anything to anyone. I think the stupid idiot was probably only playing with himself anyway and he shouldn't have even been here. Let's not be too hasty.

"I can't see anything. You must be right it's been windy all day. But maybe we should just get dressed and go, I feel a bit spooked; what about you?" said Lucy looking over at Jayne.

"I'm fine, I'm sure it was nothing but it's probably best if we get dressed like you say." Jayne replied

Jayne had practically shit herself for a moment there. She'd thought they were safe in the storeroom, now she'd have to think again about where and when they could meet. She didn't mention this to Lucy, she didn't want her to panic, or have any second thoughts about the rights or wrongs of what they were doing.

The next week Terry sneaked into the gym for his weekly peep show but was disappointed to find the place completely empty, no one about. This was a big blow; he'd been looking forward to this the whole week. There was nothing else for it, he grasped the wall bars and timed himself with the wall clock, five minutes dead, a new record.

He'd decided that without the floor show he'd just have to play with himself later when he got home and hope that his mum didn't catch him like she had two nights before. He picked up his brush and headed off to the canteen where he'd been told the floor needed a good sweeping. He enjoyed doing the canteen floor, sometimes the dinner ladies would leave him some cake and milk as a treat and he made sure the floor sparkled.

Lucy had been having real problems ever since the evening when Terry had discovered her and Jayne together naked. Sally-Anne had very clear opinions about what needed to be done with Terry, but Lucy was having some difficulty coming to terms with what she was suggesting.

All I'm saying Lucy, is that the little retard has the power to stop us ever seeing Jayne again. You'll be expelled from school in disgrace, and Jayne will be sacked in an instant. Her hockey career will be finished just as she's getting there and that's not to say anything about the fact that you're not sixteen yet! She'll be ruined. She'll never get another job. She'll be branded a paedophile; we can't let that happen.

You said yourself though, Sally-Anne, he's retarded; he isn't going to say anything is he?

He's not the sort of person I'd trust to keep it to himself though; he's hardly playing with a full deck is he? He's not the sharpest tool in the toolbox, Lucy.

Maybe not but he hasn't said anything so far, why should that change?

He's a man, Lucy. Not much of one I'll grant you that but he's still got a penis. He'll shout it from the rooftops some day soon, we can't let him, you must realise that. I really don't need your agreement, Lucy. I just thought you were ready to face up to what we've got to do. You've got to trust me Lucy, when have I ever been wrong before. Guardian angel, remember? Protecting you, that's what I do, the reason I exist, what's changed there.

Nothing's changed.
So?
I don't want to lose Jayne, you know that.
Just trust me, Lucy. You do trust me don't you?
Yes I do.

The following Wednesday Sally-Anne went directly to the gym at four o'clock, after Lucy's French lesson, and settled down in a corner. She'd been hidden from view until the gym and the changing rooms had been cleaned and the place was empty. Strictly speaking Sally-Anne was in control but Lucy was fully switched on, she'd agreed that she wanted to be part of whatever was going to happen, Sally-Anne could be very persuasive. She sat back and waited, hoping that Terry would turn up again to get an eyeful of what he'd seen two weeks earlier, it could mean a two hour wait but she was prepared for that, after all it wasn't like she was going to be lonely.

Terry didn't disappoint. At half past five she watched Terry quietly make his way towards the store room door. Just as he was about to put his face to the glass panel she swung the door open and dragged him in by his arm without a word. Terry looked like a rabbit caught in a car's headlights. He knew he shouldn't be there but he was powerless to do anything about the oncoming danger.

"Hello, Terry. I'd been hoping you were going to show up, I'm Lucy and I'm all alone and need some company," Sally-Anne said, "my friend hasn't turned up yet and I don't think she's coming, will you keep me company, Terry?"

He was struck dumb, this wasn't supposed to happen, he'd only come to watch. She was even prettier close up though, and she knew his name so she must be a friend.

"Shall we sit on the mats, Terry? We can talk if you like."

This was a unique opportunity for him, but he didn't understand that. No man had been given the chance Sally-Anne was about to offer him. He wasn't really taking much of a part in it though; Sally-Anne was like a mother leading her child across a busy road holding their hand so they felt safe, Terry just wasn't aware of the oncoming traffic, he was blind to the danger he now faced.

"Was it you who saw me and my friend in here two weeks ago playing?" asked Sally-Anne. "Do you like to play? Maybe we should take our clothes off and play. What do you think, Terry? Shall we play a game like that?"

Terry nodded, it was barely a movement of the head but he definitely wanted to play though, especially the sort of games Sally-Anne was talking about.

"Good, I thought for a moment there you didn't like me. You're very quiet, Terry. You don't say much do you? I'd have been very upset if you didn't like me."

"I like you." Terry mumbled, blushing.

"Now you've made me so happy, I'm going to take off my tie and blouse and let you see what's underneath, then I'm going to take off my skirt and let you see what's under there too, close up this time, you little cheeky monkey. Is that okay?" Asked Sally-Anne

Terry nodded quickly; he couldn't believe his luck.

"Are you going to show me what you look like, Terry? Without any clothes on, I bet you look great."

Sally-Anne could see that Terry was a big boy, judging by the bulge that had formed in his trousers when she took her blouse off to reveal a lacy bra that quickly followed suit. She walked over to the other side of the room to place her clothes on a cricket bag and then took off her skirt and knickers, kicking her shoes off at the same time.

"Come on, Terry. Now don't be shy, you do want to do this don't you?" Sally-Anne asked.

Terry wanted to do this, who wouldn't? He started pulling hard at his belt in his haste to disrobe.

"Gently, Terry." said Sally-Anne, You don't want to hurt yourself before I've even had chance to get my hands on you do you?"

Terry slowed down but quickly got down to his underpants, which were doing a very poor job of concealing his now fully erect, and some would say more than ample man hood, he was too shy to carry on.

"Come on, Terry. Everything off, don't disappoint me," said Sally-Anne, "you wouldn't like me to start getting dressed again would you?"

With that last bit of encouragement Terry shook his head, slid his underpants down to the floor and stood up proud. It was when he stood up that he could see Sally-Anne coming at him with an eight-inch kitchen knife. The knife was in his stomach and through to his back before he'd had time to react, not that he'd have known what to do anyway. Sally-Anne quickly pulled out the blade and stabbed him again; she jumped back as the blood started to flow.

Terry didn't understand what had just happened, his face was full of confusion, as he looked at Sally-Anne she was grinning back at him. Surely this couldn't be part of the game, it was too painful; he was confused, what was he supposed to do now? He wanted to go home; his mum would know what to do. Sally-Anne was picking something up from inside the cricket bag and putting them on her hands, batting gloves, she then slipped into an old discarded pair of cricket shoes before walking over to Terry's prone body, now flat on his back with the same look of confusion on his face.

The last things he saw were two cricket wickets being aimed at his eyes before they were pushed with great force into his head. He was beyond screaming at that point and went out with barely a whimper. It was doubtful that Terry could have survived much longer than that, but even without his eyes and very probably already dead he still looked confused.

Confusion was an expression that Sally-Anne didn't particularly like, she thought it was typical of a man to be confused when he thought he was going to have sex but all he got was a knife in his belly for his troubles.

She picked up a seven-pound shot put and with a rage that very rarely surfaces even in the hardest thug, for the next few minutes proceeded to get rid of the expression on his face. She didn't only manage to get rid of the expression, she actually managed to get rid of his face altogether, splintering most of his skull into the pulpy mess that was now his brain. His head now looked as if it had been run over by a steamroller.

Picking up some of the mashed up brain matter that had once resided in Terry's skull she began to rub slowly between her legs until an uncontrollable orgasm burst through her body. Laughing now, she picked up the knife once again and cut off Terry's penis. "Not such a magnificent erection now. You stupid thick waste of space" Sally-Anne shouted. She threw it behind the stacked gym mats, where a young female detective would eventually find it. From that moment on and for the following months that same police officer would question her decision to join the force. This had to have been the worst day of her, so far, uncomplicated and unremarkable career.

When Sally-Anne was satisfied that Terry wasn't going to be any more of a danger to Lucy's and her own futures she made her way into the boy's changing room. She showered, at first with the shoes and cricket gloves still on to get all the blood off them and then for five more minutes she cleaned herself off, washing herself completely, getting rid of all the blood and brain tissue that had been flying around so freely shortly beforehand. Taking care to use the wet gloves she turned off the shower, dried herself down and left, rubbing the foot marks from the floor with the wet towel as she went, making her way back to the storeroom.

Dressing quickly she gathered everything she'd used, the knife, cricket gloves, shoes, shot put and towel. She wiped the floor where she'd got dressed and cleaned off the shot put, placing it with the others on the rack. She wrapped the cricket shoes and gloves in the towel and placed these in her bag, leaving unnoticed.

Someone was in for a shock the next day, but not before the knife was back in the kitchen drawer thoroughly cleaned and the cricket gloves and shoes had been placed in a dustbin outside a house four streets away, ready for collection the following day.

Sally-Anne what happened? I couldn't watch after you'd knifed him, you totally lost it. What happened, you were just going to kill him, you didn't have to get such a buzz out of it. I didn't need that amount of protection; just dead would have been fine. Stop him talking was all we needed.

Lucy, I didn't really enjoy it that much myself, I was only setting the police off on a false trail. There's no way they're going to think that anyone other than a man could do something so gruesome. They're going to be confused about that one. It made sense to do it that way.

I'm confused too, and I did feel all your excitement, you loved it, or have you forgotten? I feel what you feel and you feel what I feel, remember?

Don't get too excited, you need me don't forget. I might have been the one beating his brains to a pulp but you try convincing anybody it was me and not you. Try convincing them I exist at all. You need me, Lucy. You need me as much as I need you. You'll never get through this life on your own; together we can do anything.

Terence's Sandford's ultimate destiny had been set when Lucy had given Sally-Anne her total trust; from that point on his future had been in the hands of a guardian angel. Unfortunately for Terry, the angel in question was Sally-Anne, Lucy Kirkpatrick's guardian angel; Terry's guardian angel had been nowhere in sight that Wednesday evening. So Terry went to meet his maker a little sooner than expected, and with his virginity still in tact.

The fact that he would never have mentioned what he'd seen to anyone else was of little consequence, Sally-Anne had decided what needed to be done, there was no point Lucy arguing about it, Sally-Anne was enjoying herself too much.

Lucy realised that it was Sally-Anne alone who'd killed Terence Sandford; she'd been only a spectator, a bystander at a game. She'd watched as much as she could then let Sally-Anne carry on alone. She had wanted what was best for their future happiness so she accepted it. She didn't have to like how she'd done it but she now trusted Sally-Anne to do the right thing as far as her future was concerned, but maybe not in the right manner though.

The school had had to close the following day, the police wanted to have uninterrupted access to all areas. It appeared from gossip that was making its way quickly around the local grapevine that a complete lunatic had run amok the previous evening in school killing at least three people. This must have been what people were expecting; after all, didn't it happen in America so often now? Lucy knew better, the complete lunatic had only killed one, and he'd had it coming anyway.

Jayne had been questioned, more out of duty than anything else, the police were fairly sure that someone as petite as Jayne couldn't have caused so much damage to a persons skull. They weren't even sure that many men existed who could have caused that much damage. Whoever Terry had upset in there, he'd done a thorough job of it.

Jayne had had a cast iron alibi though; she'd been looking for a flat close to school. She'd been finding the journey from her hometown of Wigan a little too much every day. She now needed a place of her own, a place where she could entertain Lucy in privacy and safety. Renting a flat near school would kill two birds with one stone. Jayne, Lucy and Sally-Anne were all working towards the same goal; it was just Sally-Anne whose methods were becoming a little extreme.

Two weeks later with the murder slowly fading towards the backs of peoples minds Jayne moved her belongings into her new flat. The flat was only five minutes walk from school and it meant she and Lucy could pick up where they'd left off when they'd been interrupted by Terry, not that Jayne would ever know they'd been interrupted by Terry.

The very thought of setting foot in the storeroom gave her the creeps now, she could never enjoy Lucy's company again in that storeroom for thinking that poor defenceless Terry, no more than a child really at twenty seven, had being brutally murdered there. And it had all happened only feet from their favourite stack of gym mats piled up high in the corner.

With Jayne settled in her new flat and enjoying the freedom of life without her parents once again, she and Lucy were able to continue their relationship. The truth was that they took it to another level. It had never been just about sex, even at the beginning, they'd both known that, but now it was much more.

They were in love. Had Jayne known the sacrifice Terry Sandford had paid to allow that love to flourish she would have walked away from it in an instant. She didn't know though, and if she had known she might have tried to walk away but she couldn't have done that, Sally-Anne couldn't have allowed that to happen, she would have to protect Lucy somehow. Luckily for Jayne her love for Lucy was as strong as Sally-Anne's protective instinct.

Thirteen

Marie finally decided to come clean about her relationship with Simon to Lucy and John during the Christmas holidays of 2006. A year after David's death, Simon was introduced to Marie's family. She didn't come totally clean about Simon though, she said they'd known each other for a while but had started seeing each other only the previous month.

She certainly didn't mention the fact that she'd been screwing Simon at the same time David had been doing such a good job of killing himself. She thought it would be best all round if that little snippet of information was kept under wraps, buried alongside David in the grave she hadn't yet found enough time to visit in the twelve months since his death.

Christmas was a very enjoyable time for all, John and Steph had visited for a couple of days on their way to Rome for a photo shoot and a winter break. They were such a loving, happy couple. Marie saw in them what she and David had once had; it had made her wonder when it was that it had all gone wrong for them. She couldn't pinpoint a particular time or event but looking back she now felt that Lucy's arrival on the scene in 1981 could have been the turning point.

David had seemed happy at the time but she realised now that he may well have resented having to start again after seven years having done the early years with John, with the nappy changing and night-time feeding years supposedly a dim and distant fading memory. That resentment had probably been simmering beneath the surface for David in a place hidden from view; someplace even David was unaware of until it was too late. Maybe when he finally felt unburdened enough to move up the corporate ladder he found that he just couldn't handle the pressure and one day all the bad stuff in his life that he'd kept hidden was just too much.

This was the only explanation Marie could find for him to have committed suicide. It was feasible, it could have been true, and it worked for her so she filed it deep in her subconscious and carried on living her new life. Nothing could have been further from the truth but there are some situations where the truth doesn't work for everyone.

She'd been pleased with Lucy's progress. In recent months she'd been getting out of the house much more than she'd done since moving to Manchester four years earlier. She'd said she'd made some new friends and seemed so much happier than of late. Sleepovers were becoming a regular thing these days. Marie was never going to question these too closely as they afforded her the chance to have Simon stay over. She liked the opportunity to spend nights with Simon, when they were available, in her own bed. Lucy liked the opportunity to spend nights with Jayne too; a little white lie to her mum could always give her the opportunity when she felt the need.

Lucy had been to visit John and Steph on four occasions since Christmas and enjoyed every minute of her time there. She missed Jayne, but it made their reunions extra special when they had been apart for even just a few days. She also enjoyed her time with Stein; he'd come across as a replacement father figure to Lucy, someone she could talk to. He did however shock her to her core one day when he guessed her sexual preferences whilst they'd been totally alone on a shoot, dropping it into the conversation as if they'd been discussing the price of free range chicken at the local Tesco supermarket.

"But how can you know that? Nobody knows about that, I've never said anything to anyone, only Jayne knows. We've been very careful." Lucy said nervously.

"My dear girl, it takes one to know one and believe me I should know one." Stein replied.

"But Patrick, not even my mum knows…or John."

"And they won't find out from me, my dear. Don't worry on that account. But don't forget," Said Stein, "I've been around people with a different sexual taste than society accepts as, shall we say, the norm, for the biggest part of my life. It's not very difficult to spot,

Lucy. Let's face it, dearest; there have been some of the most beautiful looking young men you could wish to meet walk into these studios while you've been here. Most girls of your age would faint at the very thought of it. With you though not even a flicker of recognition on your face. But when a beautiful woman walks through the door, well that's a different matter completely, you come alive my dear, alive."

"It's that obvious?" Lucy asked.

"Oh no, it's not obvious to everyone my precious young thing, only the ones with a well-trained eye. You'll have one yourself one day soon, just you mark my words." Stein replied with a knowing smile.

Lucy was so pleased that she now had someone she could talk to about her secret life; she practically threw herself at Stein and hugged him for everything she was worth. Most women didn't get more than a peck on the cheek from Stein but he knew he'd just given her a release that she'd needed. He was so pleased for her that he hugged her back just as hard, as if she were his own daughter, not that he would ever have a daughter. That would mean having sex with a woman and there wasn't much chance of that happening, unless she'd had a sex change. He thought he might just consider that, for the experience.

"We all have demons we're carrying around, Lucy. Now you've just got one less as far as I'm concerned. I think this girl Jayne must be a very lucky young lady, very lucky indeed." Stein said.

I bet he can't tell you what other little secret you're carrying around though, Lucy. He doesn't know about me does he? Poncey little arse bandit.

Just look who is talking, little hypocrite.

Yeah well, it takes one to know one apparently, and believe me I should know one. Not only is he a man, he also gets his rocks off with other men. He's just like the rest of them only worse; he'll let you down one day, Lucy. In the words of the great man himself; just you mark my words, my precious young thing.

Stein finding out about Lucy's secret sex life changed very little in reality; if anything it just strengthened her resolve, her desire, even more. Here was a man who had obviously lived a very different and very successful life compared to the common man in the street. And that man had just told her that he could see where her very life force was based, and that it was acceptable for that life force to come from the love of another woman. Lucy couldn't believe the acceptance he'd given her. He wasn't one to quibble about Lucy's age. Love was love after all and Lucy was much more mature than most people her age. He just wished he had his life to live again. He probably wouldn't do much different, maybe see his doctor about his headaches sooner than he had.

Jayne was just waiting for her to come of age, for their relationship to be acceptable in the eyes of the law, if not necessarily the eyes of their families, friends or colleagues. At the moment she was treading a thin line between love and legality which often made her feel dizzy thinking about it.

In June of 2007 Lucy made the fifth visit that year to John and Steph. She was becoming quite proficient in front of camera and was now attracting a lot more attention from the major model agencies. Stein personally made sure that the people who needed to know about her talent knew who she was.

Stein had become totally at ease with John's ability behind the camera; he was pushing him into situations that no photographer so young had ever found themselves in before now. John was thriving on it; his name was now high on people's lists of favourite photographers, even surpassing Stein on some lists.

Stein was slowing down, going into semi-retirement, concentrating on other projects. He'd made Lucy one of his projects. Not only was he going to give the world John Kirkpatrick, a truly talented photographer, he was also going to give them Lucy Kirkpatrick, a truly talented model, both discovered and nurtured by Stein.

Marie had other things on her mind in June of 2007. She would have the house to herself for the whole week of Lucy's half term holiday. She decided however that she didn't want to spend it on her own. Simon would stay for the whole week. With Simon being a teacher he also had the same half term holiday and they would be able to indulge themselves, however they chose to, without fear of interruption. The opportunity was just too good to pass up.

Lucy rang on Saturday afternoon to tell Marie that she'd arrived safely, John had picked her up at Heathrow as usual and that they were going out that night to see a movie and have a pizza.

"Okay, Lucy. That sounds great. Me and Simon are thinking of spending a couple of days in Grasmere at the Wordsworth, we'll have a chance to do some walking, maybe even carry on up to Scotland for a couple of days in Edinburgh."

"That sounds good, mum. You have some fun." Lucy said.

"Oh we'll try our hardest. Give my love to John and Steph. I'll speak to you soon, Lucy, 'bye."

"Bye, mum." responded Lucy

Marie had no intention of going to Grasmere or Edinburgh. She hadn't been sure how Lucy would take to the thought of Simon staying the week in her house, muscling in on her territory less than six months after they'd been introduced and only just over a year since her dad had died. Marie came up with the lie to save Lucy from having to think about it. Lucy wouldn't have minded though had she known, after all she had a much bigger secret than that, several much bigger secrets than that.

Saturday evening, whilst Lucy John and Steph were tucking into a char-grilled chicken and pepperoni pizza with anchovies and extra cheese, Marie was discussing the possibility of trying out bondage with Simon for the first time in their relationship. When she showed him the leather covered wrist and ankle restraints she'd bought the previous week he was convinced that now would be as good a time as any for life to take on one more perverted little twist. He gave a silent prayer to god that he'd found this remarkable woman at the peak of her sexuality.

She'd bought a new bed shortly after David had died. Their bed had been less than a year old but try as she might she just didn't feel right sleeping in the same bed that her husband had committed suicide in. A new bed had been delivered shortly afterwards with an antique style wrought iron headboard and footboard; perfect for the kinkier couple that might feel the need to tie each other up occasionally in order to really get the blood flowing to places where normal sex just doesn't reach. This was a real bonus since she'd only bought the bed to go with her new designs for the room.

At around nine o'clock that same evening Marie was feeling the thrill, for the very first time in her life, of giving her body up to the total control of another human being. They'd agreed that rough sex would not play any part in their little game. This was to be simply a pure voluntary submission from one to the other, the ultimate act of sexual trust between two people.

Just thinking of it gave her goosebumps. Tied to the bed, legs and arms spread wide she gave herself willingly, her only stipulation was no pain, other than that he could do whatever he pleased, she'd been trembling with anticipation for days.

Simon wasn't doing such a bad job of it either. She'd had two orgasms so far and he hadn't used anything other than his hands, his tongue, and her complete lack of control. Her total submission and lack of control was as good an aphrodisiac as she'd had in a long time. This was what she yearned for, the excitement was incredible, and inside she was screaming with the pleasure of it all. Why hadn't she discovered this pleasure thirty years ago?

When Simon did finally decide that he couldn't wait any longer and the time had come to enter her, his brain just seemed to explode, he couldn't wait any longer. But this wasn't an explosion because of the ecstasy of the situation, nor was it an explosion of joy at finally entering her; this was a different explosion altogether. As soon as he'd thrust his penis deep inside her, and she'd felt the stirrings of a third orgasm not too far away, his brain had suffered the massive and fatal rupturing of a completely unseen and unknown of aneurysm.

So it was true to say that his brain did actually explode, or a small part of it did anyway, unfortunately for Simon the explosion happened just near the part of his brain that controlled his breathing function. Simon was unconscious at the time, but it wouldn't have mattered anyway, his lungs just didn't get the signal from his brain to take in another breath. Within a matter of minutes he was dead.

It is held in popular belief that people in Simon's circumstance can die instantly. If that was the way you wanted to go I'm sorry to disappoint but that wasn't the case. Simon's body took time to shut down, for his being to cease to exist. There had been no symptoms, nothing to say he was ill in any way. Nothing to say there was any reason why he shouldn't be enjoying himself in the company of the woman he'd begun to develop loving feelings for at that particular point in his life.

He'd actually died the way most people would prefer to die, not knowing anything of his imminent passing. He was just making his way through life as normal, well maybe bondage wasn't normal for most people, and going out without too much pain or suffering. No lingering, slow, drawn out death for Simon. He would, however, have chosen a different time in life, say in forty years, and a different venue, say walking in a park in summer with the flowers in full bloom and people taking picnics whilst others walk their dogs.

As it was he died playing tunes with Marie's body, as good a way to die as any you might think, some would even say the ultimate way to die. But not when the woman you're having sex with is tied to the bed by her wrists and ankles, and subsequently lying beneath nothing more than a fourteen stone slab of meat, the soul of which has just departed to prematurely meet it's maker on a totally different plain.

So what would you do? You've just come round to consciousness after having been head butted into unconsciousness by your boyfriend in his death throes. You wake to the understanding that you're tied to a bed and can't move. You've got your boyfriends body pinning you to the bed and what's more his penis is still inside you, still in the act of making love. Only you're unaware that from now on the only thing that's ever going to make his penis stiff again is rigormortis.

"Simon, wake up. What happened? This is really uncomfortable, Simon. Please wake up you're hurting me. We agreed no pain, remember?" Marie groaned.

It was only after a few minutes that Marie realised that Simon wasn't breathing. Twisting herself to look at his face on the pillow over her right shoulder she saw the paleness of his skin and it reminded her of the last time she'd woken up to see skin so pale on the pillow next to her. David had been no more or less dead then than Simon was now, but at least then she'd been able to get up and summons help.

Marie was a level-headed woman, she did what every other level-headed woman under the same circumstances would do, she cried at the death of her lover, and then she started to scream for her own life. Normally this would have worked just fine, she would obviously have been embarrassed with the circumstances of the rescue, who wouldn't? But with your dead boyfriend lay on you it's hard to get the breath to shout very loud. It also doesn't help when you live in a detached house with your nearest neighbour situated just too far away to hear. And it doesn't help when those same neighbours have just that morning flown to Italy to catch some sun with their son and daughter during the half term break.

Basically she was fucked, and after three hours of shouting and trying to break free from the restraints she was only too well aware that she was fucked. Fortunately in early June the nights are warm enough to sleep naked with only your boyfriend's body for cover, but Simon was getting colder and stiffer as time went on.

Around two o'clock in the morning she started to cry with despair at the situation. Lucy or John could ring but she knew the phone was inches out of reach on the bedside cabinet. Why had she lied about going to Grasmere? They wouldn't think anything was wrong, they'd just think she was enjoying herself with Simon. Well, Marie and Simon were inseparable now; that was one thing that couldn't be denied by anybody.

Marie woke with a start the next morning. She couldn't believe she'd been asleep with Simon's body for company. Thirst was something that followed shortly afterwards, that and the need to empty her bladder of the two bottles of wine she and Simon had shared the previous evening.

She hadn't wet the bed since she'd been four years old but now wasn't the time to worry about her dignity, if she had any chance of surviving this nightmare her dignity would have to be challenged to its limit anyway when she was discovered. She let her bladder empty onto the bed, her piss soaking into the mattress; it was the only pleasure she could get out of the situation. She promised herself that in future she would sleep alone. This was just too much, men were good for sex but if she ever got out of this she was only doing it standing up in future, beds were for sleeping in, nothing else.

Her thirst was much worse by the afternoon, shouting for help hadn't helped. The shouting had all been to no avail. The worst moment for Marie came when she couldn't stop thinking about having a long cool drink. She could see a glass of water on her bedside cabinet but couldn't reach it. She then remembered the rule of fours. It just popped into her head like an unwelcome guest at a party you just haven't got the nerve to turn away for fear of causing a scene.

Four minutes without air.
Four days without water.
Four weeks without food.

These were the times that the average person would live without the bare necessities to sustain life. She knew she was okay for air, it was bloody uncomfortable under Simon but at least she could breathe. Food wouldn't be a problem either; Lucy was due back home the following Saturday. Water was the problem, Saturday was too far away and she would need a minor miracle to be found alive before then. She wished she hadn't remembered the damned rule of fours, it put a timescale on her life and the timescale just wasn't in her favour.

It all became too much once again and the tears began to flow with the realisation that she might never see Lucy or John again. All this because she'd felt horny after watching a programme about sexual perversion late one night on channel 4 two weeks earlier. Bondage hadn't seemed such a dangerous activity then, a little unusual maybe, but it wasn't as if there was any harm in it, it wasn't going to kill you for Christ's sake.

The phone rang three times on Sunday. If it had been Lucy she thought she wouldn't ring again until Tuesday at the earliest, thinking that they'd probably gone for the two days to Grasmere. If she phoned Tuesday and didn't get an answer she'd leave it until Thursday. By Thursday she thought she would probably be dead or close to it, unless her guardian angel was watching over her and she was rescued by some miracle.

Monday afternoon at twenty past two was a particularly low point for Marie, gasping for a drink and going out of her mind her bowels remembered how to function. She shit herself, quite literally. The bedroom now had the heady aroma of one dead person and one dying person added to which was the stink of a mattress steeped in piss and covered in shit. This was not a pleasant room to end your life in.

The phone rang again on Monday and Tuesday, once in the morning and once in the evening. By the second call Marie was struggling to swallow and was feeling uncomfortably hot, she'd not pissed since the previous evening and was getting cramps in her stomach and legs. Her body was beginning to shut down.

The cramps continued through the night when she started to hallucinate, she saw David first, sat on the edge of the bed grinning at her. She had a long conversation with him during which he told her about how he'd been murdered by Lucy, how he knew that Marie herself was a lying bitch who'd been sleeping with Simon when he'd died and how he still loved her even so. He asked her why she hadn't visited him since he died. He said it wasn't a problem because she'd be joining him soon and they'd have all the time in the world then. He told her it was her time soon and he'd come back then, to help her take the trip.

Wednesday night, just after eleven o'clock, was when Marie's body finally went into shock. She died shortly afterwards and was so glad of the release when it came. More than four days after Simon's death she also went to meet her maker, still tied to the bed where they had both died very different deaths. Simon's death had been quick and relatively painless; Marie's death very slow and very painful indeed.

John had said he'd try phoning his mum again during Lucy's flight back to Manchester but made sure she'd had enough money for a taxi home if mum didn't make it on time. Lucy wasn't worried; she'd been looking forward to seeing Jayne again and hadn't been able to think of much else for the past two days.

When Marie wasn't there waiting for her she tried phoning home, got no reply then phoned John who hadn't been able to get a reply either. With this she got into a taxi and made her way home totally unaware of the unexpected treat that fate had left for her when she got there.

When she arrived home she could see Simon's car parked on the drive, she wasn't to know it hadn't been moved in a week. She also didn't realise that anything was amiss when she saw the pile of post on the floor. The thing that hit her first, and made her stop in her tracks, was the smell.

Lucy, something's not right here.

You reckon? It smells like we've got a problem with the drains. It must have happened while mum's been away and she's only just got back. Jesus what is that smell?

"Mum, are you in? What's the smell?" Lucy shouted.

No reply, perhaps they were in the garden keeping away from the stink in the house until someone showed up to sort it out. She made her way to the back of the house but she could tell the smell was coming from upstairs when she went passed the stairs, in a rush.

There's nobody in the garden, Lucy. It's time to investigate I think. Let's go see what it is that's making that God awful smell.

Okay, Sally-Anne. Let's do it.

With that Lucy climbed the stairs, gagging twice but just able to hold it down. The main bathroom was fine. The problem seemed to get worse the closer she got to her mum's room. Opening the door slowly she was hit by a stench that made her empty her guts there and then. Gaining some composure she opened the door fully to look inside and having seen what was on the bed she fainted.

She'd only been out for about fifteen seconds but what she'd seen she never wanted to see again. The air had been thick with flies and Simon's skin had seemed to be moving. His skin hadn't been moving though; it was the maggots that were moving over his flesh, and in and out of her mother's open mouth. Lucy picked herself up ran down stairs and out of the front door to throw up again, this time though she was throwing up on empty and could only manage to dry retch, down on all fours like a dog, on the front lawn.

Lucy, I'm so sorry. You should never have to see your mother in that state, I think you need to contact John; he'll know what to do. Come on let's see if the Thompsons are back from holiday yet, they'll help.

The next few hours passed in a daze. John had spoken to Lucy briefly and decided the only place for him to be now was with his sister in Manchester. The situation was going to need some sorting out; Lucy was still a minor, only turning sixteen in six months. Where would she stay, who would be her legal guardian?

These were all questions that would need answering in the next few weeks, but prior to that he needed to make his sister feel safe again, help her to get over the nightmare she'd witnessed, if anyone could ever truly get over seeing something like that.

When John arrived Lucy wasn't home, a team from the scene of crimes unit was just finishing off in Marie's bedroom, the bodies having been moved an hour ago. John was grateful he hadn't arrived any earlier.

The police had contacted a social worker and she'd been with Lucy and Jayne in Jayne's flat for the last hour trying to find out exactly what Lucy's situation was. On top of the shitty day she'd already had the social worker was suggesting she might have to stay in a care home until the situation was clear. At that point Jayne volunteered her spare bedroom; she was after all Lucy's teacher and as such a trustworthy character. When John was offered the couch the social worker had little resistance, it would be foolish to separate her from her brother in such a delicate state.

Later that evening, John told Lucy what he'd been able to gather from the scene of crime unit. It was all speculation of course until the autopsies had been carried out, but it would appear from their inspections that no crime had been committed, Simon had obviously died earlier than their mother and she'd probably been unaware of her plight, dying in a coma. The officer was trying to be kind but it was what he'd truly believed and prayed for. He was a God fearing Christian, he couldn't believe that his God would put anyone through a fate like that fully-conscious, the thought was just too much for him to take in.

So basically he killed your mum; he might not have been able to do much about it but let's chalk another one up to mankind. Every time something shitty happens who's there waiting to claim their cigar. Bastards!

That maybe so Sally-Anne, but what's going to happen now, I'm now an orphan, fifteen years old, I've got a brother who lives in London, a lover who lives in Manchester, and my school's in Manchester. We may have to move to London. There's no chance of John coming back to Manchester, his job is London based not Manchester.

We'll be okay, Lucy. Your beauty my brains, remember?

Yeah well, there's no amount of brain going to alter the fact that we're probably going to be going to school in London soon and Jayne isn't. Relationships at two hundred miles soon fizzle out, I should know, remember?

No I don't remember, I came to you later, but I've not let you down yet have I? Trust me, Lucy. London or Manchester, with Jayne or without her, we'll be okay. Things are going to be fine, I love Jayne too, or had you forgotten about that? I don't want to be in London while Jayne is 200 miles away either.

No I hadn't forgotten. But my dad killed himself eighteen months ago and my mum died having sex with her boyfriend earlier this week. I guess you'll just have to forgive me if I don't seem too enthusiastic about my future at this point in time.

That's a fair point Lucy. All that I'm saying is that you should make your own future what you want it to be. Don't let other people tell you what it's going to be. Deal with the shit and move on. We dealt with Terry Sandford and moved on didn't we? You may not have been too keen on the method but no more problems there, you can't argue with that.

At least I know I've got one friend who I can trust, you won't let me down will you?

Never will, Lucy. You can count on me.

When the autopsy results were made available it was clear that no crime had been committed and that Marie had died because of an unfortunate and quite bizarre set of circumstances.

They were first time bondage participants whose lives ended following a serious run of bad luck. The first bit of bad luck was Simon's unquestionable enthusiasm to fix Marie to the bed so well that she had little or no chance of making an escape by herself. The second being his precise moment to die of natural causes, a genetic predisposition, and the third being the unfortunate lack of family or neighbours within hearing distance.

So what we're being told is that Simon died of natural causes while he was getting his jollies with your mum, and then she died roughly four days later through dehydration, tied to the bed and with him on top, pinning her down?

That's about it.

What a way to die. Slow and very painful I guess.

Nobody heard her screaming so they think she might have been unconscious all the time. She probably knew very little about it.

But if it hadn't been for Simon your mum would still be alive today and for a long time to come most probably, she was hardly knocking on death's door asking to come in was she?

But that's not what's being said, Sally-Anne. It was just an unfortunate set of circumstances. He didn't mean to kill her; he wouldn't be too thrilled at having died himself, I imagine. Death by misadventure is how it'll be seen. Neither Simon nor mum could have seen it coming and as such prevented it.

You call it death by misadventure if you want to. He didn't need to take total control of her like that, I'd still say Simon killed her, misadventure or not.

Yeah well I'm fairly sure there's nothing I can say that's going to change your mind on that so I'm not even going to try.

Sally-Anne wasn't to know that her submission towards Simon had been totally Marie's idea. Simon had willingly gone along with the game but he'd just been there as a tool, a method of fulfilling Marie's desires, and he'd been doing such a wonderful job of it at the time.

She would have liked the idea of Marie being the one in control though; she would have laughed at the irony of it all. Sally-

Anne liked being in control herself, she knew all about submission, but not from the submissive's viewpoint though. She liked to make people submit to her, she was much more the domineering type.

You know I'm right, Lucy. I'm always right. When it comes to men they're all complete bastards, with very few, if any, exceptions.

Fourteen

John became Lucy's legal guardian, at the age of twenty-three. He was thrust into a new role, making decisions he'd thought he wouldn't have to make for a good few years yet. At twenty-three, he'd done so much in his short life already. Being a surrogate parent to his little sister was just one more thing he needed to learn fast. He'd handled most things life had thrown at him so far, and come out smelling of roses, why not one more thing?

John, being the sort of brother that he was, made no decision without talking it through fully with Lucy first to find out what she wanted, she was after all on the verge of adulthood anyway. He was happy to go with most of Lucy's wishes, when she was sixteen she could just wave goodbye, tell him to piss off, and sail away forever into the sunset if she wanted to. He didn't want that to happen so he worked with her requests when he could and made sure she understood the reasons when he couldn't. Lucy thought he was a great brother, the best brother a girl could possibly wish for.

Lucy didn't want to move from Manchester to another school in London, particularly at such a stressful period in her life. John had come to realise only recently what the move to Manchester had been like for Lucy, he'd not been there at the time and he didn't want to be the one causing that much pain again.

The real reason she didn't want to move to London yet was because she didn't want to be torn away from Jayne. She pleaded with John to be allowed to stay in Manchester, after all, she would soon be in her final year and she would be sitting her GCSE exams at the end of it. After that time, if she wanted to carry on with her education she would have to move schools anyway. Everyone felt that this was far from ideal but in an ideal world she'd have a mother and father who were still alive so that these decisions didn't need to be made by anyone else.

With the agreement of John, the social workers, the school principal, Jayne and Lucy it was decided that Lucy should stay with Jayne for the final year of her high school. It was highly irregular but seen as the best solution. A monthly payment would be made to Jayne from Lucy's estate for food, rent and such things. Jayne was to become Lucy's surrogate mother, allowing her to stay as her lover with only both their knowledge. At the end of the year Lucy would move to London, as agreed, to live with John and Steph. Sally-Anne was sure things would work themselves out satisfactorily before the end of the year, one way or another. After her GCSE exams they were free, in reality, to do what they wanted.

Lucy's estate was quite significant after her mother's death. She had the fifty thousand pounds already in trust until she was sixteen, with half the moneys from the eventual house sale, life insurance policies, investments and bank accounts she would be a fifteen year old with a fortune nudging past half a million pounds.

Nobody would say that Lucy's life was ever going to be straightforward, but at least at only fifteen years old she had wealth behind her, a brother who loved her, Jayne who was her lover, Sally-Anne her guardian angel and a promising future in the modelling business if she wanted it.

As far as Lucy and Jayne were concerned it had been a high price to pay for Marie and Simon, but it had allowed her and Jayne to be together as a proper couple, or more like an improper couple. Even though they could only be a couple behind closed doors, the safety that the situation allowed them to feel brought them even closer together, if that was possible. Their lovemaking became less frantic, they had time now to explore each other, and their loving became much more intense. Lucy was learning things from Jayne and Jayne was picking things up at the hands of Lucy and Sally-Anne, even though she didn't know it.

Sally-Anne was sure that killing Lucy's dad had been the turning point in Lucy's life, even if she didn't know it, she just needed a little help along the way. Sally-Anne wouldn't let her down.

Marie's funeral had been a quiet affair, dignified but quiet. She was laid to rest with her husband in the same grave she hadn't even found the time to visit. This was a sad time for John and Lucy, not only did they have no parents but both were aware that neither of their futures lay in Manchester.

The grave would probably be given no more respect than it had since their dad had died, in fact once Lucy moved to London it was doubtful if it would ever be visited more than a handful of times again. A sad end for them both, the move to Manchester hadn't been good in that respect, but hey, if people thought too much about the consequences of their actions they probably wouldn't do anything in life. Consequences can be a bitter pill to swallow for the people on the receiving end.

Oh well, chin up dear, life must go on. Isn't that what they always say when the bitter pill is making it's way down someone's poor unfortunate throat, gently patting them on the back at the same time to help make sure it goes down and stays down.

Fifteen

So Lucy lifted her chin up and life went on.

<u>10 December 2007</u>

Two years had passed since the phone call about a possible job change that had sealed her father's miserably short future. She was now sixteen years old, but unless you knew her well it was almost impossible to put an age to her. She'd done so much growing up over the past two years, lived the life of a much older Lucy Kirkpatrick than the one wearing her skin.

The way she held herself, the way she spoke, her confidence, her much admired physical attributes, it all said that she was a girl not quite like any other, not an ordinary girl. It hinted at a girl with a secretive side, a girl far more mature beyond her sixteen short years. She was definitely a girl that most men would love to get to know, physically for sure. Spiritually, they would think okay maybe later, but hey, they'd be thinking, give us a fair crack at the physical side first before we get too ahead of ourselves.

The problem with men is, on the whole, they just don't know a good thing when they see it, and what this means, by implication, is that they aren't the most worldly wise at spotting a bad thing either. Not that Lucy was necessarily a bad thing. Lucy was a good girl really, but if you looked into Lucy's eyes you saw Lucy staring back at you not Sally-Anne. That's where your troubles began, especially if you're the proud owner of a penis and pair of testicles and desperate to use them the way most men think that god intended them to be used. That for a lot of men would be as regular as possible and with as many different women as possible. If a man is going to make hay then you can put your house on the fact that he'll make hay while the sun shines.

John and Steph had travelled up to Manchester to surprise Lucy on her sixteenth birthday. They weren't going to miss out on her birthday, especially so soon after Marie's tragic death, she needed them and so they were only too willing to oblige. They'd been making the trip north on a regular basis since the summer to check on how things were working out for Lucy.

Lucy had been happy enough, they saw that the situation with Jayne was working well; they were more like sisters now, John thought, rather than teacher and pupil. Jayne was good for Lucy so she was never left out of anything on their visits to Manchester. That was the way Lucy wanted it to be and John did everything he could to fit in with Lucy's wishes. He knew that at sixteen he could lose her very easily, he didn't want that to happen so he was more prone to indulge her than not.

What Lucy really wanted on her sixteenth birthday was to go clubbing in Manchester, so John, Steph and Jayne obliged. It wouldn't be a problem; Lucy could pass for whatever age she wanted to. Before they hit the finest nightlife Manchester had to offer though they decided to hit the curry mile in Rusholme. John had a few things that needed to be discussed and over a curry was Steph's preferred choice of venue to do it.

The birthday party settled down at the table with their drinks.

"Well, Lucy. There aren't many sixteen year olds with a little black Versace number they can slip into for a night on the town." Jayne said.

"I know, isn't it great I feel fantastic, but I do feel just a little too dressed up for a curry though," said Lucy "The dress must have been your idea Steph, I can't believe John picked this out all by himself."

"Well Donatella helped me actually. She did mention that it's what all the beautiful, young, and extremely wealthy girls are going to be wearing this season." Steph said.

"You're kidding, right?"

"Why would we do that, Lucy?" John replied. "If Steph says Donatella Versace helped her pick out a present for you you'd better believe it, we were in Milan two weeks ago. Steph was modelling for Versace. She's known Donatella for quite some time."

"She lost her brother 10 years ago, Lucy, he was murdered on his doorstep in Miami." said Steph, "She took a long time to come to terms with that and she was very upset when I told her what had happened to your mum. She has an artistic temperament, she may only be a clothes designer to some people, but she has the ability to be very moved by life's sad realities. She thought black was an appropriate colour."

He was murdered at home too, Lucy. Just like your mum.

"Wow, Donatella Versace." Lucy was more than a little starstruck at hearing her name.

"She wanted to help me choose something for myself too when I explained to her that I was giving up modelling," Said Steph, "I did my last shoot on Thursday."

"Giving up modelling, why?" Asked Lucy, "You're so good at it, you're only thirty, you're too young just to give up, you're just at your peak; you still look fantastic."

"Well she's not just giving up modelling for no reason; the craving for onion bhajis dipped in lime pickle at four o'clock in the morning has played a big part in the decision." John said excitedly, "Why do you think we're all sat in an Indian restaurant now?"

"Because it's my birthday and I love Indian food?" Lucy replied naively.

Jayne knew what was coming but she didn't want to steal anybody's thunder so she just sat there smiling, watching Lucy's face.

"Yes we are, that's true, and it's a very special birthday." said Steph, "But we have some news to share." Steph turned to John, "Go on, John. You tell her, you've been dying to tell her since we arrived."

She's pregnant, you Dumbo.

Wow!

"You're pregnant." Exclaimed Lucy before John could get the words out, his thunder well and truly stolen after all.

"Well I'm not," said John, "Steph's the one who's pregnant, but I suppose if you wanted to you could say 'we're' pregnant, if I'm to be included in it."

"Wow!"

"That's what we think too." Steph said. "We've been dying to say something before now but we thought we'd wait until your birthday, a double celebration."

Well what do you think of that then, Lucy? Or should I say, Auntie Lucy.

It's fantastic, Sally-Anne. Auntie Lucy sounds good too.

Yeah great, let's hope it's a girl though hey, someone we can relate to.

With the good news now finally out and everybody happy, well almost everybody, the night went with a bang. Steph could now eat what she wanted without thinking of her career and so she attacked the meal with gusto, especially the onion bhaji's and lime pickle. Lucy on the other hand ate like a model in the making, she enjoyed all she ate but in much smaller portions than the others, she now wanted the sort of life that Steph was giving up more than ever. John and Jayne gave the meal what it deserved on such an occasion, they thrashed it to within an inch of its life and a good time was enjoyed by all.

Getting into a nightclub, any good nightclub, in Manchester isn't always easy. That night it was a doddle. Let's face it, how many doormen were going to turn away Stephanie Wilkins and still have a job to go to the next day? Nightclub doormen are many things, but on the whole they aren't stupid. Steph could enjoy free entrance to any nightclub being a VIP of head turning quality, and of course everyone in the party gets in free, and a table in the VIP section at whichever club they choose to grace with their presence.

Any nightclub in Manchester worth visiting would usually have a VIP section. There are lots of famous footballers, actors and musicians who carry a certain amount of kudos in Manchester on any night of the week. To have that kudos in your club allows some of the kudos to rub off. It also brings in a regular flow of stargazers; it's good for business, so long as you can keep the riffraff at a reasonable distance.

"Well it certainly has its benefits, the modelling game." Jayne said to Steph, "I've never seen people more eager to have someone in their club. They were practically drooling when you turned up."

"Don't believe it, Jayne." Steph replied. "The times I just want to be able to walk down the street without having to put on a thick coat and a woolly hat to not be recognised. The celebrity status has certainly started to outweigh all the benefits. I feel as though modelling has had my best years, I want to have kids, and I want to eat real food again. Don't get me wrong it's a fantastic way to earn money and travel the world at someone else's expense. But when I see girls who look like Lucy coming up snapping at my heels it makes me feel old at thirty, it was time to make a decision, getting pregnant just made it very easy to make."

Just at the time Jayne and Steph were discussing the modelling game Lucy was being chatted up by someone in the VIP lounge. She didn't know who he was but she was fine with it, she knew the guy, whoever he was, had no chance but he obviously thought otherwise.

What a boring tosser this guy is. Let's lose him, Lucy.

What's wrong we're only talking, it's not like he's got his hands all over me.

Give him a chance and he'll try to be there, just watch his eyes, he wouldn't need asking twice.

Sally-Anne, I think it's fair to say that very few men in this place would need asking twice. My beauty your brains remember? I can't help it if god made me look this good, and if you've got it why not use it?

The conversation soon fizzled out, he could obviously sense he was getting nowhere with Lucy. He cut the conversational tether and disappeared, there was something about her that scared him anyway, something in her eyes, he couldn't put his finger on it but his brain was telling him to back off. Matt Daniels would never know it but his senses had been on high alert that night, his defence had done him proud.

John then came over and asked her what Matt Daniels' chat up technique had been like.

"Matt who?" said Lucy

Matt who?

"Matt Daniels... Manchester united... England... Oh forget it." said John, "I've just remembered you wouldn't know who he is, you are a woman after all's said and done, you wouldn't know anything about the beautiful game. If only dad could see you now though, he'd be so proud, his daughter being chatted up by one of the Manchester United living legends."

Lucy then realised that John had called her a woman. She was no longer his little sister. She'd been chatted up by Matt Daniels, whoever he was, and she did now feel mature enough to be called a woman, in her own mind she was a woman, no longer a girl. She'd grown up on her birthday by realising her position on the ladder of womanhood. She didn't understand yet, but she'd been standing on the same rung of that very same ladder since her first shower with Jayne some eighteen months earlier.

The same thoughts struck Sally-Anne at the same time. She'd been waiting for this day. She knew she could have some fun now. Lucy was confident, she was a woman and men wanted her, grown men, not boys like most of them at school. Well they were never going to get her, but they could at least try, and then they'd have some fun, her and Lucy. Really do some damage to the collective male ego, and why not, it wasn't as if they didn't deserve it.

That night Lucy showed Jayne how much more mature she was for having reached sixteen. She took control of their lovemaking. Jayne made her own decision that night and it had been their lovemaking and talking to Steph that had made it an easy decision to make.

She was going to follow Lucy to London at the end of the school year. What they had together was too good. Being with Lucy was like taking a drug, a very strong very addictive drug, Jayne knew it was wrong to have a relationship with someone so young but she couldn't help herself, she was hooked. And she also knew she wouldn't be able to handle the withdrawal symptoms if they were ever to break up.

Sixteen

The run up to her high school exams had gone well, she'd revised as if she actually needed to pass them. She already knew she didn't need a certificate saying she'd passed so many GCSE exams, and achieved such and such grades. She'd already signed up with what was felt within the industry to be one of the best model agencies, and only weeks after her sixteenth birthday. She was already on a retainer; Stein had made sure of that, 2008 was going to be a good year for Lucy. She'd actually go on to get nine GCSE passes; mostly grade A. The future looked rosy for Lucy from whichever angle you looked at it.

The future was looking good for Georgie Dunston too. Georgie had been head boy at school, captain of the football team and an under 17's county cricket player. He was made of the right stuff, or at least that's what everyone said.

It couldn't be denied, Georgie was a good-looking boy. He was a bit of a lad too, he fancied himself with the girls and quite rightly too so he believed. He'd had more than his fair share of success. He lost his virginity at fourteen and just continued on from there. Never a steady girlfriend in Georgie's life, he liked to sow his oats far and wide, he was a very giving person was Georgie; he saw it as one of his best traits.

Sowing his oats was easy for Georgie, in more than one sense; he lived on a farm, not a big farm when you think in terms of the farms say in America. One hundred acres in America is more like a hobby, not much bigger than an allotment relative to a big farm over there, but over here on such a small, over populated island it's big enough.

Georgie was an only child; eventually the farm would be his. That would be quite some inheritance, but Georgie would never sell, he was a farmer through and through, he had farming in his blood.

A-levels next, then agricultural college, he'd then show his dad what intensive beef production was all about. He had big ideas for such a young lad, and although foot and mouth disease nearly devastated the whole of the Dunston's farm livestock a few years ago the farm had risen from the ashes of the dead livestock. So why not have big ideas, they don't cost any more than little ones.

Farming wasn't the only thing he'd had big ideas about in the summer of 2008; he'd seen Lucy Kirkpatrick as one of his, so far so young, life's major challenges. She'd been the only girl able to make him shoot both barrels into his pants at school just by looking at him, and she been fully clothed and at least fifteen feet away from him reciting poetry at the time. To give her the benefit of his cock would be a pleasure for them both. He didn't like to fail in life's little challenges; it was almost alien to him. She'd have to say yes sooner or later, and when she did he'd be there, cock at the ready, eager for some action.

What exactly was god thinking when he allowed men to reach their sexual peak some twenty or so years before women do? Georgie had his way with Susan, the neighbouring farmer's wife, last summer when both farms had combined forces for silage making. Susan was as randy as a bitch on heat all the time but she knew when Joe was bringing in the winter Barley she wasn't going to get any from him. Eating, sleeping and driving one piece of farm machinery or another was really all he was fit for at that time of year.

Susan had obviously been at her prime last summer and it was her who'd made all of the running. What exactly was Georgie supposed to do? He certainly wasn't going to turn down an offer like that. He was like most sixteen-year-old males with their lust meters set to maximum. He couldn't have said no, even if he'd had a mind to try, which he hadn't.

It had happened when they'd been alone stacking the bails in one of the barns, he couldn't even remember which barn now, both sweating with the heat of the work, both thinking that there must be something better to do on a Saturday afternoon.

Once they'd got past the awkward preliminaries, they didn't have long before they'd both be missed; his cock was barely able to touch the sides. This was a woman with one hell of a capacity for men. Having said that though she'd seemed happy enough, but he couldn't help thinking how he'd have loved to have had the pleasure when she'd been his age, and a hell of a lot tighter, and maybe carrying a little less around her waist.

The experience, enjoyable in the end, had left him disappointed, not with himself but with Susan. Surely, he thought, it just isn't right that she should let herself go like that, like some old milker down there. She'd always had a glint in her eye for him though from then on, and Georgie tried to make sure he and Susan were never left alone, especially anywhere near a barn on a summer afternoon, if it could possibly be helped.

Lucy had always seemed just out of reach to him. Uninterested would be the word most people would use if they saw them talking, but not Georgie. He could never believe she wasn't interested, and that she could just keep on blanking him at every opportunity she was given.

He was, after all, one of life's ever-eternal optimists, and he was sure it had been his optimism that had helped him into Suzie Johnson's knickers the previous month. It was well known that in a poll of all year eleven boys, she was voted second best looking girl in the entire school, teachers included. How many people could say they'd had the second best looking girl in the entire school? Chalk one up for Georgie boy. But Georgie boy might have been disappointed to find out that Suzie Johnson had a track record that made him look like a monk in comparison. There were more than a few boys who could say they'd had Suzie Johnson. Now he wanted to do the poll winner while he still could, and who wouldn't?

He thought that if he could get his leg over Suzie Johnson so easily he must at least stand a fair chance with Lucy. He only wanted her body for an afternoon of fun that was all, it wasn't like he wanted to marry her and start a family for god's sake, just a bit of fun for them both. He knew if he could crack her they'd both enjoy it, after all that was what usually happened.

Georgie also knew he was running out of time, He'd heard that Lucy was moving to London during the summer to be with her brother and that meant failure was looming on the horizon for him. It wasn't that Georgie minded failure so much, it was just that it didn't happen to him very often. Failure was just something that he thought happened to other people.

Georgie took the opportunity that he was given after the finish of the maths exam on Friday afternoon. Walking out of the exam room, with Lucy by his side, Georgie asked what Lucy had planned for the weekend.

"Not much really, more revision I suppose." Lucy replied.

"The next exam is the last one and that isn't until Wednesday of next week," said Georgie, "plenty time to revise, why don't we spend tomorrow afternoon together? I can show you round the farm where I live, I know you've never been bothered before now but it's going to be too hot to be cooped up inside revising all day and with you leaving soon we might not get another chance."

Lucy stopped to bend down and tie her shoelaces by the school entrance. Her hope was that he'd be gone when finished.

Oh Christ, Sally-Anne, here we go again. When will this loser ever learn that no really means piss off?

Why not humour him, Lucy? He'll be like a dog with two dicks. If you say yes, you can always tell Jayne you're going into town to buy her birthday present, she needn't know.

You've changed your tune all of a sudden. Thought Lucy, wouldn't what you're suggesting be against everything you've ever preached before, or believe in, he is a man after all, well nearly a man more of a boy.

Don't worry, Lucy. I know what his intentions are and he isn't going to get his grubby little fingers on your merchandise. No I'm here to guard against the likes of him, what ever he wants isn't going to happen, trust me.

So why should we go then? Pointless exercise isn't it? Let's face it, Sally-Anne; I wouldn't even like him if he were a girl.

Come on, we could really use some entertainment at the minute. Exactly why you're putting so much effort into these poxy exams when London awaits, whatever the outcome, is beyond me. Let's have some fun, say yes and we can teach him that yes, in this case, really means piss off. It's been a long time since we enjoyed ourselves, just you and me. Let's do it Lucy. Trust me, it'll be a giggle.

Do you mean the same way that Terry Sandford was a giggle? You don't need to protect me from Georgie Dunston; he's never going to cause me any problems is he?

Not like poor, simple, little Terry, no. But you need to put your own mark on this life; it's your destiny, our destiny. If this guy keeps pissing you off it's time he understood the meaning of the word no. Trust me, Lucy.

Lucy stood up again, her shoelaces firmly fastened; Georgie was still there. Nobody could ever say he wasn't persistent. A stupid bastard maybe, full of himself obviously, but persistent most definitely. It is generally thought that persistence is a good thing in one as young as Georgie, but it can also be bad, very bad, especially if the persistence comes with a lack of regard for the very real dangers that exist in Sally-Anne's world.

"So come on Lucy. What's your answer? You won't get too many offers like this when you're in London." Georgie said.

What he actually meant was that there aren't too many farms in London. Lucy thought he'd meant something else completely. "Up himself." just wasn't strong enough to describe Georgie Dunston. That made for an easy decision, she wasn't going to be patronised by a little prick like him. She had no hesitation in accepting his offer; she and Sally-Anne were going to have some fun on the farm tomorrow.

This guy is a total prick, Sally-Anne. He's completely up his own arse. You're right; I could just handle some fun just now, a day off exam revision is exactly what I need.

I'm very rarely wrong, Lucy. I've never let you down before, and I don't intend to start now. Just concentrate on that feeling, Lucy. Let it grow.

Sally-Anne had been right; a dog with two dicks had been a very apt description. It seemed like he just couldn't keep still. His only thoughts seemed to be about which one of the two dicks he was going to take his pleasure with first.

…

Georgie Peorgie pudding and pie,
Kissed the girls and made them cry.
When the girls come out to play,
It's Georgie who should run away!

...

The walk to Dunston's farm took about fifteen minutes from Jayne's flat. Georgie had been right; the weather really was too good for her to be cooped up inside all day revising. She heaved her bag over her shoulder and walked onwards, with a spring in her step and a smile on her face.

When Lucy arrived at the farm it was a very impressive farmhouse, more like a manor house looking at the size of it. Georgie was very excited. He'd looked like he was going to wet himself he was so happy to see her. He couldn't wait to tell her that she'd just missed the two farm hands, they'd just finished for the day and weren't due back until nine the following morning to help feed the cattle and take delivery of a load of feed pellets. His second piece of news was even better, he said, his mum and dad were in Northumberland for the weekend at an agricultural show and wouldn't be back until the Sunday evening.

He really was like a dog with two dicks; he'd been given the run of the place for the first time ever. He was at home on his own, with no parents to stop him doing whatever he wanted, wherever he wanted. Add to that the fact that Lucy Kirkpatrick had just shown up with a smile on her face and he was most definitely in blood pumping, erection inducing, teenage heaven. Georgie's intentions were obvious even to a blind man; it took all the willpower he could muster to stop himself from jumping her bones right there and then. Why rush he thought? He had time, lots of it. There was no need to rush what was going to be the best afternoon of his life, and Lucy's. That was Georgie's view of the situation anyway.

Georgie couldn't help thinking that Lucy was like a fly, a very beautiful fly it had to be said, and he was a spider, and how lucky can a spider be? She'd just landed on his web and was powerless to escape. He wasn't to know, however, that he was playing the part of the fly and it was Sally-Anne playing the part of the spider.

What Lucy was teasing him with would have had most grown men on their knees, let alone a seventeen-year-old. A young lad who'd been trying to get into this position for the last two years and who was now, as far as he could tell, within sight of the finishing line for completing yet another one of his life's personal challenges.

> *Run, Georgie boy, run. Like the sad loser you really are. Oh no, my fault, I forgot, you can't actually hear me can you, Georgie boy? You can't even see me can you, Georgie boy? Well never mind. That's just got to be a real pisser hasn't it, Georgie boy?*

"Well, Georgie. Are you going to show me around this farm before we start? Before we get on with the real reason we're both here today." Lucy said.

Georgie felt the blood start to flow, 'before we start', she was obviously thinking along the same lines as he was, 'the real reason we're both here today', straight to the point, what a girl! She was going to be even easier than Suzie Johnson was, and she'd been all over him in no time at all.

"Only I've brought my biology books to revise from," said Lucy, "when you said it was going to be too hot to be cooped up all day revising you were spot on, it's lovely out here though. I thought we could revise outside in the sun on such a nice day. We don't want to miss out do we? What is it they say in America? Oh yeah, we can be study buddies."

Jesus Christ, Georgie thought, this wasn't going to be as easy as she'd first given him the impression it would be. She obviously couldn't read the situation for what it was. No wonder he'd got a blank for the past two years, he was thinking to himself, she must keep her knickers in the freezer compartment overnight. Still, there's plenty of time yet, ever the optimist.

"No we shouldn't miss out, Lucy, not at all. Come on I'll show you around, before we get down to it." Georgie said, biology revision being the last thing he wanted to get down to.

Did you see his face? I didn't think it was possible to actually see that much dejection on only the one face. You're good, Lucy. You're very good.

He makes it very easy though. What a loser! Does he think I'm just going to lie down for him?

"Come on, study buddy. We don't want to waste too much time do we," Lucy said, "lots to do, especially with biology. There's a lot of biology I haven't got a clue about yet."

Yeah, thought Georgie, that's just become much less of a surprise to me than you could guess. He was still an eternal optimist though; he could give her a practical biology lesson later he thought, concentrating on the male and female organs of reproduction and how they function together. That was if she still insisted on revising for exams.

Dunston's farm was impressive, even Lucy had to admit that. This had been her first time on an actual working farm. This wasn't one of those farms that have a few livestock and barely ekes out a living on the back of school trips, weekend family visits and a shop selling sweets and toy farmyard animals. This was the real deal, an eight hundred-head intensive beef production unit. This was no game they were playing this was big business, and according to Georgie it was doing well.

It was doing well enough for them to have a top of the range New England harvester that looked as though it had just been delivered, and enough John Deere equipment to look like they'd opened a franchise right there on the farm.

But the smell, Lucy just couldn't handle the smell, seven days a week, fifty-two weeks a year; bullshit everywhere you turned. At least she now understood where the saying "hanging around like a bad smell" must have come from. She had to giggle at Georgie being linked to hanging around like a bad smell, it was more than apt. That was after all what he'd done for the previous two years; he'd hung around her like a bad smell.

Georgie Dunston hadn't been a major concern to her, no big problem, she'd coped with most of the crap at school without much of a fuss, she just blanked it out, or Sally-Anne helped her out and she got on with life. As often and as hard as she tried though, this bad smell just wouldn't take the hint and piss off.

Some people just can't take the sensible options in life, make the tough decisions; they just aren't able to realise their mistakes and leave well alone. Sally-Anne thought that now was the perfect time for Lucy to wash away the smell that was Georgie Dunston, once and for all. He'd unwittingly set up the perfect opportunity, his untrained, over active and immature libido had finally caught him out. The irony of it all was just too much for Sally-Anne, she wasn't just having a giggle now; she was splitting her sides with uncontrollable laughter.

During Lucy's tour of the farm she couldn't help but think what a dangerous place it actually was. Safety wasn't really the main issue in a place like this; competence was what counted. Incompetence coupled with that environment would be a dangerous combination. Safety would be a secondary feature in those circumstances. And here she was with Georgie, left in charge of a potential bloodbath in the making, alone with Lucy and Sally-Anne, a guardian angel with a sense of protection more than capable of producing a bloodbath in her pursuit of what she believed to be Lucy's happiness.

Run Georgie, run. Run run as fast as you can!

The plough attachments he showed her that could turn over soil at some ridiculous rate could make easy work of slicing through human flesh at the same rate. He showed her harvesting machines so powerful that they could make a man unrecognisable in mere seconds. The bailing spike attachment Georgie had shown her could kill a man effortlessly, but very painfully, and if you got him in the right place it could take hours to die. These were barely scratching the surface of possibility for harm on a farm.

*Georgie peorgie pudding and pie,
Kissed the girls and made them cry.*

Lucy despised him, hated everything about him. She hated everything she saw in those eyes, eyes that couldn't bear to be off her for too long, undressing her in his mind, a mind filled with his dirty little desires. She despised his intentions, his need for self-gratification at her expense, his total unwavering self-belief.

*When the girls come out to play,
It's Georgie who should run away!*

She weighed up her options carefully, so much choice. She felt safe with Sally-Anne there in her head; Sally-Anne wouldn't let any harm come to her, whatever she decided.

No rush, you take your time. This idiot's going nowhere so treasure the moment. We've given him plenty of opportunities to run; now it's payback time Lucy, the very best time of your life.

Lucy couldn't do it though; when it came to it her capacity to take another life just wasn't there. Lucy couldn't kill him; as much as she hated him, he'd done her no harm. He hadn't threatened her life; she despised him and everything he represented, but killing him wouldn't make her feel any better.

But it would give us a giggle, Lucy. Don't forget that.

But he's just a man with big ideas, Sally-Anne. He just wants to get his grubby little hands on me, have his bit of fun. His intentions aren't exactly honourable but he probably wouldn't harm a fly. If you see every man that wants to get his hands on me as a corpse just waiting to happen then there won't be many men left in this world soon, especially if you believe what Stein says.

You mean we've actually come here so you two can study?

It didn't set out that way and he might not like it but it's his safest option, he should be grateful that's all we're doing. And that is all we're doing, Sally-Anne. Understand?

No reply.

It appeared that Sally-Anne was sulking, sat in one corner of Lucy's mind with her bottom lip stuck out like a child who's been caught with her hand in the biscuit jar just before dinner. They'd never fallen out before, they'd had differences of opinion but Lucy had always trusted Sally-Anne in the past.

Lucy had come to Dunston's farm with every intention of ending Georgie's short life. The hatred was there, but when the crunch came she couldn't do it; it wasn't in Lucy's make up. If Sally-Anne didn't like it Sally-Anne could sulk all she wanted. Lucy was no more a killer than mother Teresa. Unfortunately Sally-Anne was no more like mother Teresa than Saddam Hussein.

Lucy didn't want to stay any longer than she had to. She didn't want to be there any more, even though she'd actually enjoyed the tour of the farm. She couldn't bear to be with Georgie; the requirement for being there had gone so she made her excuses and got the hell out of there, her sanity just about still in tact.

Chalk another one up for Georgie boy.

He might well have been self obsessed, his mind on just one thing that Saturday afternoon, but he would never know just how lucky he was to be watching Lucy walking away from his little fantasy forever. Deflated ego or not, some people are destined to benefit from the rub of the green, they're born to be fortunate, they have the luck of the Irish, others just don't have any Irish blood they can count on in a crisis.

Jayne was at a fund raising barbecue that night at the hockey club. Lucy, not really into the hockey scene, settled down to watch a video and maybe get the biology books out for one last time that day. She was all by herself, no Jayne, and definitely no sign of Sally-Anne. She didn't mind though, she was tired and not feeling very sociable anyway. The day in the sun had left her physically and emotionally drained; she'd probably just get an early night, recharge the batteries and hit the books again tomorrow.

Sally-Anne had failed to convince Lucy that Georgie's life was better off being ended for their enjoyment. Maybe Lucy wasn't beyond saviour; it was after all Sally-Anne who had the killing instinct. Lucy was beyond reproach.

...

It was Monday evenings Manchester Evening News that confirmed what Jayne had just said to Lucy about the boy from school.

Local farmer's son brutally murdered-
In his own bed

Lucy went cold.
Could it just be a coincidence?
Could one person be so unlucky to have escaped murder on the afternoon and then be brutally murdered the same evening by a different person, someone with a different motive?
Lucy's head was spinning; she couldn't believe what she'd just read. Her mind then went back to a conversation she'd had with Sally-Anne. A conversation she'd shoved to the back of her mind and forgotten about until now. It was something Sally-Anne had said before she'd murdered Terence Sandford. Sally-Anne had been particularly persuasive that day but the words she'd used were just coming back to her, she hadn't questioned the words, just filed them away neatly.

I really don't need your agreement Lucy. I just thought you were ready to face up to what we've got to do.

Sally-Anne hadn't spoken since Saturday afternoon. Lucy needed her to speak now though, she wanted to know what she'd meant when she said she didn't need her agreement. Could it be possible that Sally-Anne could act totally independently of Lucy? Lucy couldn't believe it, Sally-Anne was supposed to be her guardian angel. If Sally-Anne had just packed up and gone it meant she was on her own again, no guardian angel. Life had taken a turn for the better since Sally-Anne had come into her life, would it now all turn back to shit without her?

Sally-Anne, talk to me. What's going on?

No reply.

Since when did a guardian angel just pack up and leave without saying anything, Sally-Anne? You're there somewhere, I know you are, talk to me, you can't do this to me!
Yes I can.
I knew you'd be there. Stop acting like a spoilt child and tell me what's going on.

No reply.

Sally-Anne!

But nothing came back.

That was as much as she got out of Sally-Anne that evening but at least Lucy knew she wasn't alone. Thank God for that, Lucy knew that Sally-Anne was hard work to be with at times, but without her she wouldn't feel complete anymore.
Sally-Anne knew Lucy couldn't cope with the shit life threw in her direction without having someone there to help, she just wanted to make sure Lucy understood it was Sally-Anne she needed in her life, above anyone or anything else.

When Lucy went to bed that night she didn't sleep well, she was too warm and restless. When she did finally slip into a deep sleep Sally-Anne played back to her what had happened the previous Saturday evening when Lucy had fallen asleep on the sofa with her revision book lying on her chest.

- 119 -

Lucy dreamt that she'd woken up, stood up from the sofa, got herself ready to go out and picked up a carving knife from the kitchen. Looking at the clock she could see it was half past eight in the evening. The carving knife was slipped into her coat and she was through the door into a hot, quiet evening carrying the coat; it's only purpose to hide the knife. She felt good about the knife, it made her feel safe in her dream, she knew no harm would come to her even though no one had ever been attacked, really attacked, in a dream.

The walk had been the same one she'd taken to Dunston's farm the two days previously. This time though she was being especially careful to hide her presence from other people she might otherwise have passed; jumping through hedges to hide when she sensed people approaching, waiting until the coast was clear before resuming her journey.

Lucy felt somehow detached, as if it wasn't her walking along the road, as if she was being given the privilege of observer rather than actually being there. She could see though that the person in the dream was herself, no mistaking it to be anybody other than her detached self.

When she arrived in her dream at the entrance to Dunston's farm it seemed only right that she would turn right and walk up the long driveway towards the farmhouse, out of view of the road and all other prying eyes.

At this point in the dream Lucy began to feel uneasy, she didn't know if this was a dream of her own making or if Sally-Anne was there pushing all the buttons. No matter who was in control of this dream, she had a good idea what the outcome was going to be, and she hoped above all else that a dream was all that was happening.

She approached the farmhouse door and knocked. Georgie answered after only a short time and was confused to see her. Sally-Anne didn't like that look, Lucy was aware of that; she'd seen what Sally-Anne could do to a face that looked at her like that.

"Hi, Georgie, It's only me again. You were right; it's time we got physical with each other, we may not get this opportunity again. That is unless you've got anyone else in there with you."

Lucy knew that Sally-Anne's 'opportunity' and Georgie's 'opportunity' were completely different things. Georgie wasn't to know that the person suggesting that they should get down to it was anyone other than his number one fantasy girl. Lucy knew right away though that she hadn't spoken those words. She was fairly sure at this stage in her "dream" that at some time on last Saturday evening those words had been spoken, but not by anyone Georgie Dunston wanted to get physical with. No man alive would want to get physical in the way Sally-Anne was about to get physical.

She watched the rest of the dream as she'd been made to, not because she particularly wanted to, she didn't have much choice in the matter.

The dream culminated with Georgie, whose body she actually thought might have been worth getting to know a little better had it not been dead, losing his penis. Terry Sandford had lost his penis to Sally-Anne too, but at least she'd only thrown that to one side as if it was discarded because it was of no use to any body. Georgie's penis ended up being pushed up high inside his arse, and Lucy knew exactly why Sally-Anne had felt the need to play out this final insult on poor Georgie.

Georgie peorgie, pudding and pie,
Kissed the girls and made them cry,
Georgie's life was one big farce,
Now Georgie's prick is up his arse.

The newspaper had been correct about one thing; Georgie Dunston had been brutally murdered in his own bed. Lucy knew at least one fact that the newspaper didn't disclose though, and that was because the police wouldn't let information like that out to the reporters. But Lucy knew. She was well aware that Georgie still had his penis when he died; she also knew he only had it because it had been stuffed up his arse for safe keeping.

Lucy realised in her sleep that she couldn't live without Sally-Anne. She probably could live without her in reality but she came to understand that she was never going to be given that opportunity. Sally-Anne was all powerful and it was only in Lucy's best interest to play along. How could Lucy explain to anybody what she had living in her head? At best she'd be seen as unstable at worst a complete murdering basket case.

Lucy woke up late in the middle of the night sweating; it was as if she didn't want to face reality, but face it she did.

You said he was up his own arse, Lucy. I only made sure the rest of his family knew too.

No reply.

Come on now, Lucy. You must admit it; life can be quite a giggle if you want it to be.

No reply.

Have it your way, but remember this sweetheart, I really don't need your agreement Lucy. I just thought you were ready to face up to what we've got to do. I was wrong, so I had to take things out of your hands.

Lucy knew this now but she wasn't going to give Sally-Anne the satisfaction of admitting it. She stayed silent, and settled down again to try and get some sleep, she wanted to forget what she'd just dreamed of, but the visions of Georgie pleading for his life wouldn't go away. Sleep was going to be very difficult that night.

You do trust me don't you, Lucy? One way or the other, it doesn't really make an awful lot of difference to me. But it might make your life a lot easier if you do.

Trust me, Lucy. I'm right on this one.

TRUST ME!

Seventeen

Wednesday was Jayne's birthday, twenty-six years old and life felt good. It was about to feel much better though. Breakfast was usually a rushed affair on a school day in the Parkinson / Kirkpatrick household, not today though. Today was a special day, Lucy slipped out of their bed early, she never did manage get back to sleep, breakfast was prepared and she returned with a tray just as Jayne's alarm clock made its presence felt.

Hot croissants, Strawberries and cream, bucks fizz and coffee, better than a quick piece of toast just before leaving in a mad panic, their usual breakfast fare. There was also a birthday card on the tray which Lucy insisted be opened before anything else was even considered.

"I couldn't think what to get for your birthday so I hope you'll like this." Said Lucy, picking up what looked like a birthday card and handing it to Jayne.

"I'm sure whatever it is I'll be more than happy with it," replied Jayne, "after all we know each others minds very well, I know I'll like it."

She doesn't know your mind as well as she thinks she does, Lucy? But I think we can forgive her that, after all she's very good in bed, what do you say, Lucy?

No reply.

Jayne was more than a little intrigued though, sitting on the bed in just her skin. There weren't any bottles of perfume or antique silver necklaces that could fit inside a birthday card. These had been the things she'd been dropping hints about for the last month whenever they'd been out shopping together, hints she'd hoped Lucy would tune into. She wasn't disappointed, but how could Lucy have missed such blatant unspoken requests?

With the card now out of its envelope she could feel that there was something else in there too when another envelope fell out of the birthday card landing on the bed between them.

"This is exciting," said Jayne, "the suspense is killing me. Don't you just love birthdays?"

"Not all of them, but I'm liking this one so far, come on Jayne, open it and see what it is. I hope you'll like it."

"Okay okay, here goes."

Jayne opened the envelope like a child on Christmas morning, there was no finesse about it, and she was more than a little confused when she found air tickets for the British Airways shuttle to London. To be more accurate, an air ticket, singular, Manchester to Heathrow, open ended.

"It's an expensive present to buy someone for a birthday present, Lucy. I'm sure I'll love it," said Jayne, "but I'm a little confused, can you help me out a little?"

"Well," said Lucy a little nervously, "I've no choice in the matter. If I want to be a model I need to be in London. If you wanted to be with me though, permanently, you could use that ticket. It's only one way though, I've torn the return ticket up, no turning back, and that goes for both of us."

"You really can read my mind, this is what I really wanted all along but I couldn't bring myself to say anything because I didn't want to hear you say no. This is the best present I've ever had, the very best." Jayne now close to tears hugged Lucy as if her life depended on it and at that point they both burst into floods of tears. Not tears of sadness, that couldn't have been further from the truth, they'd both never felt so happy in their lives.

After a short while Lucy, wiping the tears away, reached under the bed and brought out another package. "I've got you these too, just in case you didn't like the first one."

An antique silver necklace that looked like it could have been made specifically to go round Jayne's very pretty delicate neck and a bottle of her favourite perfume. Life couldn't get much better as far as Jayne was concerned. Kissing Lucy passionately on the lips she decided that school could handle her absence for half an hour at least, she owed it to Lucy to show how appreciative she was.

So Jayne showed Lucy exactly how appreciative she was, and Lucy showed her own appreciation back at the same time. By the time they'd finished appreciating each other the croissants and coffee were cold, but lying back on their dishevelled bed, they enjoyed the strawberries and cream and bucks fizz just the same. Claudine had taught Jayne a few things about cream during a skiing trip once, she did enjoy cream, not just the taste of it; the feel of it on her skin was what she enjoyed most.

And who was it that brought us three together, Lucy? Don't tell me you've forgotten that. When have I ever let you down?

No reply

Don't keep blanking me, Lucy. You know you can't hurt me. If you try you'll be the only one who ends up getting hurt.

Some guardian angel you are! A big sister but with added menaces, is that how this thing works now?

That's not how I meant it, Lucy. You know I wouldn't hurt you. You'll just end up hurting yourself. Trust me. But at least you're talking to me now.

Trust is a two-way thing, Sally-Anne. It appears that I have no choice in the matter!

You're not still going on about Georgie Peorgie are you? Move on, Lucy. Get over it, it was just a giggle and he really did deserve it... Trust me.

When Jayne did eventually reach school she wasted no time in trawling the Internet sites, educational papers and anything else she could get her hands on that might lead to a job as a PE teacher in or around Central London.

Having been given the opportunity to move south with Lucy she was going to embrace it with both arms and everything else she had, no turning back for either of them.

Eighteen

Lucy's new life began at three o'clock on Thursday 28th June, when the exam invigilator asked everyone sitting the biology exam to stop writing, put down their pens and please remain seated while all the exam papers were collected. That was to be the last thing Lucy did as a schoolgirl.

She didn't celebrate with her classmates. Even though Georgie's murder was to put a bit of a dampener on proceedings, the last exam had come and gone and they were going to enjoy themselves. Some of the boys couldn't help expressing their joy in the types of celebrations that often follow the last exam of the last high-school year. Some tore up shirts and ripped the arms off their blazers while others were much quieter, looking inwards at how much they'd matured once they'd been allowed to leave the school hall after the last piece of work had been collected.

There were tears, as you'd expect, mostly from the girls, some were for Georgie Dunston, and some were for the sudden realisation that a big part of their own life had just passed them by, and like Georgie, they could never have it back, no matter how hard they tried. Most wouldn't understand that yet; that type of understanding only comes with experience for most, when they look back and realise those years really were the best years of their lives.

The first thing Lucy did was to find a phone and ring John. Steph had gone into labour very early that morning, she was still two weeks early but it seemed that just as Lucy's new life was about to begin so was the life of her niece. Lucy was so excited, with school already fading into a dim and distant past she picked up the receiver and called John's mobile.

John had been in the hospital canteen taking a breather while he could and had just turned his mobile on to check for any messages when the phone rang.

"Hi, Lucy, finished your exams?"

"Forget exams, what's happening there?" Lucy said impatiently. "Am I an auntie yet or not?"

"I wish you were," replied John, "Steph's been in labour for over twelve hours now and no sign of an heir apparent just yet."

"Don't worry, John. These things take time, so they tell me. How's Steph bearing up?"

"I've seen her looking better," said John, but then everyone knew twelve hours into labour wasn't the time to re-apply your make-up just in case the paparazzi are waiting outside. "They're actually giving her an epidural at this very moment to deaden the pain. They're telling me we'll be parents before the evening is out."

Promise me you won't let a man, any man, cause us so much pain just by using his sweaty little dick. No forget that, you just stay irresistible to women, I'll take care of the men.

"Good, keep me informed, John." said Lucy. "As soon as I'm an auntie I want to know, okay?" it wasn't really a question, more of a threat to John if he kept her waiting any longer than was absolutely necessary. "And the exam went very well thanks, now go back to Steph big brother, or I'll poke your eyes out when I see you next."

"Okay okay I hear you, I'm going, little sister. I'll speak to you soon… hopefully."

"Give my love to Steph, and tell her to keep pushing," said Lucy, "that little niece of mine is going to be just fine, trust me."

Lucy had sounded so sure that his soon to be firstborn was going to be a girl. John didn't know how though, not even he and Steph knew that. The opportunity had been there but they didn't feel the need to know, a healthy child was all they wanted, girl or boy it didn't really matter to them. It had probably just been wishful thinking on Lucy's part, like wanting the sister she'd never had.

She's going to be a beautiful baby when she's born Lucy, let's face it, beauty plays a big part on both sides of her family.

At eighteen minutes past nine that evening Lucy got the call, John had just stepped out of the delivery room to make the call. Rosie Marie Wilkins Kirkpatrick had come into this world at four minutes past nine, a healthy six pounds seven ounce baby with powerful lungs if the noise she was making was anything to go by.

John and Steph both felt that she was the most beautiful thing they'd ever seen, but then they should, she was their first born.

Lucy couldn't believe how good life had just become when she took the call. Apart from the Georgie Dunston incident she was really happy. There wasn't much she could do to alter Georgie's fifteen minutes of fame.

It seemed that now was as good a point as any to move onto the next stage of her life. Before she could do that though she needed to see John and Steph to explain to them that the next stage of her life would be spent living with Jayne in a loving relationship and not living with them as she'd agreed twelve months earlier. And any way, she could now see that three's a family, four's a crowd. She was also desperate to meet Rosie, her new niece.

The following Saturday morning, two days after Rosie's birth Jayne's Vauxhall Astra pulled into John and Steph's driveway and parked up behind John's 1962 Aston Martin DB4.

John's love of classic British sportscars had come from Stein, "If you're going to turn up anywhere by car, make sure you do it in style. You won't go far wrong buying British, nothing less than twenty five years old or it's barely broken in." Stein would say.

Stein had owned plenty of cars over the years, most of them worthy of a grand entrance. Of late he restricted himself to two of his all-time favourites, he owned a 1959 Jaguar XK150 fixed head coupe for everyday use, and for special occasions he would bring out the Rolls Royce Silver Cloud, a two tone, two tonne lump of motoring history. A car that the spirit of ecstasy could have been made for, a car fit for a queen. This last point had attracted Stein to it in the first place; he thought it was quite appropriate under the circumstances. It tickled him to think that a member of the royal household wasn't the only queen being driven around London in a Silver Cloud.

Stein's first British sports car had been a 1967 Triumph TR4 bought new and thrashed to within an inch of its life, it was well past ever being driven on the road again, he just couldn't bear to see it go. He'd knocked the restoration idea on the head shortly after being told about the cancer. He knew he didn't have the time or the energy to get into a project so big. The Triumph would meet its maker at the same time as Stein, it was written into his will. It could never be said that Patrick Stein didn't have a true sense for history and drama.

Steph drove a twelve month old Porsche 911 Turbo, bought new, German engineering at its finest. John and Stein thought she was a philistine when it came to cars.

Jayne felt a bit intimidated in her four-year-old Vauxhall Astra diesel, nice enough car as it was she just couldn't see herself turning heads in it. Lucy thought Jayne could turn heads driving anything, and she was probably right.

John and Stein both thought most women were philistines when it came to cars. They'd both made it their profession to photograph things of beauty, why shouldn't they surround themselves in a thing of beauty every time they put the key in the ignition? They believed most women would never understand this guttural urge, so they didn't get into an argument they knew they could never win. After all, women buy clothes, men buy cars. In John and Stein's world they cost roughly the same anyway, so who's counting?

"I hope you know what you're doing, Lucy." Said Jayne, sat in the car, unwilling to go any further at that particular moment. She'd been dreading Lucy's 'confession' to John since they'd set out at six o'clock that morning.

"Don't worry, Jayne. I know what I'm doing." Replied Lucy with confidence, "John only wants what's best for me, and you're what's best for me. I know how to handle my brother, he'll be okay. Trust me."

You do trust us don't you, Jayne?

"I do trust you, Lucy. I just don't think John's ever going to trust me again after you've dropped your little bombshell in his lap, that's all." said Jayne. "After all is said and done, he trusted me to look after you in Manchester and now he's going to find out what's really been going on, he'll probably throw me out of the house and I wouldn't blame him."

"There's no denying you looked after me though," laughed Lucy, "taught me everything you know, took care of all my needs. Wasn't that what you were supposed to do? Come on let's see this niece of mine, check out the family gene pool of the future."

With that they both got out of the car just as the front door opened to show mum, dad and daughter Rosie waiting patiently. Not exactly your average family, when you looked at who they were, but as John was going to find out shortly that same day, very few families are average, especially when you're brother to a person such as Lucy.

"Oh wow, look at those chubby little arms and cute baby feet." Lucy had never held a baby before, never been so close to another human being that was so dependant on her. That is unless you counted her dad, Terry Sandford and Georgie Dunston. They'd all been totally dependant on her; they just hadn't known it at the time.

"I know," said Steph "I could just put her feet in my mouth and suck on them for hours, they're so cute."

"Not if she's inherited John's feet you wouldn't." said Lucy.

"Oh well, I see Jayne's not been able to cure you of that dreadful sense of humour then." said John turning towards Jayne "I was hoping you might at least have done that while you've had the chance, Jayne."

Jayne uncharacteristically blushed, not a good sight in most red heads, no matter how beautiful they might be.

"She'll have plenty of opportunity in the future, John." said Lucy, "Jayne's moving down to London when she changes job."

"Great," said John, "but teachers are always complaining about the cost of housing compared to wages down here though Jayne, It's not the cheapest place to live London, make sure it pays well."

"She'll be okay on that front, John. She's coming to live with Me." said Lucy, "we'll rent a flat."

"I thought you were going to stay here with us," said John, "for a year or so anyway, until you find your feet."

"Find my feet in what sense?" said Lucy, "Financially? I've got more money than most people dream of, remember, the same amount of money that you got left."

"Yeah I remember, Lucy. I'm not likely to ever forget." John said trying desperately not to raise his voice and just about managing.

"One bedroom flats are cheaper than two," replied Lucy, hoping that a light would suddenly come on in John's head and he'd realise what she was trying to tell him without actually having to say it outright. "We won't need more than one bedroom; we haven't for a while now."

The light did come on in John's head, he realised what she'd been trying to tell him. Steph had just had her suspicions confirmed, suspicions she'd held for a couple of months but hadn't mentioned to John, thinking she might have just been "experimenting" as girls Lucy's age sometimes do.

You've dropped the bomb, now run to a safe area and watch it go boom.

I don't need to, Sally-Anne. I know my brother better than you do. It's time for you to trust me.

John got up out of his chair, said nothing and made his way out of the room, his face expressionless. Jayne was speechless, not because of John but because of Lucy. She'd seen her opportunity and jumped on it; no subtle "John can I have a quick word alone" like she'd expected, it was the full on we're here so you're going to hear this now or never approach.

It didn't take too long before John re-entered the room, Jayne couldn't bring herself to look at him. She knew it would be her he'd be aiming his fury at now, and rightly so.

"I was saving this for later, we were going to wet Rosie's head with it, but we've got something else to celebrate first." Said John turning to look at Lucy, "I'm not mum or dad, Lucy. I never will be, your life's your own and if you're happy I'm happy. I felt like I was turning into a bad parent for a minute back there and I never want to be anything more than a brother to you, that's enough for me. Okay?"

"That's all I could ever wish for." replied Lucy just as the cork popped out of the bottle of Krug and the champagne began to flow.

I'll never fail to be surprised by your brother, are you sure he didn't start off life as your sister?

He's all man, Sally-Anne. You just need to trust me when I say I know him better than you do. Not all men are the lowlife pond scum that you think they are.

Okay, just the majority. He must have been a woman in a previous life then. I can't think of any other reason for it, there's definitely some woman in there somewhere.

The relief on Jayne's face was palpable; she wasn't being thrown out of his house like she'd thought she would be; she was being firmly welcomed into it.

Life was picking up its pace for Lucy, but at least she had the backing of her brother, the only real family she had. No more fibbing to John when she needed to hide a relationship, not regarding Jayne anyway. Sally-Anne was a different prospect altogether, she'd never lied about Sally-Anne before, she didn't need to, nobody knew Sally-Anne existed apart from Lucy. And if she did tell John about her 'guardian angel' what would he think of his little sisters state of mind?

Least said soonest mended.

On the Sunday morning John took the opportunity to drive Lucy and Jayne to some areas where they might consider renting a flat, the sort of locations with excellent access to the underground system. Owning a car in London wasn't necessarily a good thing, the DB4 was nice to look at and Lucy and Jayne were enjoying the experience but parking could be a bitch in the capital city, and Lucy couldn't drive yet, she wasn't even old enough to take a lesson yet.

In the afternoon Stein glided up the driveway in his Silver Cloud, this was after all a special occasion. Everyone thought he'd come to pay Rosie a visit, and in part that was true; his main reason for visiting John and Steph that afternoon though was to visit Lucy, and the fact that Jayne was also there made the visit so much more of a pleasure and less of the chore it might otherwise have been.

He'd heard so much about Jayne since the day he'd guessed Lucy's sexuality nearly twelve months earlier, he was dying to finally meet her in person. After he'd spent a politely long enough time congratulating Steph for looking so fantastic on only her fifth day 'out of prison' and cooing over Rosie he was able to give some attention to his 'big girls.' John and Steph didn't mind this, they knew he wasn't a baby type of person; if he couldn't hold an intelligent conversation with the person in his company he became bored very quickly. These days conversation was all he could manage. He was becoming more tired. The cancer was certainly making him slow down. He had never realised the value of his health like he did now.

Lucy enjoyed her time with Stein, she could talk freely, confide in him, and the female side of his persona enjoyed being Lucy's confidante.

He doesn't know everything about you though does he Lucy?

Some things are best kept secret.

"Patrick, come and sit between us so we can talk, we've got lots to talk about." Said Lucy, "and I want to introduce you to Jayne properly. By the way John's been showing us where we might rent a flat, me and Jayne, together."

"So the cat's out of the bag is it?" whispered Stein, Lucy nodded with a big grin on her face, "I can't tell you how thrilled I am for you both, at last."

"Yes, at last, I don't think I could have managed without our little chats, you've been like a surrogate father to me Patrick, thank you, you big old fruit." Lucy then gave Stein a kiss on the cheek and a big hug.

"Something I missed?" said John.

"Not at all, dear boy." said Stein, "It's just us three ladies having a girlie moment."

Turning to Jayne, Stein ran his professional eyes over her face feeling not the slightest bit tempted to rush because of any embarrassment Jayne might be feeling. "Jayne, my dear, you're everything I expected and more, you could certainly straighten out a few of my friends in no time. Let me tell you, I've been in the company of many beautiful women and your face is up there with the best."

When she was able to overcome her initial embarrassment, he was after all far more full-on than anyone she'd ever met before; they got on like a house on fire. Stein's feminine side always put women at ease in these situations, what a pity for them he'd been gay; when he was younger he must have been every woman's dream man.

Just as he was leaving Stein had a thought about accommodation for "his girls." He'd have to check it out first but he thought it was probably an ideal situation just so long as John agreed, he didn't want to cut John out of the decision making process on this one. No more secrets, life was too short for secrets and keeping Lucy's sexual preference from John for the past twelve months had been hard enough, he didn't want to put himself in a position where he could lose John's trust. He'd discuss this one with him first, if it was a non-starter Lucy need never know.

Nineteen

John turned up at the studio mid morning on Monday; it had only been five days since Rosie was born but he was loyal to Stein, he owed him that much and more.

"John, you needn't have come in today," said Stein, "there are other people here apart from you and me you know. I thought we'd discussed this already. "

"Steph wanted me out of her way to be honest, too much fussing. She says it's not good for Rosie." replied John. "To be honest I think she just wants some time alone with her."

"Ah well, who can see what's going on in a woman's mind? Certainly not I dear boy. But while you're here I've got something to show you," said Stein. "The thought struck me that I could solve Lucy and Jayne's flat hunting nightmare before it even begins, come on follow me."

John was intrigued, the thought of his little sister in the big bad world had been disturbing him since she'd left with Jayne to go back North the previous evening. It wasn't that he didn't trust Lucy; it was all the low life scumbags that London seemed to attract by the thousands he didn't trust.

"Stein studios has been at this address for twenty years now, I don't own it I lease it, from a friend of mine shall we say." said Stein, "I've just signed the lease for the next ten years, this friend has more money than he could ever spend in ten lifetimes so I get a very favourable rate, always handy to know the right people. Anyway where was I? Oh yes, the studio, I lease it all you see, three floors and a basement of which the studio takes up two floors and two thirds of the basement was darkroom before the digital age and the rest storage as you're aware. The building is far too big for what I need but I've been too lazy to sub-let the top floor. It would need some work doing to it but come and see for yourself, tell me what you think."

When Stein unlocked the door to the top floor John could see just how much work would need doing.

"What exactly was this place before it became Stein studios?" John enquired, able to anticipate Stein's reply but just wanting it to be confirmed anyway.

"A club, surely you can see that, a club for the more sensitive members of society, people who liked to be dominated and to whom a little humiliation was an everyday pleasure." said stein, "In its heyday this was a little goldmine, it ruined some politicians and Judges along the way I can tell you."

The cage in the corner of one room, the butcher's hooks hanging from the ceiling, the two beds with rubber sheets and the fine array of manacles and whips on the wall, all now covered in many layers of dust, they'd been a bit of a giveaway really.

"So how come you know it was such a goldmine, Stein?" asked John jokingly. "Don't tell me you owned this place when it was whatever it was back in those days."

"It was called 'the humble pie' to the club members and I was only part owner, it was more of a business proposition than a personal pleasure, my sexual tastes have never included humiliation. You know where my sexual preferences lay, John. Being caged up, whipped and given the golden shower were never the type of activities that captured my imagination for too long. But like I said, it was a little goldmine, the landlord used to spend more in the club than we gave him every month in rent for the building, so I could have no complaints."

John had to laugh to himself; he'd not been expecting that answer, Stein part owner of a domination club. Well it takes all sorts, but it did strike him that shafting another mans arse had to be a sexually violent act in itself and more than a little humiliating for the person on the receiving end. He'd never tell Stein that though.

"So what do you think, John? It could be a splendid apartment."

John had just had the same thought. It would also mean Lucy could be in close contact with either himself or Stein on a regular basis. The more he thought about it the more he liked it.

"It's certainly got a lot of potential, and I like the location." said John.

"Good I'll speak to a friend, get some plans together take it from there," said Stein, "shall you tell her or can I?"

"It's your idea, be my guest. I just want to see how quickly she'll be back to look at this place and tell you how she wants it, you know what she's like."

"My dear boy, I could kiss you." replied Stein.

Only if I'm pissed thought John, he liked Stein, owed him a lot, but he was never going to kiss him. He'd seen how Stein kissed men before and it wasn't for him, no thanks. Tonsil hockey is a game best played between man and woman; woman to woman was just about acceptable, and he'd have to get used to that now anyway, now that Lucy was picking her partners from the same team sheet.

Lucy and Jayne were back in London by the following Friday evening. With the end of school year quickly approaching Jayne had applied for three possible teaching vacancies in the area and had interviews lined up on Monday and Tuesday of the following week for all three positions. Like John had said, teachers did complain about having to live in London on the wages, it seemed getting an interview for a teaching position in London was easy, and living in London was going to be easy too according to Stein.

Stein met them at the studio at ten o'clock on Saturday morning. John had told them that the building had once been a club and that the top floor hadn't been touched in twenty years. He didn't tell them what type of club it had been; he wanted to see their faces when they walked into their potential new apartment.

The look was one of awe and amazement and finally realization.

Wow, Lucy. Look at this place. We'll take it as it is; cage, hooks and all.

Isn't all this stuff about controlling people, just like when mum died?

No way, this is nothing like that it's completely different; this is about you. This is about how you should be in control. This is about protecting yourself when shit happens. It's about you and me, Lucy. People came here because they knew what they wanted, they needed to be controlled. In this life you can be controlled or controller, the choice is yours. I'm only here to help, to guard you and keep you safe.

"This place is huge," said Jayne, more to herself than to anybody in particular, a little embarrassed to ask the obvious questions like 'what the fuck is this place?' and 'how much did it cost to be a member?'

"Yes it is," said Stein, "the studio has the two floors below which are the same size as this and that's more than enough space for us. I'd almost forgotten about this floor, it was the place to be if your tastes were a little different than usual shall we say. This floor was what was known as the punishment zone."

"You used to come here, Patrick?" asked Lucy not really too surprised having spoken to him about his love life often enough.

"Not exactly, my dear. It was more of a business venture, a retreat for the better off clientele who found pleasure in humiliation. We had over six hundred members in the club's heyday. I heard it said once that area for area it was probably one of the highest earning clubs in the city."

"I say we keep the cage Jayne, just as a memento of its former glory, what do you say?" said Lucy laughing.

Good idea, Lucy. Cages can be a giggle, just so long as you're not the one trapped on the inside. Let's keep the cage.

I was only joking; the cage goes, along with the hooks the chains and that red rubber floor.

Rubber is very easy on the knees you know and red such a lovely colour; and if you fall on your arse in here you bounce right back up again, it's going to be your loss if it goes.

Stein was excited by the prospect of making the top floor into an apartment. The cost could actually be relatively small, the building was sound and the main work would be room partitions a bathroom, toilet and kitchen. Stein knew a friend of a friend who could fix the place up at minimal cost and since the buildings lease was already being paid by Stein Studio's Ltd the cost to 'his girls' would be peppercorn. Stein loved Lucy; he wanted to give her something while he was still around to do so.

By the following Tuesday afternoon Jayne had the choice of two teaching posts and had been told she'd come very close on the third. The trip back to Manchester that evening had been less of a chore than usual as life started to take shape nicely. With only two more weeks to the end of Jayne's school term Lucy decided to stay in London and become better acquainted with her own future career.
Visits to the modelling agency to update her portfolio were done, all in the company of Stein, and agreement reached that she would become available from September. Steph had told her how busy she'd probably be when she jumped on the modelling merry-go-round so she wanted to enjoy her freedom while she still could.

Within one week Stein had people working on the upper floor. He'd been right when he'd said it was handy to know the right people, he'd also known that in a city where money is king it also helped to have the cash to flash. Stein had plenty of cash and a project he wanted finishing, quickly. He'd consulted with Lucy on one or two things but as far as he was concerned John and Steph had Rosie but this was his baby, and he was going to enjoy himself. Lucy could have the keys when it was finished and he hoped she'd enjoy it. If he'd ever had a daughter of his own he would have wanted to do just the same for her. In a way he was compensating for the child his lifestyle had never allowed and the life the wretched tumour he was carrying would prematurely bring to an end very soon.
By mid September the money spent on the apartment would have bought Jayne's parents semi-detached house in Aldershot twice over. Stein could have bought a very nice house anywhere in the country several times over in cash before his bank manager would have even raised an eyebrow. The cash spent on the apartment was a drop in the ocean to Stein and he knew anyway that where he was going to end up there was no need for it.
A three bedroom, two-bathroom 3000 square foot apartment with an Italian kitchen and bathrooms was not what anyone had expected when Stein had started out on this project, anyone except

Stein that is. Stein was not a person to settle for second best, he didn't think Lucy and Jayne should have to either.

They finally saw the apartment for the first time after Stein had spent some time fixing everything just how he wanted it, getting all the little details just so. This is something that most women are very good at, but at which they genuinely lag behind when compared to a truly gay man.

The apartment was stunning and Stein knew it, very modern and he was so pleased with what he'd created he believed he'd missed his real vocation in life. Stein was good, with a truly artistic knack for getting things correct, no question there. Had he, however, been asked to design an apartment for two sixteen stone bricklayers from Bolton he would have always been well wide of the mark, even if he'd been given the rest of eternity to work on it. An apartment for two girls of a certain sexual persuasion, now that was like trying to turn on a light switch in the dead of night, he could do it blindfolded.

"Wow, Patrick. Look at this place!" said Lucy, "It's fantastic. How did you do it so quickly?"

"It's mostly superficial really, new kitchen, bathrooms, some electrical work and then get the decorators in," replied Stein waving his hand around as if to dismiss the achievement as anything other than adequate. "I really enjoyed myself picking out the furniture, and the rest, as they say, is history my dear."

"Patrick, you must have spent a fortune," said Jayne, "just on the furniture alone."

"A mere trifling amount relative to the joy I've had seeing your faces when you walked in. Do you really like it? Stein asked."

"I think it's fantastic," said Jayne.

"Make that two, Patrick. We love it." Lucy jumped in.

Make that three, Patrick you soppy old tart.

Stop it, Sally-Anne.

No I mean it; the place is just like my idea of heaven. Now ask him what he's done with the cage and all the other fun stuff.

"Apparently it was the devil's own job to get the 'voyeur's cage' and the iron bedsteads into the basement, the market for that type of 'specialist equipment', shall we call it, is bigger than ever." said Stein, "I'm sure I've got some friends who might like it as a special present, a memento maybe. After all, it was the best stuff money could buy at the time, better than the local police cells for keeping people in their place."

"Look at the bed, it's the biggest I've ever seen" said Jayne.

"I've seen bigger, much bigger, but not for a long time" said Stein, "Orgy beds, you can't get them anywhere these days. Do you like what I've done with the lighting above the bed though?"

The lighting in the main bedroom was a genuine one-off. The finest mood-lighting system on offer in Paris, strung between three gilded butchers hooks. The bedroom lighting wouldn't have looked out of place in the Tate modern gallery. Stein remembered the price he'd paid to have the hooks installed so many years ago, a small fortune with all the reinforcement needed to the roof beams. He wasn't just going to rip them out, and the final effect was very pleasing.

Stein showed them where everything was and some of the vagaries of the kitchen before pulling out a bottle of Bollinger from the fridge.

"I'll just have a quick glass of the fizzy to welcome you in then I'll be on my way, I'm sure you girls will want to 'christen' the place by yourselves soon anyway," said Stein, "and I wont stay and spoil your fun, maybe a different lifetime and who knows what fun we could have had together?"

It was true, they were dying to christen the place as Stein had put it, and the bed was easily big enough to lose themselves in, they'd never had the advantage of such a vastly oversized bed before with the finest Egyptian cotton linen, they were itching to give it a try. But first though they had to try the double size bath. Stein was truly a wonderful man, he'd thought of everything a girl could need. He was like a dad, only better. Maybe he was more of an elderly uncle. But definitely not the type who'd try to walk in on you when you were getting undressed, acting all innocent and apologising at the same time as copping an eye-full. Lucy felt safe in his company; he was truly one of the girls.

Lucy and Jayne were both busy during what remained of 2008.

Jayne was finding her feet at her new school and had finally faced up to the fact that her international hockey career was going nowhere. Being on the fringe of the England squad was okay as a temporary state of affairs but she'd been on the fringe for far too long now and had seen other girls leapfrog her from what appeared to be mediocrity straight into a first team place. She'd just enjoy her hockey at club level from now on; one rising celebrity in a relationship was plenty.

Lucy's celebrity, however, was definitely on the rise. Judging by the amount of work she was being requested for. Her face and body fitted precisely the image that designers wanted their names to be associated with.

The lifestyle wasn't always as glamorous as she'd expected, and some of the cutting remarks doing the circuit didn't help while she was a newcomer, a novice just starting out. It was pure jealousy that started the rumour that she was Stein's love child and only days after that the remark that she was 'Our Child of the Immaculate Conception' was also doing the rounds, the first child to come into this world who could walk on water, or so it seemed. Steph had been right when she said it was a bitchy world Lucy now lived in. People who thought they knew her thought she must be too busy and maybe too naïve to hit back, but she was enjoying herself too much and she had broad shoulders; shoulders built in Aldershot but toughened in Manchester and reinforced by her fair share of misfortune.

Sally-Anne wasn't too bothered. That amount of jealousy showed just how well Lucy was respected by the people whose opinion really counted. She couldn't help but laugh though the first time she heard the Immaculate Conception comment. It just went to show how people were so ill-informed; she wondered how the religious authorities got away with some of the crap they spouted at times. Immaculate Conception! Surely everybody should realise that Mary had been well and truly caught out in that age-old fashion. And when a woman is cornered like that she says the first thing to come into her head.

Let's face it, if Mary was your daughter and she said she was pregnant and still a virgin would you really believe her?

...I didn't think so.

And what if she said she'd been screwed by the very Devil himself?

...

Whenever their busy schedules allowed it Lucy and Jayne would baby sit Rosie, even if it was just to give John and Steph a quiet night in to themselves. Shitty nappies and baby sick on her shoulder, it was all worth it to be with her niece. She really was a beautiful baby, even though it hadn't looked too promising for the first couple of weeks.

Twenty

Some of the things that life throws your way can sometimes be pleasant; you accept them and with a smile and carry on. These things don't necessarily change the course of your life. They're just the good things that sometimes happen. They are sometimes a good marker as to whether you're generally lucky in life or not.

Some of the things that life throws your way can be really shitty, but even these, for the most part, you can accept and carry on with life, waiting for the good things to come along again.

Lucy had had lots of good and bad in her life. For the greater part the people that mattered the most to her loved her unconditionally. Her father had supposedly killed himself, but then he was the bastard who wrenched her away from her previously happy life. In the overall scheme of things he'd been no real loss to her. Her mother had died in unpleasant circumstances, but they'd said at the time she didn't suffer too much and it was purely accidental. Not a thing easy to accept but then at the same time there was a lot of good happening at that point in her life too, Jayne for one thing along with John and Steph and Stein. She came to accept it, after all Simon couldn't have known what was about to happen; he had no real choice in the outcome.

She'd been witness to two murders, Terry Sandford and Georgie Dunston. Terry had to die according to Sally-Anne. She'd said she was only protecting her that time, ensuring that life with Jayne could continue. Sally-Anne had convinced her that the world was no worse a place for Terry's loss, convinced her he'd been no great loss to mankind. Georgie was a different matter altogether, he hadn't needed to die but then again Sally-Anne was only protecting Lucy from the sort of shit life had to throw in her direction; nothing too specific with Georgie, just life's shit, and she was very good at that. Sally-Anne could deflect most things that came Lucy's way if she needed to, the shit that originated from men especially, and Lucy thought Sally-Anne was right about most things; she was after all her 'guardian angel.'

Sometimes though, usually just as life gives you the impression that everything is just fine and dandy things happen which make the whole of your world shake to its very core; these things can have no benefit to your life; they have the destructive effect of an earthquake and begin to tear at what, for some, can already be an unsteady grip on reality.

Unless you're the one being affected you won't feel the earth shaking, you won't necessarily see a life tearing itself apart. At such times the people affected sometimes pray to god, any god, for a guiding hand to help them through, maybe a guardian angel to see them safely to the other side. Luckily for Lucy she didn't need to ask any god for assistance, she had the benefit of Sally-Anne her very own guardian angel. Sally-Anne wouldn't let her down, she trusted Sally-Anne.

The first of Lucy's 'earthquakes' struck in the late summer of 2009, just when things were fine and dandy, and everything in the garden was rosy.

...

One thing Stein could be sure of after four years of inactivity was that the Triumph engine wouldn't be inactive for much longer, not once he'd pulled on his overalls and got to work. The faithful 2.1 litre Vanguard based four-cylinder engine that sat under the sculpted bonnet of his TR4 might not have the finesse of a modern engine but it had been built in an era when things were built to last, a time when tinkering with your car was an hobby that had lately been negated by engine management systems. In Stein's mind engine management systems should come as an option, like air conditioning or alloy wheels, it was a case of technology gone crazy, a modern day disease. Stein was no technophobe; he just didn't like losing the ability to choose, something that was happening all too often for him as time went on.

The engine was never going to let him down; he knew he just needed to stroke it back into life. It was the bodywork that had forced this car off the road and Stein's experience told him only too well that when the body starts letting you down you don't look as good as you used to. It's very easy to become a disgruntled motorist, especially when you're as fastidious as Stein.

Stein's mind had started to let him down. He'd seen what brain cancer could do to him. He'd wanted to know what he could expect from life when he'd been discussing his future with his consultant. He had a good idea of what to look out for. When he looked at a car he had a good idea of whether a particular problem was going to be terminal or not, whether or not he'd get another year out of it. In Stein's eyes you could only go on driving a car for so long before it fell apart in front of your eyes unless you treated it with care, gave it the respect it deserved.

Stein had a real sense of history, an unflappable desire to do things right, to do things in style. That was why the TR4 had to run, he wasn't taking it for a last drive, a relived thrill on the roads of his younger days, but it had to run, he was absolutely certain of that.

After an hour tinkering under the bonnet he was pleased with how she sounded, he'd had no doubt that when he'd bought the car he'd been living the best days of his life. The sound of the engine when he pulled on the throttle cable having just cleaned out the carbs and set them up to his liking reopened a memory bank he hadn't taken a withdrawal from in many a year.

Those memories were good but the feelings they stirred were ones of sadness, and the feelings were complete and unshakable. He'd tried many times in the recent past to convince himself of his immortality, the thing people always feel about themselves when they're still in the prime of life. But the feeling of inevitability was too strong now.

He'd been finding it harder to stay focussed on life of late. He knew what the next month or two would entail. He'd seen it before in one or two friends not to know what was happening. His body was letting him down, and no amount of drugs, drugs which had thus far worked so well at coping, could work forever against a disease which would ultimately claim him if he allowed it.

For Stein this really was a living nightmare, he felt like he was now on death row but the phone could ring all it wanted, he knew there was no Governors reprieve coming his way, it was far too late for anything like that.

The car was washed and polished and looked good enough to go out in for a spin along some country lanes. Stein knew though that most of the rotten metal was out of sight, a rotten chassis you could poke your finger through in places and bodywork fixings that would never make it past even the shoddiest of MOT inspectors.

Stein could see the irony of working on his beloved car; he was just a person rotting away working on his rotting car. Stein also looked well enough on the outside, he even scrubbed up fairly well, for now, all of his cancer was out of sight but if someone were to give him a close inspection, started poking in the wrong places, he knew he'd be condemned to the scrap heap in an instant. A car could be left to rot for several years and still be brought back to production line condition; unfortunately mankind begins the process of dying as soon as they emerge from the comfort of the womb and there really is no going back.

With only a few more adjustments and alterations to Stein's precise specifications the ignition key was hung on the hook and the garage light switched off. Stein went to shower and change, happy with what he'd achieved in just one afternoon's tinkering; the young men of today's world just didn't know what they were missing, driving their ultra-safe, ultra-boring 'euro boxes.'

Stein entered the garage again after his personal tinkering time. He looked like a man with tickets to the opera, a man who could afford his very own personal box. He was carrying a book that he intended spending some time with, escaping from the realities of life, if only for a short time at least, remembering the freedom he'd once had earlier in life.

Taking the keys to the TR4 he got himself seated in the familiar leather surroundings of his old friend. Turning the keys the engine caught first time and a smile of satisfaction settled on his face, he'd known his old friend wouldn't let him down; there were at least some things in life you could count on.

He'd managed only half of the first page of the book when the fumes made it difficult for him to carry on. At least he'd made the effort, closing the book he settled down to let the carbon monoxide do its job. It was very efficient; taking full advantage of the fact that haemoglobin is over two hundred times more likely to attract carbon monoxide than oxygen when given a choice between the two.

Strange is the unlikely attraction between one thing and anything that has a natural capacity to ensure that thing its ultimate destruction. But then again, looking around maybe it's not so strange; it's just like the need to shoot a drug into your vein for the temporary high it affords or maybe even as simple as smoking a cigarette to help calm the nerves. Both have the capacity for death yet some people can't live without them.

Stein went out in style. The double exhaust pipes, one on each side of the car, had caused him an initial problem, but once he'd overcome that it was a single entry insulated pipe via the plastic rear screen of the soft-top car, sealing any gaps with a mastic gun. The car could have had articles written about it in the motoring press, it was such an 'effective conversion of a classic two seater in British racing green.'

The engine had died after barely fifteen minutes; Stein had made sure there was the barest minimum of fuel in the tank, just enough. He wasn't discovered until mid afternoon of the following day, looking healthier than he'd looked in a good while, but then Stein had wanted to look good. Just like Cleopatra prior to her own death Stein had put a lot of thought into how he was going to look in death. He'd known that the colour of his blood would be much brighter because of the carbon monoxide resulting in him looking in the pink; some would even say the best he'd looked in years. Stein was very particular, even in death.

Reading a signed first edition copy of Arthur Ransome's classic novel, 'Swallows and Amazons' was also Steins idea of style. His parents had presented him with it on his tenth birthday and it was still one of his most treasured possessions. He'd had a real sense of history; he'd wanted to do what was only right and befitting. When he was found the next day the book was open at Chapter 1, 'The Peak In Darien', as if he'd put it there to read during his next journey. The book had been carefully placed on the passenger seat next to the note explaining why he'd done what he'd felt was necessary to maintain some semblance of dignity, and his last will and testament. A neat little adventure story finally brought to a close, motive, opportunity, and evidence.

If he'd had the foresight to understand what a devastating effect his actions would have on Lucy he would have probably taken the slow, lingering, painful way out and bugger the expense. But then foresight is a truly wonderful thing, a thing few of us if any are blessed with.

Stein's will was a simple enough matter considering the wealth he'd been able to accumulate during the long years at the top of his profession. June, his younger sister, was his only family and as such she inherited the greater part of his wealth and his home. He had however made provision for Stein studios to continue under the hands of his 'capable assistant and worthy successor' John.

John had ceased being Stein's assistant many months before and was now the real heart and soul of the business, the building was leased and still had a good few years to run before the company would need to renew it but all the equipment was bought and paid for.

The will made provision for John to inherit all the stock and take over the business and 'do with it as he sees fitting.' This gave John complete control of a successful business in which he himself now had his own celebrity status. He'd believed this would happen one day; he had after all been groomed for it from a very early age, he just hadn't wanted it to happen so soon. John also inherited the Silver Cloud with the proviso that Stein's ashes be stowed in the voluminous boot and taken for a drive at least twice a month. Stein knew his man well enough to know that John wouldn't have a problem with this request. It was typical of Stein, and John did after all love the Cloud, Stein had taught him well.

Stein stipulated that Lucy would have the apartment rent-free for as long as John could ensure the building was in his control. Stein knew John would do anything he could for Lucy, and if a little proviso such as Lucy's comfort were to help ensure the future of Stein Studios then so be it. Lucy was to also become owner of his much-cherished 1959 Jaguar XK150. As Stein explained in his will, the XK150 was a thing of exceptional beauty; it deserved an owner with an equally exceptional beauty. Lucy had earned her right to drive the car only three months earlier, but she didn't think she'd ever be able to drive one of Stein's cars; she felt he'd let her down, in the worst possible way.

I told you he'd let you down, Lucy. All men let you down eventually. They can never be trusted to do things correctly in the end.

I thought he was a good friend, Sally-Anne. More like a dad than the real thing ever was. I thought he was somebody I could trust, who'd be there when I needed him, I thought he understood me, really understood me and I thought I understood him. Apparently I was wrong, again.

There aren't too many people who really understand you, Lucy. Otherwise they wouldn't keep letting you down. I'll never let you down, Lucy. You know that don't you?

It's people that disappoint me most in life, when you think you know someone, really know them; they just disappoint you, no 'sorry Lucy'. Who cares a fuck about Lucy? Nobody, that's who cares about Lucy!

That's overstating it a bit, Lucy. I care, you can always trust me, and I won't ever let you down. Men, Lucy, it's always men who really let you down. Your dad for one, Simon for another and now the biggest taker, steals your trust and abandons you when the going gets tough. Oh he leaves you with 'possessions' but that's not what you need. You can trust Jayne, you can trust me, and now you have to start trusting yourself, do what your head tells you, not just your heart.

Stein's funeral had been a grand affair; all instructions even down to the flowers he wanted on his coffin and the hymns to be sung were as per Stein's instructions. The whole of the industry turned out or so it seemed, some people would never baulk at the opportunity of making it onto the ten o'clock news, no matter what the circumstances. Along with these lower level creatures Stein would have been pleased to see some faces from the past, faces John had believed would never want to make it onto that evening's news broadcast, along with a couple of what people would call 'minor' royals.

Stein's circle of friends had been large and far-reaching, and to John, in many cases, most surprising. The worlds of fashion, photography, gangsters, politicians and royalty all turned out to mourn Stein's death under the one roof. Maybe not in the least bit surprising when you knew Stein, but then there were few people who got close enough to Stein to really know him.

There was however one person missing from his wish list, and that would have made Stein weep into his bloody Mary if he'd been watching from his hallowed perch on high. Lucy wasn't there. She'd been unable to forgive him for his last living act, an act Lucy saw as one of pure selfishness. She'd thought she'd known him. Now she'd come to realise that whoever she knew, in one way or another, would probably let her down at some stage in her life. Trust was something to treasure, it was in short supply as far as Lucy was concerned.

Men had let her down since she was eleven years old, men who were supposedly close to her. Stein had died because of a disease in his head, not directly the disease but because of what the disease had made him do. Eventually the diseased mind had been all powerful. If Lucy had thought about this too much she may have seen the irony in his situation compared to hers. She didn't think about it at all though.

It seemed that the only man in her life who hadn't let her down so far was John; in her mind this was now just another fuck up waiting to happen. Lucy had the world at her feet; she was becoming a household name at just eighteen years of age but what people couldn't see was how bitter she was inside. With a lifestyle like hers what could she possibly be bitter about?

Sally-Anne knew the answer. Sally-Anne was after all inside Lucy's head, advising and making suggestions as to how she should live her life. Lucy trusted Sally-Anne; she'd never let her down before.

Twenty-One

The mind, it could be said, is like a corridor, a long corridor with many doors off it. No two corridors are ever the same. Some people are destined to have more doors in their corridor than others. Some, such as Terence Sandford are born with few doors and have even fewer opportunities in life to build any more. Behind each door is one of life's opportunities, maybe a desire, a dream maybe a particularly good memory or a particularly bad one.

During our lives we open these doors when we're made to, or when we want to, sometimes when we need to. On other occasions the doors just open by themselves, when you least expect it, and you can't help but see what's behind them.

When Rosie was born she was the inspiration to build many doors in John and Steph's minds, she had been building them since the day they'd found out Steph was pregnant. She had also closed a few, but on the whole both John and Steph were richer for the experience. Both of their corridors had been lengthened and the new doors were made of some of the best quality, richest and most inviting wood they'd ever seen.

Doors in the minds corridor are generally unlocked; you are free to wonder in and out at will. Sometimes the corridors are very long and there are doors you haven't opened in many years, but that's not to say that the opportunity, memory, desire doesn't still exist. Maybe your legs just aren't as fit as they were in the past and maybe you've even forgotten some doors ever existed.

When certain doors become hard to enter we start to lock off these doors and enter doors that are easier to go through. A problem occurs, however, when we have to pass the locked off doors every time we want to open a 'good' door, we can still see the locks and we know the door has things behind it we'd rather not see.

One thing is certain in life though, the more doors you have in your corridor the better off you are, and the fewer of those doors with a big ugly padlock on the outside the better.

Lucy's corridor was quite a long one considering her age, but she had too many padlocks in her corridor for someone so young, far too many. Sally-Anne was also behind one of the first doors Lucy came to on her particular corridor and Sally-Anne's door was always open. Well almost always, she could restrict access when it suited her purpose.

Sally-Anne was also free to wander the corridor in Lucy's mind, oiling some door hinges and continually pouring water on others, and even on occasion taking a big sledgehammer to some of those padlocks, when it suited her purpose.

Sally-Anne had also built another door next to the one she herself was behind; this door was padded on the inside and had a straight jacket hanging from a rusty nail. She used this door very rarely but should the occasion merit it the door was ready and waiting and she had one of the biggest, most ugly looking 'fuck-off' padlocks you've ever seen, ready and waiting for when the occasion merited it. Sally-Anne had made this door one of her first priorities following her introduction to Lucy, in 2004, outside a school in Manchester when Lucy was struggling with the unfortunate Gemma.

A day filled with much relief for Lucy. It really was pissing down in Manchester that day. Poor Gemma, she really didn't know what hit her.

...

After Steins suicide Lucy had felt the need to find some happy doors to look behind, and as with most toddlers it was clear that Rosie was a fine carpenter when it came to doors. She worked with only the finest materials and tools. Everybody who knew Rosie was gifted with at least one happy door to look behind when times were a little tough.

The modelling was good. A models life isn't all glamour and to reach the top of the trade is like anything, it is very hard work. When you saw what Lucy was earning you'd have to say modelling was very good. If you'd been gifted with the look designers were looking for they were prepared to lay money down for you to walk on. Lucy had the look.

The bitchiness was still present in her life, just like it had been since the age of thirteen. Much of the recent bitchiness coming from Stein's Legacy of grooming, his desire to assist Lucy become the model that in reality she was always going to be anyway. Other, lesser models don't take kindly to 'special treatment' in the very competitive world they live in. Just as in every walk of life though there has to be a fair share of mediocrity, it's the nature of the beast, if you don't have mediocrity how do you know when someone's truly good?

Lucy just couldn't see beyond the manner in which Stein had died. Most people had seen it as typically Stein, and he was even praised in some circles for 'not letting himself down'. It was said by many that he'd stayed true to himself and, oh yes, boy did he look good in the chapel of rest when people came to pay their last respects. Wherever Stein was watching from for those three days he would have been tickled pink to hear the comments being made.

He may well have not let himself down but he'd certainly let Lucy down, and at an age where you can't appreciate any death staged to look good.

Rosie was the distraction that allowed Lucy to place a less than stable padlock on that door. But even so the bitterness never fully went away, because to reach that happy door she always had to pass by several padlocked doors on the way. Sally-Anne could always open doors, padlocks or no padlocks. A little gentle persuasion with the sledgehammer works every time, and let's face it, Lucy's mind wasn't built like a bank vault, her weak points were well known.

With Sally-Anne to guide her though life though Lucy appeared to the outside world like she could take on anything thrown at her and beat it. Most people weren't looking at her mind; if her mind had been lodged between her breasts then they may well have had a good look. But it still would have been low on a list showing the order of things they noticed about her, having just met her for the first time.

Twenty-Two

Keith Waterson wouldn't forget Christmas Eve 2010 in a hurry; one that brought with it his first six figure bonus. For Keith that was a clear sign that he'd finally made his mark on the City's financial merry-go-round.

Keith hadn't been educated at Eton or Harrow like an awful lot of his colleagues; he didn't have the necessary qualifications to be part of the old school network, but even so, there was nobody who could accuse him of not being good. He was better than good, after the last twelve months people were calling him 'golden dick'. Everything he touched seemed to turn to gold and since the majority of his colleagues thought he was a wanker anyway the name just stuck.

Keith didn't mind the nickname. He'd known from the start that his life in the city wasn't going to be one of permanently open doors and shared memories of a particular housemaster. He'd had to work hard to get to where he now was. His local high school hadn't had housemasters; in some places it barely had a roof to keep the rain out.

His lowly beginnings hadn't hindered Keith too much, he'd had a focus when it came to money, and he understood its true value. That was why he was driving a four-year-old Range Rover whilst most of his colleagues changed their cars every twelve months. They would never dream of buying a car unless it only had delivery mileage on the clock and was most probably German or Italian in origin, British built vehicles were a definite no.

Keith liked to look down on other motorists from his lofty leather seated driving position. He took the tube into the office most days but at the weekend he would pull his trusty workhorse onto London's roads and cruise around the country's Capital. During these drives he would meet his friends for a drink, maybe a meal and of course drive to Stamford Bridge, home to his beloved Chelsea

Football Club, where he hadn't missed a home game in nearly two seasons.

Keith loved going to Chelsea, he enjoyed the football but he saw Stamford Bridge as a place where he could let his cloak of respectability drop for a short while and let his life's frustrations dissipate. Unfortunately for the visiting fans he would usually let his frustrations show via his fists and his feet or those of his so called friends.

Keith was part of the new breed of football hooligan, fighting was now being orchestrated by highly respected professionals out to satisfy their own needs for violence and thuggery. He was one of the highest-ranking members of an army where opposing armies would gather all over the country every week to fight battles. Battles that were so called in the name of football.

If you passed him in the street you'd think that by the way he dressed and held himself that his hobbies were probably brass rubbing and train spotting, probably of the diesel variety. Just like everything in life though, just because a dog doesn't appear to have much of a bark it doesn't necessarily mean it won't bite your leg off, given half a chance…

Christmas Eve of 2010 saw Lucy and Jayne packing overnight bags and Christmas presents, ninety percent of which had Rosie's name on them, into the limited available space of the XK150. The car had become Jayne's. Lucy didn't like the car, there was too much of Stein in it, but Lucy had seen Jayne fall in love with it the first time she'd seen it.

Lucy's mood was as good as it had been for some time. The sun was shining for the first time in what seemed like months, but even so, the temperature was a long way from anything that could be remotely thought of as warm. As they were waiting for the XK150 heater to warm up before setting off though, they were both eagerly anticipating their first Christmas spent together with Rosie. John and Steph would play a part in proceedings too, but waking up on Christmas morning to watch Rosie unwrap her presents had been the inspiration for the relatively short trip to John and Steph's, and the reason for them both spending the next few days there, following Rosie's ever so formal crayoned request.

For Rosie, now two years old, this would be her first truly exciting Christmas. It would be a Christmas where she could understand a little of the fuss being made, and be the centre of the attentions of all her favourite people in the whole world. And those same people all under the same roof. She was probably looking forward to this almost as much as her two aunties. Not to be outdone, Rosie had even wrapped up her own presents, with the very least amount of assistance possible, and placed them carefully beneath the tree.

Chelsea hadn't played since 12th December when they had drawn 1-1 at Tottenham Hotspur. A hard fought local derby but outside the ground the away team had won the battle. A difficult thing to put a score to, hooliganism, but going by opposing fans hospitalised, the Chelsea fans had won four-nil. An excellent result as far as Keith was concerned and one that made time spent organising a battle army for the Arsenal game on the 27th well worthwhile.

It was the Arsenal 'away day' organisation and planning meeting that saw Keith Waterson climbing into his Range Rover to head off towards a pub within throwing distance of Stamford Bridge. The meeting with three of his, so called, Generals would be to discuss battle tactics. Christmas time matches were usually well over subscribed by away fans, and could there be a better way to get rid of those Christmas day frustrations than causing havoc at Arsenal? If you were to ask Keith Waterson the answer would probably be no. The only thing that might beat it for Keith would be an England international. Fans that had battled each other all season coming together to join forces to take on a bunch of foreigners! Even hooligans feel pride in representing their country.

At thirty-two years of age Keith still lived with his mother. A sad state of affairs for any thirty-two year old man, but then Keith was a man's man. He liked to have his meals cooked and his clothes washed and ironed by someone who wasn't looking for commitment.

Physically and mentally he had little to offer any sensible woman but he had enough money to his name, especially with his latest bonus. Keith had many frustrations in his life. His sexual frustrations were taken out on the prostitutes he visited regularly. Otherwise his frustrations were taken out dictating events on the Chelsea battlefield.

Today would be a good day, he'd get the boys motivated for the Arsenal game first then he'd spend some of his hard earned bonus buying an hour of Vickie's time, maybe even two hours if he was feeling up to it.

Driving down Fulham Road Keith's good mood made the decision an easy one; he was definitely up for the second hour with Vickie, maybe the whole afternoon. He reached into his jacket for his mobile phone. Scrolling through his directory for Vickie's number his concentration was momentarily broken. A moment was all it took though.

Keith Waterson's car, veering from its previous straight line, because of his inattention, was like a missile aimed directly at the bus stop. The people innocently standing at the bus stop, waiting for the number twelve, a bus that should have been there five minutes earlier, were supremely fortunate though. Keith noticed them just in time. He was able to wrench his steering wheel and miss wiping them all out by a fraction of a second.

Fortune favoured seven very lucky people that day, the oncoming car wasn't so lucky though. If you'd been watching events unfold from a position of safety you would have been surprised at how like a guided missile a car can move when it's travelling at speed. In that short instant in time Rosie's Christmas was ruined, her presents would stay under the tree unopened, forgotten about. It wasn't going to be the best Christmas Lucy had ever had either.

A 1959 Jaguar XK150 fixed head coupe wouldn't score high on any modern day safety test. Safety wasn't as big an issue in the motor trade of 1959 as it is today. If you're unfortunate to be involved in a car-to-car accident though, a Range Rovers isn't a bad car to be driving. Let's face it the Royal family and police forces all over Britain have been using them for years, and for good reason.

When it comes to potential for damage however, a Range Rover is a real beast. With their height, weight and power they're a modern day battering ram, the perfect vehicle for all budding ram-raiders to cut their teeth on. Keith Waterson liked his car, it suited his image.

Heritage doesn't in any form equate to safety. The XK150 was a mess. The brunt of the force had been taken on the driver's side; with no air bags to deploy, unlike in the Range Rover. The only things available to cushion Jayne's head had been glass, steel, the polished wooden dashboard and eventually Lucy's lap.

The people crowding around the car following the accident were reminiscent of the paparazzi in the Paris tunnel where Princess Diana's life was ended; stunned silence was the general reaction. When they found their voices again they would have to say that Lucy was the most fortunate of the two people in the car. They didn't recognise who Lucy was at that stage. Recognition would come later when they saw her photographs in the national newspapers and on TV. They could be forgiven for not recognising her though. She wasn't exactly looking her best with Jayne's head sat in her lap.

Jayne's pain was short, sharp and quickly over. Lucy's pain wasn't ever going to pass quickly. Looking down at Jayne's face in her lap, her flowing red hair tinged with blood and her eyes wide open looking directly into her own, Lucy already knew her lover was dead. Lucy was no paramedic but she did know that having your head very nearly disconnected from the rest of what was once a beautifully slender neck would usually have that effect on a person, no matter how much you wished it was otherwise.

The full realisation kicked in quickly and this was shortly followed with Lucy screaming her way into the oblivion of a safety zone. The same place that people often go to when faced with a shocking trauma such as Lucy had just witnessed.

Fortunately, for most people they will never witness anything bad enough to require their whole system to cart itself off to the padded cell and lock the door from the inside; to simply power down and switch itself into stand-by mode. But then as with everything in life there are many varying degrees of fortune.

Let's face it, if you were to ask anyone alive today who was born into a pre Second World War Hitler ruled Germany what life was like for them growing up, most people would probably say it could have been a lot worse, a hell of a lot worse. Ask the ones who were born to Jewish parents and you'll get a different answer. They'll be capable of telling you about trauma and fortune, but you may not relish hearing the story they have to tell.

Man's inhumanity towards its fellow man continues and will always continue, probably until man has caused its own extinction. Some of the world's most powerful leaders seem intent to ensure its continuance. But then the problem with the world's leaders, these people we place on a pedestal and put all our trust in, is that they are just like you and me. They're no super heroes; they're only human, just as fallible as the rest of us. And who knows what paths the voices in their heads, their 'guardian angels', are advising them to take, all in the name of world peace?

One of these days it's going to happen, trust me. One brain, two minds, one big red button, BOOM! Chain reaction time. Perpetual motion at it's most destructive.

And by the way, Superman doesn't really exist. When the bombs start flying there won't be anybody from the planet Krypton to save our sorry little asses. Flash Gordon, 'saviour of the universe', he won't be there either. Super heroes are the figments of some very talented imaginations. World leaders of dubious character who have access to the big red buttons of the world are unfortunately very real.

How good is the 'intelligence' used regarding the whereabouts of the world's so-called 'weapons of mass destruction'? Not very good, it's been proven, but our leaders ask us to trust their intelligence. And for the most part we do. They ask us to trust every word they tell us, and accept it as fact. And for the most part we do. But do we really ever get the choice not to? Do we really have any intelligence at all?

All that Sally-Anne asks of Lucy is her trust. Sound familiar?

When evil sets out to find a mate it searches out potential for harm and vulnerability. When people are at their most vulnerable they want to be able to place their trust somewhere, anywhere. At that point they are potentially at their most dangerous and at the same time in the most danger.

Twenty-Three

Lucy missed Christmas day that year. When you're in an intensive care ward, heavily sedated and in total ignorance, days tend to pass by quietly. Not only did she miss Christmas day, she missed the rest of that year and most of January 2011.

Lying in a sterile world where she was safe Lucy had locked herself away from the outside world. She'd place the straight jacket on immediately and sat in a small corner of her mind, sucking her thumb. Lucy's only company was Sally-Anne. The modelling world and the British public held their breaths and at the same time crossed their fingers.

It would be said by most people that Keith Waterson was a very lucky man. Too lucky most would say if they knew the man. He'd walked away from the crash without a scratch. Physically he was no worse off than he'd been minutes before the crash. In his own mind he knew though that he and he alone had been the cause of Jayne Parkinson's death.

The police also knew he'd been the cause of Jayne Parkinson's death. What could they do though? He'd been stone cold sober when they breathalysed him. Even though he was about to use his mobile phone the police couldn't do anything about it, he hadn't even been speeding. Driving without due care and attention was the most the police could expect to prosecute him with. The loss of one life, another traumatised beyond a full recovery; and what would Keith Waterson's penalty be? Probably something that wouldn't be a major burden to him, when and if it ever came to court.

Yes, most people would say Keith Waterson was very lucky indeed. For Dawn Waterson, Keith's mother, however, this was to be a turning point. She had believed for so long that her boy was a good boy. She'd realised early on in his life that he wasn't the easiest son a woman could wish for, especially without a father figure to look up to. She would accept whatever punishment the court felt fit to give. What she would never be able to accept though would be the stories, dragged up by the press, of his life beyond the bounds of which she was already aware. The hooliganism, which she felt reflected directly on the job she'd done of raising him. Or as she now saw it the poor job she'd done of raising him.

Most women would have given anything to have had a life like Lucy Kirkpatrick. She had money, glamour, adoration, all at such a young age.

That wasn't the case now. Most women were glad they weren't Lucy Kirkpatrick now.

Come on, Lucy. Let me in. You need me now more than ever. I know what you're feeling. Let me help you. Please.

Lucy's mind had needed to switch itself off. A defence mechanism against what it knew to be life's ugly reality. Some people, in similar circumstances, never wake up again. They have no reason to go on living so they remain in the twilight zone. Somewhere between life and death, slowly fading away, until years later their candle just burns itself out.

Sally-Anne didn't want Lucy to slowly fade away. She knew Lucy could be so much stronger for the experience. Strength, true strength, comes from the shit you have to endure in life, or at least your perception of that shit. Going through the experience that Lucy had just endured was enough to kill some people. Sally-Anne believed that the same experience could be the catalyst for so much more.

Let's at least talk about it, Lucy. I loved Jayne just as much as you did. I was there too. I saw what happened. It isn't easy to carry on, but you've got only two choices at this time. Stay here, fester and die, or move on. If you want to die then I'm out of here and you're on your own, all alone. If you want to move on we can do it together. Two choices, the decision is yours.

She's dead, Sally-Anne. Why did it happen? Why Jayne? Why not me instead?

I've asked myself the same question so many times. I don't know the answer. Nobody knows the answer to that question. Maybe it was her destiny, who knows? At least now you're talking, we can discuss it, see where we go from here.

So; Come on Sally-Anne. You can do better than that, Why did it happen? You're supposed to be here to protect me. Wasn't that the deal? What happened? Where were you when I needed you? Jayne's dead. Where were you when we needed you?

It doesn't work like that, Lucy. I can't be everywhere, protecting you from everything. I'm here for you Lucy, you're still alive. This is the worst thing that could possibly happen to you. Don't you think I know that? Don't you think I would do anything in my power to prevent that if I could? Turn back the clock, do whatever it takes? Unfortunately life very rarely gives you a second chance.

So what is the point, Sally-Anne? What's the point in any of this? Jayne's gone, what's the point in carrying on without her?

The point is, Lucy, that you can fade away into this self-imposed exile of none-life or you can move on, try to make things better, try to make things right.

Same question, Sally-Anne. What's the point?

Revenge, Lucy. Getting even, not letting the bastards, whoever they are, think they've got away with it. We'll be doing it for Jayne, doing it for you, doing it for us, Lucy, you and me Lucy, you and me.

Now rest Lucy. But think about this, I'm not going to give up on you until you decide otherwise. Trust me, let me redeem myself. Give me the chance to at least try. Let me make this right.

...

Sally-Anne and Lucy talked long and often. Not that anybody could see Lucy in conversation. Lucy was still, motionless; any monitors she was attached to were picking up nothing of what was happening in her mind, Sally-Anne's domain. Her guardian angel was talking her through it, helping her come to the correct decision. A regular little psychiatric nurse, in a slinky red PVC nurse's uniform. She was much more Sally-Anne than Florence Nightingale.

...

John, Steph and Rosie visited Lucy everyday in hospital. They were, after all, Lucy's only family; her nearest and dearest, now. As much as they talked to Lucy though there was no change, she wasn't making any progress. The doctors were grim faced when speaking to John, none of them willing to offer any hope where they couldn't see it for themselves. Time was the only thing John could cling to. Lucy had lots of time on her hands, a whole lifetime virtually.

With Lucy in hospital and with no sign of any immediate recovery, it was decided that Jayne's funeral should go ahead without her. Not knowing when or if Lucy would make a recovery the decision was made to bury Jayne in the Parkinson family plot.

So on 15 January 2011 Jayne was laid to rest in a small graveyard just on the outskirts of Wigan. On a wet and windy Monday in winter; hers was just one amongst many funerals taking place in the North of England that day. The only difference between this one and the rest of them was the discreet presence of a handful of photographers. People whose only reason to be there was to collect the very latest images for the continuing editorial saga currently being played out in the broadsheets and tabloids that make up Britain's national newspapers. The saga that was currently strumming the nation's collective heart strings being the continuing story of Lucy Kirkpatrick's recent heartbreaking misfortunes.

The newspapers were working on the nation's subliminal feelings. They were doing a very good job at showing Lucy in an exceptionally good light and at the same time highlighting the injustice of her recent predicament. In the eyes of the British public she was becoming worthy of being canonised. She was being made into a heroine for the whole country to rally behind and pray for. It could have gone either way, the media decided that the story would sell more newspapers this way so it went in Lucy's favour.

As they followed the story of her past family misfortunes and her current situation the whole nation was unwittingly being dragged along on a wave of sympathy. If they were to ever know the real truth about Lucy Kirkpatrick the British public would turn on her in an instant, demanding her head on a platter. This, of course, is a very British tradition when it comes to celebrity. A pound of flesh is a pound of flesh after all, and celebrity flesh tastes so much sweeter, celebrity flesh sells newspapers.

But how could they ever know the truth about what went on in her pretty little head? How could they know she had Sally-Anne watching her back?

So what's it to be, Lucy? Do we part company here or do we show the world what you're made of? It's your choice. No pressure, but any time soon would be just fine and dandy.

So we can have our revenge?

Eye for eye, tooth for tooth, hand for hand, foot for foot, burning for burning, wound for wound, stripe for stripe… **Life for life***.*

For Jayne?

Of course, wouldn't that be the sweetest revenge of all?

What about for us, Sally-Anne? What about for you and me?

Absolutely, revenge for you and me.

And how exactly do you suggest we get our revenge?

Don't you worry about that for now, let that be my concern, I have a very active mind, or should I say we have a very active mind.

Revenge like the revenge we had on Georgie Dunston and Terence Sandford? Is that the sort of revenge that concerns you? Is that what you want? Is that what we want?

A life for a life! One life for Jayne! One life for you and me! Is that enough for what you're going through? Is that enough for what you're feeling? Don't you deserve more than merely a life for life?

I do the way I feel now, yes.

Good, that is exactly the type of revenge that concerns me. That is exactly what I want too. Vengeance is ours, Lucy. We will repay, just trust me.

Good. Thank you, Sally-Anne. That was all I wanted to hear.

There's just one more thing, Sally-Anne. Pain, will they feel pain? Pain like we're feeling?

It will be a different kind of pain, Lucy. But that depends on you, you and me. But we can make it as painful as you want. How much pain are you feeling now?

I'm feeling a little better now, not as much pain now. Thank you, Sally-Anne. You really are my guardian angel aren't you?

Yes I am. The money isn't great but the job comes with some great fringe benefits. So come on, I want to start earning again.

Lucy's vital signs immediately began to improve. She was coming round, John was called and within twenty minutes of John reaching her bed she was awake. John had wanted to be there when she woke. He wanted to be the one answering the questions about Jayne.

Nobody had been able to tell him what she may or may not remember about the accident. Doctors were unsure as to whether or not she'd remember the accident at all, and if not, whether she'd expect Jayne to come walking through the door at any minute. She may not even remember who John is, or that he's her brother. She may not remember who she is, let alone John. He would have to play it as it comes and hope that it didn't all come too fast and furious.

When it did come it came calmly. Lucy told him that she already knew Jayne was dead, explaining how she'd seen that for herself at the time of the accident. No real chance of making a mistake when her head was barely attached to her body.

"Lucy, we've all been so worried about you," said John, "the doctors couldn't tell us much. You've been out for twenty nine days in total. We've just been waiting, hoping and praying, it's so good to have you back with us."

"Don't worry about me, John. I'll be okay from now on. I've already accepted that Jayne's no longer here, but I've still got you, Steph and Rosie. You're what matter to me now."

With that a solitary tear slid down Lucy's cheek. That tear was the first and last tear John would see shed by Lucy following Jayne's death. He obviously wasn't aware how many boxes of 'virtual' tissues Lucy had been through in the previous twenty-nine days.

"By the way," said John nonchalantly, "Who's Sally-Anne?"

"Sally-Anne, Why do you ask?"

"You must have been talking to her in your dreams just before you came round." replied John, "I didn't pick up much of what you were saying to each other but I'd like to thank her personally, whoever she is, her memory must have helped bring you out of a coma, and I for one will be eternally thankful for that."

Be careful, Lucy; our secret, remember?

"Sally-Anne James do you mean? I haven't seen her since we lived in Aldershot." replied Lucy. "And that seems like it was a long long time ago. It feels like a whole lifetime ago now. I probably wouldn't even recognise her if I saw her. She was a dumpy little fat girl with scruffy greasy hair back then, but then I think we've probably all changed a lot since we lived in Aldershot."

A Dumpy little fat girl with scruffy greasy hair? Thanks Lucy...I think not.

There's just no pleasing some people, Sally-Anne.

Good to have you back baby girl.

I wish I could say it was good to be back.

But you will do, trust me.

...

The British public loves a happy ending, and Lucy coming out of a coma was about as happy as it could possibly get under the circumstances.

Not everyone was happy though. Keith Waterson was finding life as the nation's pariah, the man people love to hate, more than a little tiresome. He couldn't walk down the street without being recognised. Inevitably, with recognition came the verbal abuse. He didn't dare go near a football ground on match day for fear of the mob mentality. The hunter finally becoming the hunted, his own friends, such as they were, refusing to be drawn into his private battle. People he knew well and who he'd fought alongside, in the name of sport, turned against him. A small justice... of sorts.

Lucy meanwhile was coming to terms with a life without Jayne. She spent the first two months of her convalescence with John, Steph and Rosie. It was too soon to move back to the apartment, too many memories.

There had been no physical damage to Lucy on Christmas Eve. She could have glided down the catwalk with the rest of the models in any major city in the world. But people would know something was wrong, something was different. Not enough pain, not enough grief, they would comment.

Those same people would never realise that twenty-nine days to relive the horror, twenty-nine days to ponder a life without Jayne, twenty-nine days to weigh-up your options, is a very long time. As mere words, pain and grief just don't come close.

Lucy knew what she craved, but she also knew that now was too soon for that. She could wait, time meant very little to Lucy now. Lucy was with the people she loved most in the world, the living ones anyway.

Twenty-Four

As much as Lucy hated her new life without Jayne, and swore revenge, Sally-Anne was only too aware of Lucy's fickle nature. Georgie Dunston had highlighted her feeble side, her ability to 'give in when the going gets tough'. Sally-Anne knew that living with Rosie's innocence could be the downfall of Lucy's rage. She would become soft in the head before too long. Rosie could do that to most people just by being with them for any length of time. Sally-Anne was only too aware of Rosie's virtuousness, her mesmeric nature.

The first of April 2011, all fools day, saw Lucy's anger restored. At Sally-Anne's suggestion, that was the day she decided to face the challenge of moving back into 'their' apartment.

It would always be their apartment. Even though Jayne had been dead for over three months she was never going to be totally alone. Sally-Anne lived there too. Wherever Lucy set up home in the future, it would always be 'their' home. There could be no show without Punch.

We should send Jayne's clothes to a charity shop, and send some things back to her mum and dad. We need something to keep us busy, keep us occupied. Do you think you're up to that?

Truthfully, Sally-Anne; I don't think I am, I don't think I ever will be. But then I know it has to be done, and we're the only ones here now, so I guess we don't really have any choice. I don't want anyone else delving into her privacy, our privacy, so it's just you and me.

When we've finished I want to show you something. I've had an idea for the spare bedrooms.

Revenge?

Eye for eye; tooth for tooth; hand for hand.

Show me now, Sally-Anne. The way I'm feeling right now, revenge is a very appealing topic for discussion.

Okay, before we start on Jayne's things just lift up the edge of the carpets in the spare bedrooms. If I know Stein it won't be just wooden floorboards looking back up at us.

Lucy struggled against the carpet grippers but eventually pulled up the carpet to reveal what was hidden beneath.

Red rubber, just as I thought. The pervy old bastard just couldn't bear to see it go. I wonder if he kept anything else from the 'good old days'.

The basement, if it's anywhere it'll be in the basement.

Get the key; let's see what hidden treasures the old tart stashed away for us down there.

Lucy took the basement key from a drawer in the kitchen, she'd needed it only once before now, to restart the building's gas boiler in November. She made for the door.

Come on then, let's take a look.
You lead the way.

...

The part of the basement not being used by Stein Studios was tucked away in one corner room. It was very rarely entered, if at all, since Stein's death. It was like stepping into a junkyard full of someone's past life. To John it was just a roomful of tat that he'd get around to clearing, someday when he wasn't so busy. He was a very busy young man at the moment.

He obviously didn't get chance to pass any of this stuff on to his old fruity friends, 'for old times sake'. It looks like he kept it all, cage, bedsteads, manacles, whips, chains, everything. Killed himself before he got chance to move it on. Oh well, wouldn't you just know it, his loss is our gain. You know what I'm thinking?

Eye for eye; tooth for tooth; hand for hand. When can we start?

Lucy restricted herself to 'reorganising' the first of the two spare rooms during weekends and evenings only. No need to let John know what was happening. Least said soonest mended.

It gave her mind a focus. She needed to buy things, decoration mostly, tools, and a few other things. But then the Internet is a wonderful place for a virtual trip to the shops.

You needed no disguise when you went shopping over the web, no chance of some nosey plebeian looking over her shoulder to see what she'd just placed in her shopping basket. Impersonal shopping, a celebrity's dream come true. You could buy tools, clothes, furniture, weapons, a pair of soiled knickers worn by a thirteen-year-old Philippino slave girl currently living and working in Woking; something for everyone.

Lucy was busy assembling equipment to build her very own web. This one wasn't for shopping on though, or for downloading paedophile porn from, this was the kind of web a spider uses to catch a fly, a poor misguided fly.

Lucy wasn't ready to return to modelling just yet, it was too soon. Everybody understood; everybody sympathised. Lucy's face still fit that ideal the modelling world was always striving for. The accident had caused no blemishes to appear, no scratches, no broken nose, no stitches required, no permanent damage, not even a spot that might need concealing beneath extra make-up. As far as the modelling world was aware there was nothing wrong with Lucy that time couldn't heal.

Lucy could have returned to the catwalk any time she wanted to. If anything, the accident had made her more marketable, every fashion house worth its salt would love the kudos of coaxing Lucy Kirkpatrick back onto the catwalk. The television cameras and world press would all be there to witness that event; the free advertising alone would be worth hundreds of thousands.

Lucy Kirkpatrick was quickly becoming the David Beckham of the modelling world; everyone wanted a piece of her, and soon she'd also be able to name her own price. Lucy, however, had decided to take a sabbatical from modelling, and under the circumstances nobody was going to question her wisdom. A good break was what she needed, come back strong.

But Lucy was busy. To the outside world it seemed that she was busy, desperately trying to get over Jayne, and she had everyone's sympathy there. She was busy though, reworking the spare bedroom, but she'd get no sympathy for that, not if they understood. But no one else knew. Sympathy wasn't what drove Lucy on. Sympathy was the last thing she required at that particular point in her life.

Deliveries came thick and fast. If Lucy was expecting a delivery on a particular day she would stay in her apartment or spend time with John in his studios downstairs. She would just lend a hand mostly, one of the most instantly recognisable photography assistants in the world. John thought it would be therapeutic. It also enabled him to have daily contact with his little sister, without having to knock on her door every five minutes acting like some sort of mother hen. It even allowed Lucy to keep in contact, of sorts, with people in the business. And she was also well placed to keep a lid on the number of deliveries destined for upstairs.

Often Steph would bring Rosie to visit her Auntie. When this happened Lucy would lock the spare bedroom door and give Rosie her complete attention. Rosie, this mesmeric little child who, in Sally-Anne's eyes, had also lost someone very special to her, and just like her Auntie Lucy, it was through no fault of her own.

Revenge for Rosie, wound for wound.

Yes, Sally-Anne; revenge for Rosie too. We are after all her Godparents; the least we can do is avenge some of the wrong.

And who better to assist in God's work than an angel? An angel sent to protect, sent to advise and sent to guard.

She's innocent now, but one day she'll understand. Vengeance must be the way now. Sally-Anne, she needs us now. I need you now.

I'm here, Lucy, forever and ever.

Amen!

24 June 2011.

Lucy collected her tools together, swept the floor and surveyed what had once been one of the spare bedrooms, in what had once been hers and Jayne's home. No longer would anybody be using this room as a bedroom though. There was a bed in the room, but nobody would ever sleep in it.

Twenty-fourth of June, six months to the day after Jayne's death, had been the date she'd set herself to finish the room. June 24, Jayne's birthday, she would have been twenty-nine years old on that day. Lucy's gift to the memory of Jayne was to be this room. Not what most people would call a shrine, but still a place where she could come in memory of Jayne. A place built to honour her passing.

In reality though this wasn't a place to remember Jayne and Jayne alone; when she was in this room she remembered so much more.

She remembered her mother, death by misadventure, Simon's misadventure.

Bastard!

She remembered her father, killed himself by overdosing on his own brand of paracetemol, when she'd been fourteen.

Selfish bastard!

She remembered Stein, the nearest thing she'd ever had to a mentor and someone she could talk to, really talk to, death by carbon monoxide poisoning, while he sat in his garage.

Stupid selfish bastard!

Keith Waterson, murderer of Jayne. Jayne, the singular most important part of her life. Except maybe for Sally-Anne.

Dead man waiting to happen!

Twenty fourth of June 2011; she'd finished in time to enjoy the afternoon picking out a present for Rosie who would be three years old the following day.

Men, her life had been plagued by men since the age of eleven. Sally-Anne had been right, Georgie Dunston and Terence Sandford had to die; they were, after all is said and done, men. They were poor examples of the so-called 'stronger' species, but they were men never the less. Sally-Anne had never been wrong before, Lucy understood that now. Why had she ever doubted her in the past?

She'd had her fair share of bitchiness directed at her by other women. But bitchiness she could handle. Bitchiness doesn't kill your mother. Bitchiness doesn't cause your father and your mentor to commit suicide. Bitchiness doesn't place your lovers nearly severed head in your lap. No, bitchiness she could handle, it was men who gave her a major problem. All men except John that is, but then John wasn't like other men.

Sally-Anne was always there to reinforce her view. She was there to help her fight the cause, and she would turn it into a crusade whenever the time was right. That time was quickly approaching.

Sally-Anne, please forgive me for ever having doubted your word.

You know you don't have to ask me for forgiveness Lucy. To err is human, to forgive is divine. You just carry on being human and I'll just carry on being divine.

Having finished the first room it was now time to start work on the second room. An easier task by far the second room, remove the carpet and bring in some equipment, no big deal. Ordering over the Internet, and with weekend deliveries she would see the job finished sometime in July. She'd need to spread out the deliveries though; she didn't want to raise any suspicions from nosey neighbours.

She knew exactly what she wanted, and she could wait. Waiting was good for the soul. Most girls were being told to wait over one thing or another, sex, drink and even the latest fashions. What was the point in buying the latest fashions if they weren't the latest fashions anymore? Being made to wait just strengthens a girl's resolve. She already had the motive and the means now she just needed the opportunity.

...

In August of that year Sally-Anne and Lucy decided that the time was right. Lucy had been 'in mourning' for long enough, now was the time to show the people what Lucy Kirkpatrick was capable of. It was after all what the British public had wanted to see since the previous Christmas, Lucy back on the world's catwalks, Lucy back in the world's top fashion magazines, Lucy just being Lucy again.

Lucy would never be Lucy again though, not now, not the old Lucy, not the pre 2011 Lucy. The Lucy that the press, public and even her family would see from now on would look like the old Lucy, even act like the old Lucy, on the big stage. But this Lucy was a whole new Lucy, a reinvented Lucy. Still with four months before she reached her twenty-first birthday this was a Lucy with more secrets than any sane person should have to handle in a whole lifetime.

Just as with fortune, there are many varying degrees of sanity. Psychiatrists faced with the pre-accident Lucy and then the post-accident Lucy may well have said that she had been before, and was also now, showing all the signs of sanity expected of an average person under her particular set of circumstances.

But could there ever be an 'average' person with Lucy's particular set of circumstances? A twenty year-old supermodel with the world at her feet, who had recently lost her lover, her lesbian lover, in a most horrific car accident. Her last memory being her lover's dead eyes looking blankly up at her from her blood soaked lap.

None of those same psychiatrists would ever accuse her of having a split personality, an alter ego. She wouldn't suddenly turn into Sally-Anne and speak in a different accent, or even a different language. As far as Lucy was concerned she was Lucy and Sally-Anne was Sally-Anne, and Sally-Anne was her personal guardian angel.

Of course, Lucy knew Sally-Anne existed. Sally-Anne made no secret of her existence, not to Lucy anyway, she'd known for eight years. But she'd never tell John or Steph or Rosie or anybody she knew, let alone a psychiatrist. So how could they ever accuse her of having an alter ego, a part of her that comes to the fore to handle the stress at times of greatest need?

As far as Lucy was concerned she had a guardian angel that went by the name of Sally-Anne. And Sally-Anne may well have advised her to get back onto the catwalk, and to appear to be moving on with her life, everything back to normal.

But it was Lucy up there strutting her stuff.

It was Lucy taking the standing ovation when she made her first appearance on the stage since Jayne's death.

It was Lucy whose image the TV cameras were there to catch.

It was Lucy who'd make the national evening news.

It had been to Lucy that the nation had sent their love out last Christmas.

It was for Lucy that the nation was happy now.

Sally-Anne was always there though, in the background, advising, thinking of the next move, and waiting.

Twenty-Five

The waiting didn't last too long…

<u>12 October 2011</u>

The opportunity just seemed to present itself out of nowhere. Lucy had donned her now much needed disguise, which she tended to wear when she needed to get out, and get some fresh air in her lungs. A black wig, a woolly hat, oversized scruffy jeans, an oversized parka and the very minimum of make-up.

It's just so much easier to disguise yourself with the British weather. It's hard not to draw attention to yourself when you look like a supermodel wearing a disguise of T-shirt and shorts. October in Britain, you could fool your own mother.

Five minutes into her walk, barely four hundred metres from where she lived, she walked past a decorator's van, a van that was currently being loaded by Steve Summer. Job done, finished, and only the middle of the afternoon.

Steve Summer, Painter and Decorator, six feet two inches tall, sixteen stones of muscle. A man truly worthy of the male gender, the same man who had given her a look as he was coming out of the house carrying a bundle of dust sheets. A look that said haven't I seen you before somewhere, and if I haven't then give me a chance, you don't know what you're missing.

Lucy, walk to the end of the street, cross the road and get the mobile number from the side of that van. Painter and decorator, he must be a one-man band, and we just decided we need to decorate a bedroom.

Did we?

Yes we did. Come on quickly, get the number then back home and call his mobile. Tell him we saw this number on the side of his van, we're not too far away and we'd like him to come and look at a job. He should come right away if he's got any sense. He isn't going to start a new job at half past three in the afternoon. Come on, Lucy; opportunity knocks at our door.

Revenge?

Revenge!

When Lucy got back home she called the mobile number and arranged for him to call round at four o'clock. Sally-Anne had been spot-on, he was just finishing off a job in the area and while he was so close he'd call in and have a look. He was a one-man band, happy for any job opportunity that came his way.

When Steve eventually rang the intercom Lucy didn't hesitate in buzzing him in, and told him to just keep climbing the stairs. When he made the top floor the door was just being opened by Lucy, now back in her regular attire, without the black wig, unmistakably Lucy Kirkpatrick.

When Steve saw her stood there a big grin stretched across his face.

"Hello, I'm Steve Summer. We spoke earlier, about some decorating." Steve's Welsh accent giving away the fact that he'd spent the first twelve years of his life just outside of Cardiff. "And I already know who you are."

"Hello, Steve. Thanks for dropping by; I hope it's not too inconvenient. Come in, I'll show you what I want," said Lucy, "it's in the bedroom."

'If only', thought Steve, but the whole country knew where Lucy Kirkpatrick's sexual preferences lay.

"This is a fabulous place you've got here, Miss Kirkpatrick." Said Steve looking around, a little embarrassed by Lucy's presence. He had seen the inside of a lot of people's homes in his thirty-one years, but this was a bit special. As a decorator he was feeling a little out of his depth, but then he thought this was maybe his chance to impress somebody with lots of cash rich friends, not the tight wads he usually worked for. A recommendation from Lucy Kirkpatrick in the circles she moves in could make his life so much easier. Her model friends must need decorators, and who knows? They surely couldn't all be Lesbians, could they?

"Please call me Lucy. You make me sound like some dowdy school mistress."

An image of Lucy, barely dressed in a skimpy school uniform, and brandishing a whip flashed into his mind at that point.

Where did that thought come from I wonder? Thought Steve, grinning to himself; a chance really would be a fine thing. Come on Steve concentrate on the job.

"So where did you say you want me to look?" said Steve, trying not to let his mind wander too far into that particular cul-de-sac.

"Oh yes, decorating, the bedrooms. My mind was beginning to wander for a minute there. There are two I want you to look at," said Lucy, "the master bedroom and the playroom."

"Okay", said Steve, thinking that she must have only recently moved in and never likely to need a playroom was looking to re-decorate.

"The playroom seems as good a place to start as any." Said Lucy, "Follow me."

Like lambs to the slaughter.
Live in my thrall.

Steve couldn't help but watch Lucy's arse as he followed her, mesmerised by the thought of what a man like him could do to a body like hers, given half a chance.

Lucy opened the door to the spare bedroom and walked in. Steve eagerly followed her in. When he was able to tear his eyes away from Lucy's arse, just for the minute, he couldn't believe what he was seeing in front of him.

"Bloody hell, when you said playroom I thought you meant a playroom, you know, toys and games and things." Steve said. "For children."

Lucy laughed out loud, "I don't have any children Steve, not yet anyway."

"But..." It was out before he could stop himself. Both he and Lucy had known what hidden meaning that particular 'but' carried with it. Meanings like:

But aren't you a Lesbian?

But you can't have children without there being a man involved.

But the newspaper stories said...

"You shouldn't always believe everything you read in the newspapers Steve." said Lucy to a dumbstruck Steve.

"And anyway", continued Lucy, "this is a playroom, an adult playroom, it is lots of fun."

"What's the matter, Steve?" she said, "Cat got your tongue?"

"No", said Steve, "no, it's just that I've decorated lots of playrooms before now, but none of them have been like this. This really is a first for me."

"Come on, Steve," said Lucy turning to face him and moving a little closer. "Are you trying to tell me that a big strong man with a beautiful body like yours has never wanted to feel the thrill of being dominated by a woman before?"

Steve looked Lucy in the eyes for the first time since he'd walked through her door, not sure of what was happening to him, but happy to play along. "No, I'm not saying that." He replied "But look at this place, it wasn't exactly what I was expecting, that's all I'm saying. Who lived here before you?"

"Nobody, this is all my own work."

"So you really like all this stuff do you?" Said Steve quizzically, "You're absolutely right; you really shouldn't believe all you read in the papers." The bed was what interested him the most. He was interested in the chains, the whips and what could only be described as the tools of the torture trade, circa 1400AD, hanging on the walls. It was just that the bed was much more likely to deliver what he wanted. And what a bed it was, four-poster wrought iron bed frame complete with four spikes on the uprights and enough chains festooned off it to tie a whole rugby team up.

"Oh, don't get me wrong, Steve; I do love women, the newspapers got that right," Lucy said, "but I'm not exclusive, if the right man comes along I can still enjoy myself, I'll just never fall in love with him."

Steve stood looking round in awed amazement at the room.

"So have you ever thought what it might be like, tied to a bed, no control whatsoever?" asked Lucy.

"It's got to be every man's dream hasn't it?" replied Steve, "Giving yourself up to a beautiful woman like that."

"Not every man's dream, Steve. You'd be surprised how many men are scared of giving control to a woman. Would you be, Steve? Scared? Scared of losing all control?"

"No, not at all," replied Steve too quickly, "I think I could handle it."

"Big men are usually all talk." Lucy Said, "When it comes down to it they can't do it. That's my experience, get so far then beg for mercy. It's only a game for Christ's sake, purely hedonistic fun."

"What are you saying?" asked Steve.

"No bottle, most men don't have the guts. Not until they've tried it once, then they just want more." Said Lucy. "Anyway, let's concentrate on what you're here for shall we? The ceiling needs painting, red I think, and there's a couple of small cracks need filling in this room."

A vision of Lucy stood over him teasing him with a cane, suddenly came into his mind. He would love to fill Lucy's small crack; right here right now.

"Hold on a minute. No guts? That's a bit of a sweeping statement isn't it?

"Are you telling me you're a man with guts?"

"Yes."

"So prove it you snivelling piece of shit, lick my boots... RIGHT HERE RIGHT NOW!"

Steve was down on his knees in a flash; his only problem was deciding which one to lick first.

...

...*Yes, yes, yes, thank you God,* thought Steve, ***this is actually going to happen.***

Steve had let her talk him into being tied to the bed, but the truth of it was that he hadn't taken much persuading; he'd practically offered himself up there and then thinking the lads wouldn't believe him when he told them. The reaction would most likely be, "Lucy Kirkpatrick You lucky bastard!" or more likely, "Lucy Kirkpatrick? You lying bastard!" He could imagine the lads cheering his exploits over a beer in the bar at the rugby club later, when he'd revel in telling them exactly what he'd got up to with Lucy. Would they ever believe him? Probably not, but at least he'd know the truth.

When he'd agreed to be tied up all he was thinking about was having his kinky little sex fantasy fulfilled, at last, after so many rejections. Not only that, it was with Lucy Kirkpatrick, and she was making all of the running. Okay, so in his fantasy he wasn't the one being tied up, but he'd get his chance too, she'd promised. This must be a dream he thought, it has to be. Lucy suddenly reached under the pillow and brought out a gag. Smiling at him provocatively, she slipped the gag over his head and tightened it around his mouth. Steve was not overly concerned at this, *whatever floats your boat Lucy* he thought. There wasn't much he could do about it now anyway he was in this for the excitement of the journey, he was just hoping as he looked at Lucy that he'd be able to make the journey a long and memorable one and not the quick drunken fumble it usually ended up being.

Ever the optimist, Steve offered up his usual quick prayer of thanks to the God of sex. This was a prayer collectively written over a few beers one night after training. He knew that seven of his mates were still in the habit of offering up the same prayer on a regular basis; the guys who had managed to remain single.

> *For this and every other beautiful liaison thou shall ever grant to me,*
> *My heartfelt thanks and gratitude I offer up for free,*
> *I ask only two things O lord in this my hour of need,*
> *Let it be that all my women are a nice tight fit,*
> *And please ensure my condoms never split,*
> *Amen.*

She got to work on him then. She brought him to a full and, even Steve would have to admit it, glorious erection. In no time whatsoever he was stood up proud and ready for action so to speak. Steve was as ready as he'd ever been, Lucy was not going to disappoint in any way. After making sure Steve was well tied to the bed, leaning over him and giving him a brief taste of what he thought was to come Lucy reached under the bed and brought out a toolbox. Giving him her most seductive look yet she started taking the tools out of the box, one by one. She showed each one to Steve before lining them up on the end of the bed. These were not the sex toys Steve had imagined they would be when he saw the toolbox. She brought out a hammer first followed by pruning shears, saw, electric drill, heat gun, Stanley knife and chisel.

Steve was now more than a little concerned at his total lack of control, his inability to influence what was happening. But wasn't that what she'd said being tied up was really all about? Losing control, "you've never felt anything like it until you've tried it", those were her very words. So here he was giving it a go, no control, his life in Lucy's hands. Lucy, the woman he knew well but had met for the first time that day.

He started to sweat, started to test the strength of the bindings that made him so vulnerable. Not to an extent that made him seem desperate, he hoped, but such that she thought he was playing along with the game. He wasn't playing along with the game. He could take a joke as well as the next man. But this, come on! It just wasn't funny anymore. Wait until he found out who had set him up, he'd pay them back for this, with interest. He'd set many of his team members up before now. Not like this though, whoever had thought of this had done a really good job. This one would go down in rugby club history, very funny. He wanted to say "good one, you got me, really, can we stop now?" but he couldn't he was bound and gagged he had no control at all.

The thought then struck him that none of his mates knew he was here, in fact, nobody knew he was here, only Lucy. His heart felt like it was going to give up on him, right there and then. Strangely enough though, even in a crazy situation like this, he was still fully aroused. Even with his total lack of control he was still standing proud, he was definitely still up for it. Lucy had been spot on. Sexually, he'd never felt anything like it. He just needed her to put the tools back in the box, point proven and they could screw each other's brains out. When they finished whatever debauched sexual activity she had planned they could have a good laugh about her scaring the shit out of him and how he never lost his appetite for it. That was what he was hoping, praying for even. He'd forgive her everything for that. *Please Lord let it be that,* he said to himself.

When she picked up the pruning shears with a crazed look in her eyes Steve tried to scream but it was useless, Lucy was in control, screaming was pointless. Steve knew then that he was losing his cock, not yet though, and not because of excessive use. Quite the opposite, he wasn't going to use it at all.

Lucy was in the room with Steve but there was somebody else in there with her as well as Steve. The person with the shears was Lucy Kirkpatrick, but Sally-Anne was guiding her, helping her fulfil what she'd set out to do. Sally-Anne was a different proposition altogether. Sally-Anne was about to float her boat in one of several of her favourite methods. Lucy was there taking advice as the game unfolded.

Before she'd finished with him all the tools had been used and what had been left tied to the bed didn't look very much like Steve any more. His mother would have been hard pressed to recognise anything of the pulpy, slimy, stinking mess Lucy and Sally-Anne had made in that room as once ever having been her son.

Sally-Anne had been thorough in her advice; nobody could ever accuse her of being anything else. But then they wouldn't ever get the chance to accuse her of anything, never mind being anything other than thorough. It was a strange relationship that existed between Lucy and Sally-Anne.

...

Come all you sinners,
Come one come all,
Like lambs to the slaughter,
Come live in my thrall.

...

Wow, Lucy. You're good, do you feel good?

Yes I do. Like you said revenge is sweet. I'm tired though, I feel like a rest now.

Not yet, sweetheart; no time. We need to move his van, get rid of any sign that he might have been here. Just leave him here for now, he isn't going anywhere in a hurry. Lock him in though, just in case we get burgled. That really would be unfortunate, for the burglars.

Lucy showered, and then she checked in Steve's pockets for car keys and mobile phone. Lucy donned her disguise again and with rubber lab gloves on her hands she slid behind the wheel of Steve's three-month-old transit van.

Well it's hardly a Porsche, but then I don't suppose many decorators use their Porsches for work. Can you see a notepad, anything he would have written our address on?

Shifting the copy of last Tuesday's newspaper from the passenger seat she found a notepad and pen.

Here it is, Sally-Anne.

Good, put that in your pocket and drive this to the Golden Lion. Park it as far from the road as you can. It's only twenty minutes on foot so we can walk back. Okay?

Fantastic, hold on tight.

Slow Lucy. Nice and slow, don't draw any attention to us.

Half an hour later Lucy was back in her state of the art kitchen, making a drink as if nothing had happened.

When shall we move the body, Sally-Anne?

No rush, the door's locked, leave it until tomorrow. Are you still tired?

No, not now, I'm on fire.

Ring for a take away then. That new Italian, maybe get it delivered, a small celebration.

You read my mind, Sally-Anne.

...

That night Lucy drifted off to sleep, carried along, high above the clouds of consciousness, in the warm embrace of her very own avenging angel. Both were grinning like Cheshire cats, both felt sated by their evening's work. This had been the first chance Lucy had had of seeing what Sally-Anne looked like, not just hearing her as a voice in her head. When she woke later she wouldn't remember Sally-Anne's face; just the memory of looking deep into her eyes and seeing her own reflection smiling back, reassuringly.

Jayne had been there with them as they drifted along. No words were needed to express her gratitude. Lucy hadn't felt love so strong since before that fateful day when Jayne had left them. All three of them drifted along on a sea of love. It was good to have her back, even if it was for just the one night.

Lucy woke the next morning rejuvenated, happy, the sun was shining, the birds were singing and she felt set for the task ahead. A task that was a pre-requisite of the last evening's entertainment. At least she wasn't alone though, that really would have been too heavy a cross to bear.

As a child she had always been tidy in her habits. She had never been the sort of child whose parents would always need to 'encourage' her to tidy her bedroom. Lucy had a place for everything and would keep everything in its place. She wasn't like any normal child in that respect, any normal child seems to enjoy the constant war being fought against them by their parents because of their untidiness. But then Lucy had never really been a normal child, she didn't fit the rules. She never would.

For Lucy to have left the mess that she was now surveying wasn't normal. To anybody else looking at what had once been Steve Summers in the cold light of day, they would have to say that making the mess in the first instance was as far from normal as you could ever imagine.

Stage two, Lucy; let's move the stupid bastard. As if we'd ever be interested in a dumb fuck like him.

Looking at her handiwork, Lucy could only agree with Sally-Anne's description of her talents. She really was good.

He was a big lad wasn't he? I'm thinking we should do this in more manageable chunks. Legs, arms, head and a torso should do it.

I'll fetch the angle grinder.

Lucy's skilled hands got to work on Steve once again. Within thirty minutes he'd been reduced to six component parts, lumps of meat and bones. There were many more than six, if you counted his toes and his penis, but she wasn't counting them. They were Insignificant; you could fit them in the palms of your hands. And anyway, she'd taken them while he was still alive, they were hers now.

Torso first, Lucy; wrap it up in the polythene sheet then drag him next door.

Lucy did exactly as Sally-Anne suggested. She wasn't too surprised at the ease of the process. In her mind she did have justice on her side. Twenty minutes later Steve Summers body, each and every component part, was neatly packaged away. She didn't know how long it would take for the chest freezer to turn him into just blocks of frozen meat. In reality it didn't matter to her, she'd moved him from one bedroom into the next. She was disposing of Steve Summer in her second spare bedroom. Disposing was maybe the wrong word, storing him for remembrance sake was what she was doing.

Steve Summers had been innocent of every crime on which any judicial system could possibly be asked to preside. To Lucy, however, he'd been a man, he'd been available, and he'd been stupid enough to believe her. That had been enough reason to convict.

She was able to squeeze him into just the one freezer. Covering him was the bloodied black silk bed sheet he'd been lying on during the attack as well as the rubber mattress protector, which had been beneath it. On top of that she placed a plastic carrier bag. A carrier bag, which now contained his clothes, mobile phone, notepad, which contained Lucy's address, and the latex gloves she'd used when she'd driven his van away the previous evening. Steve Summer, rest in pieces.

If he'd been too big to fit into the single freezer it wouldn't have been a big problem. Sally-Anne had made sure there was capacity enough. Lucy had followed Sally-Anne's instructions to the letter, walking into Lucy's 'remembrance' room was like walking into your local Iceland freezer centre. You would have been disappointed though if you were a vegetarian, this branch only stocked meat, and red meat at that.

Lucy returned to the playroom with mop and bucket, disinfectant, polish, air freshener and new bed sheets. Before the afternoon was through, anybody walking into that room would have thought only of Lucy's kinky habits. To the naked eye there was no evidence of what had happened only twenty-four hours previously. The only evidence was residing in a freezer next door. And nobody but Lucy and Sally-Anne would ever be allowed in there.

The first thing anyone knew about Steve being missing had been when the owner of the Golden Lion reported a van, which had been parked on his car park, probably stolen, to the police. This had been on the fifteenth of October, two days after his death. The police couldn't find any sign that the van had been stolen. When Steve's mobile phone failed to respond they had the van removed from the car park. After a further three days, and with no sign of Steve at his home, the police began to ask questions of his neighbours.

There was no sign of Steve but nobody had reported him missing. The Spencer's had been more than a little pissed off when he didn't turn up to decorate their living room. After three days, and with Steve not taking any calls, they sacked him in absentia. Mr Spencer decided he'd decorate the room himself. He hadn't much liked Steve Summer in any case. He'd only given him the job because he was cheap.

After three weeks the police decided to launch an inquiry into Steve's apparent disappearance. Three weeks had been plenty of time for him to return from a last minute, bargain holiday he might have decided to go on at the spare of the moment.

With no body turning up, and no one coming forward yet to report him missing, the police had little to go on. It was a mystery for sure, but the police are much more likely, in a capital city, to try solving murders where they have a body than a missing person. He was a missing person who may turn out to be a murder victim, or he may well have run off with some wealthy lady for a life in the sun. Any possible clues were quickly fading away into history, Steve's trail wasn't only going cold, and it was positively freezing.

Means, motive, opportunity.

Twenty-Six

Eighteen British magazine covers in the six months since August of 2011, her return to modelling. She was told by one of the editor's that such coverage was unprecedented. She was setting new records for magazine sales. Lucy's return was still stroking the nation's feel good nerves, her picture on the cover of a magazine practically ensured full sale of that particular issue.

She was the girl that Hugh Hefner was willing to pay five hundred thousand dollars to appear as cover girl for Playboy magazine. Hugh Hefner didn't pursue it for too long though, he knew women; he knew when he was wasting his time.

Late February 2012, more than twelve months after Jayne's death, Keith Waterson finally had his day in court.

Motoring organisations the land over were hoping that, with such a high profile case, the courts would at last show their guts. They were hoping that justice would be seen to be done and an example made of the punishments that could be expected for causing death and destruction on the roads. How else were people ever to learn?

But what could the courts do? It was to come to light that he had no alcohol in his blood, he had swerved to avoid a far worse collision, he wasn't speeding at the time of the accident, he had admitted to being about to use his mobile phone but that he hadn't connected with anybody at the time of the crash, and he had assisted completely with the police at the time of his arrest, wrongful arrest. These were the facts.

As much as the police wanted the scumbag hooligan to get what he deserved, the courts weren't there to judge his skills for riot organisation. The law found him guilty of driving without due care and attention and gave him six points on his hitherto clean driving licence. A fine of six hundred pounds was also felt to be sufficient, payable in instalments if necessary. In reality Keith Waterson wasn't a bad driver, he was only guilty of driving without due care and attention. His mother privately wished they'd locked him up and thrown away the key, not for Jayne's death, for just being himself, his true self.

Keith was publicly very sorry to everyone who had been touched by the tragedy, and he explained how he would never get over the guilt he felt at being involved, in any way, in the events leading to another person's death. But the people who knew him knew what he really thought. If you take the risk of driving a fifty plus year old sports car in modern day traffic then you must accept the increased risk when something goes wrong. In Keith's eyes he was the innocent victim of a very old and unsafe car design.

When his employers found out the truth about his life away from work however, they felt duty bound to dispense of his services forthwith. Keith made his intention to sue for wrongful dismissal clear on his departure. He had had the law on his side once, why not again?

Lucy's public life had been hectic since Steve Summer came a calling. She had felt appeased by his death, she'd finally done what she realised she should have been prepared to do some time ago. She'd finally got one over on the male race.

Sally-Anne knew better though, she knew that Lucy's real target for revenge would always be Keith Waterson. In truth Sally-Anne didn't mind who it was, she had her playroom and a room full of shiny white coffins just waiting to be filled. Sally-Anne was just waiting for a trigger.

Driving without due care and attention; six points on his licence and a fine. Keith Waterson, aided by the British legal system, had brought shame upon Lucy and Jayne's life by valuing it so low. Shame somebody in public and they are far more likely to want revenge.

Lucy didn't sleep well the night of the verdict. Reporters had wanted her view on the outcome of the judgement that very afternoon. They were finally putting to bed the story that started on Christmas Eve 2010, putting the final nail in Jayne's coffin. Most people in the same circumstance, maybe with the benefit of foresight, would view this as the moment to move on, a turning point. Lucy just felt terribly sad.

At a little after four o'clock the following morning Lucy had reached the point where her body finally overcame her mind, she fell into a fitful sleep.

She was back at school, running a cross-country race; training for the inter-schools athletics championships. Five girls and Miss Parkinson on a rain soaked course. Conditioning Miss Parkinson had called it, Sally-Anne had called it an opportunity. Lucy's memory was playing tricks on her though, she knew this day had been significant for some reason; she just couldn't quite grasp it out of the ether. She thought this was maybe the day she and Jayne had kissed for the first time, she couldn't be sure.

The dream started just as it had been in reality. Lucy's long legs were once again giving her an advantage over her shorter team-mates, she found herself out in front, running by herself. What was it about this day that was so significant? She couldn't remember; then she tripped on a tree root. Now it was coming back, slowly, the fall had been manufactured, purposefully at the furthest point out on the course.

That was where the dream had started to deviate from reality. The four girls, who had been following, just like when she'd been a fourteen year old, didn't stop to show concern. They just carried on in their stride, jumping over her as if she didn't exist, not even giving her a second glance.

When Jayne did exactly the same she couldn't believe what was happening, it was as if she wasn't there. But they must have seen her; they'd avoided her skilfully enough. Jayne, whose job it had been on cross-country to run at the back, to make sure any stragglers made it back safely, stopped after a further twenty yards and walked back to where Lucy was lying. Lying in both senses of the word; on the floor and through her teeth. Leaning in closely, as if she was having trouble seeing who Lucy was, Jayne said, "Oh, it's only you Kirkpatrick, come on there's nothing wrong with you, get up and finish the course or you'll be off the team. There are no places for stragglers on my team." At that point Jayne turned round and continued running, leaving Lucy to pick herself up off the floor.

This wasn't the way it was supposed to happen. This wasn't what had happened before, was it? Her brain was trying hard to recall what had happened next in 2006. As hard as she tried though nothing was coming through, it was as if what she'd had with Jayne, from that day onwards, had never existed.

She couldn't remember the dream when she finally woke, but she still felt quite depressed about the previous day's events. The dream was lost to her conscious mind, but her sub-conscious mind was still trying to figure out its meaning, giving consideration to it while Lucy got on with her day.

Lucy continued, unknowingly, to have the same dream at regular intervals. And barely a day went by without the word revenge popping into her head at least once, and the vision of Keith Waterson's grinning face, captured for the newspapers, outside the courtroom.

...

24 June 2012

The day had been a difficult one for Lucy. Jayne would have been thirty years old, had she lived. She'd spent the day at home, their home, thinking about what could have been, if only.

If only that jerk hadn't nearly decapitated her.

If only we'd driven in my car, not the one Stein had bequeathed her in his will.

If only it had been me instead of Jayne.

If only, if only...

The last thing she did on Jayne's thirtieth birthday was to place a single red rose inside Steve Summer's 'coffin', in memorium. She vowed to herself and Sally-Anne that there would be more next year.

It's what she would have wanted, Lucy; blood for blood.

Yes, Sally-Anne; I want him to pay the price. I want him to suffer just like he's made us suffer. I'm sure it's what she would have wanted, revenge worthy of her memory. I feel like I'm beginning to forget.

Blood cannot be paid for by a simple fine, there is always a higher price to pay. Blood for blood, it has to be Lucy. I think it's what Jayne has been trying to tell us.

No name was mentioned, they knew who it was they both spoke of. No more words were needed.

25 June 2012

Rosie's fourth birthday. Lucy couldn't help but wonder at the double celebration they should be having. It had been the cruel hand of fate that had allowed Rosie to be born on the day after Jayne's birthday. Lucy would never be given the opportunity to get over Jayne, not that she would ever want to. Every year Rosie's birthday would be a constant reminder of Jayne's birthday; every day her own home would be a constant reminder of when she had been her happiest. She wouldn't change her home though, not for the world.

It hadn't been fate that had guided Keith Waterson that day. She didn't believe, like many people do, that you go 'when your time is up'. She didn't believe that the sand in Jayne's life-timer was pre-ordained to run out at that particular time, on that particular street. Lucy would never allow herself to forget. She decided that she was going to stay faithful to her lover; she would never again enjoy the intimate company of another woman. She was a one-woman woman. That is of course, apart from the intimate companion she'd been living with in her head these past seven years and more.

John and Steph had decided to celebrate Rosie's fourth birthday by giving her the option to choose whatever she wanted to do. This was a risky strategy to play with a four year old. Four years old, is an age where few, if any, boundaries apply when given the option to choose for yourself. Luckily for John and Steph she chose well.

She chose a trip to the zoo on a beautiful summer day. She did specify a proviso though, as the brightest children of that age frequently do. If her auntie Lucy couldn't come with them, she didn't want to go anywhere. Within ten minutes Lucy was in her car, driving to her brother's house. She had a big smile, lighting up her whole face, and a teddy bear so big it needed the whole of the passenger seat, all to itself.

She was just as happy as Rosie to be going to the zoo. She didn't care how many people she saw pointing in their direction, and nudging each other, she was with the people she loved. It was her niece's fourth birthday; no amount of public gawking was going to spoil the fun.

Rosie was thrilled with the teddy bear. She told Lucy she was going to call her Jayne. Different people have different methods of dealing with grief. Rosie had her own shrine to Jayne's memory, six teddies, all lined up in ascending order of size, all called Jayne.

Dawn Waterson, fifty-four year old single mother of Keith, couldn't believe her eyes when Lucy walked through the door of the gift shop. The same gift shop she herself managed, at the same zoo where Rosie was enjoying her fourth birthday.

This was the same woman she had wanted to speak to ever since the accident. The same woman she had wanted to apologise to for what her son had done. The same woman, who it appeared, was more beautiful in the flesh than on TV or on the glossy pages of the magazines. That same woman stood no more than fifteen feet away from her at that very moment. Dawn Waterson was a great believer in the hand of fate.

The gift shop was relatively quiet compared with other times during the day. Dawn was able to get close to Lucy by pretending to restack the miniature farm animals into some sort of order while Lucy picked Rosie up to show her some stuffed giraffes and elephants on the top shelf. From her lofty position Rosie spotted her dad near the ice cream freezer and immediately wanted to be with him. As soon as Rosie had her feet on the floor she was off like a shot.

"They can be a hand full at that age can't they?" Dawn remarked, as a means of an introduction to a conversation. "Enjoy your kids while they're young, sweet and innocent I say. Believe me they only cause you heartache in the end."

"Oh she's not mine, I'm only her aunt. At least I get to give her back when I'm tired." replied Lucy, happy to be discussing Rosie with this total stranger.

"I wish I could give mine back," said Dawn, "but he's thirty three now."

Lucy laughed at the comment, thinking that this woman she'd never met before, this woman with the kind face was just being friendly.

"Let me introduce myself, dear. I'm Dawn, Dawn Waterson." When that produced no reaction, "My son is Keith Waterson."

Lucy stopped dead, frozen to the spot. "This is some sick joke, right?"

"No, unfortunately I am Keith's mother."

Lucy turned to leave, the conversation now finished.

"I'm sorry," said Dawn, "I've wanted the chance to say sorry for so long. When you walked through the door I knew I just had to say something. I was wrong, I'm sorry."

Lucy turned on Dawn with thunder in her eyes. "Sorry? Sorry? Well thank you, Mrs Waterson; that makes me feel so much better now. Maybe now I'll be able to sleep at night!" At that particular moment sarcasm wasn't Lucy's strongest suit, but Dawn had known exactly what she'd meant. Now had not been the time or the place. There would probably never be a time or a place. Sorry could never put right what her son had done to this poor girl, she had only been thinking of her own selfish needs. She had wanted to get something off her chest and all she had done was to become the cause of more pain.

Lucy stormed out of the shop. Fortunately, for Rosie, the others had been concentrating too much on which ice cream to choose to pick up on the conversation. The last thing Lucy wanted was to spoil Rosie's big day. She put the conversation out of her mind, for now. Back in the safety of her home, however, she was able and most willing to discuss the day's events in full.

…

26 June 2012

At 10.00 am, on the day after Rosie's birthday, Lucy was making her way back to the zoo. Sally-Anne had made the suggestion; they'd talked long into the night. This woman was a way to get to the real prize, why waste the opportunity?

Wrap around sunglasses, her hair worn up beneath a baseball cap, and an extra large sweatshirt, went some way toward fooling the public away from instant recognition. She wouldn't be hanging around today though; she only wanted to speak with Dawn Waterson.

People usually make the gift shop their last port of call when they visit the zoo. The zoo's efforts to squeeze the last few pounds out of the public's pockets were invariably well rewarded; children can be very persuasive at the end of a long day.

The gift shop was usually very quiet for the first couple of hours. When Lucy walked through the door she was the very first customer. Dawn was the only member of staff there at that time; Emma who should have been there too had called in sick. Dawn was always first to arrive and last to leave, her staff was mainly made up of casual seasonal workers, students usually.

Dawn was surprised to see Lucy enter the gift shop for a second day running. Like waiting for a bus, you stand in the pouring rain for an age, and then two come along at once.

"Hello again," said Lucy nervously.

"Hello, you're the last person I expected to see in here today." Replied Dawn, not sure of what was happening.

"Look, I was angry yesterday, I'm not going to apologise for that but maybe we should talk. It's obvious that you've got things you want to say to me and I've got a few things I should probably get off my chest too, maybe we could do each other a favour, kill two birds with one stone?"

"I have got things I need to say to you," replied Dawn, "I've tried speaking to friends about the way I feel. God only knows I've tried, but they don't understand."

"Can you come to my place, tonight? I've thought about it since yesterday and I now think you could help me," said Lucy, "I think that's what you want isn't it? To help repair the damage your son caused."

"That's exactly what I want to do," replied Dawn, "I realised after we spoke yesterday that it must have been a shock to you when I told you who I was, but the last thing I wanted was to cause you more pain. My son has caused us both enough pain already, I can't forgive him and I don't expect you to, I just want to talk."

Lucy drew a map of where she should come from the tube station and asked her to use her discretion. "Obviously I'd rather the papers didn't find out about this, they'd have a field day if they knew. Neither of us would come out of it unscathed but I think I might just fair better than you when it comes to the headlines, trust me."

"Okay, whatever you want." Dawn said.

"Thank you. I'll' see you later." replied Lucy.

That was more than Dawn could have ever wished for, a real chance to explain her resentment toward her son, and to somebody who had good reason to understand exactly how she was feeling.

That evening Dawn Waterson rang the ground level buzzer to Lucy's apartment. She was buzzed in and Lucy was at the top of the stairs waiting.

"I came straight here, I hope you don't mind."

"No problem, I invited you, come in, let me take your jacket."

Dawn entered the apartment and followed Lucy through to the living room.

"Thank you for letting me do this," she said, "I was worried you may have changed your mind and told me to go away. I would have understood if you had."

"No I needed to see you, when you introduced yourself yesterday I thought it was probably destiny that brought us together. You can't ignore your destiny," Lucy said. "Would you like a drink, coffee or tea?"

"Tea, please"

"I'll not be long."

Lucy went into the kitchen, made a drink, composed herself and came back to the living room. Dawn had picked up the copy of the bible that Lucy had left on the coffee table.

Come into my parlour said the spider to the fly.

"Are you religious, Mrs Waterson?" asked Lucy, nodding towards the bible. "Can you turn the other cheek? Let somebody take a second shot?"

"I used to go to Sunday school when I was a child, but that was as far as it ever went," she said, putting the book down again. "I'm sorry about yesterday, I must have shocked you. I hope it didn't feel like a slap in the face, it wasn't a cheap shot if that's what you're thinking."

"Well." Said Lucy, "At the time I was angry, I must have sounded awful, but now I think we could help each other. I don't exactly feel like turning the other cheek yet, but there must be something in the bible that can work for us."

"I hope so. As I said yesterday, I've wanted to contact you since the accident, to tell you how sorry I was. Still am. When it first happened I wanted to ask you to forgive Keith for what happened but I soon realised I couldn't ask you to do that if I couldn't forgive him myself."

"But why would you need to forgive him, he never did you any harm did he?"

"He'd been lying to me all his life, I didn't know at the time," said Dawn, "you see it's like he has two sides to him, a good side and a bad side, two personalities. I only ever saw the good side until the newspapers uncovered his other side. I'll never be able to forgive him."

"And what do you want me to say? Good? Or maybe thank you for your support, it's much appreciated? What exactly is it you want from me?" said Lucy, her voice rising in pitch.

"I don't know," said Dawn, "This doesn't seem like such a good idea now. I'm sorry, I should go."

"Does he know you're here, your son? Is he out there waiting in his car, getting some thrill knowing you're in here now asking for my understanding, wanting me to bear my soul?"

"No he doesn't know I'm here, nobody knows I'm here, and I'll keep it that way. I can see that all this has done is to bring all the pain back for you. I'm sorry if I've upset you again, I shouldn't be here. I'll leave now."

"No, please, it's me who should be sorry." Said Lucy lowering her voice, "Jayne didn't die at your hands, you're only crime in all this, as far as I see it, was to have given birth to him in the first place. Stay, please. There is something I want to show you, if you want me to feel better you'll stay for a little longer."

"Okay, if you think it will help."

"I just want your opinion on something that's all, it won't take a minute. Then maybe you'll understand me better."

"Okay."

Lucy and Dawn finished their tea. If you knew no better you would have said they were mother and daughter sat there, chatting over a cup of tea. That was unless you could have listened in to the conversation.

"I'll just go and check that everything is in order before I let you see what I've got. It helps me get over the pain, I think everyone who has felt pain like I have should have one." said Lucy, "Back in a tick."

Dawn Waterson was intrigued. She had been feeling pain, not as much as Lucy, but maybe this could work for her too. Maybe she had been right to come here after all, hadn't Lucy said they could help each other? Maybe it had been destiny when they were thrown together yesterday.

Lucy was back in no time, "Okay," she said, "I'll show you what I've got that helps ease the pain, come on. Follow me."

With that Dawn was on her feet following quickly behind Lucy.

Entering the room Lucy said, "It's the second one along, take a look."

Dawn hadn't known what to expect, maybe a specially designed darkened room for meditation or a gym to help her relax. A room full of chest freezers would have been number one hundred and one on a list of the top one hundred of her probabilities.

"Don't be shy," Lucy said, "as I said earlier, I thought we could help each other out. Take a look."

Dawn pulled up the lid and looked inside. "But it's empty." She was about to say, just as the hammer struck the back of her head. Not a killing blow but one that would put her out for ten or fifteen minutes under normal circumstances. She slumped over the side of the freezer, her head and shoulders already inside. She looked like she'd fainted trying to find the last pack of chicken fillets or frozen peas. It was no effort for Lucy to lift her legs and finish the job. Lucy arranged her so that she was laid on her back, her legs pulled up to her chest.

"Now didn't I say we could help each other? You won't feel any more pain and I feel better too. Do you see? We all win." said Lucy.

With that Lucy shut the lid and flicked the switch to the on position. A satisfying hum followed as the unit started removing any heat from its internal compartment. A single ratchet strap secured the lid, ensuring that Dawn wouldn't escape her makeshift coffin, not unless she could put five tonnes of upward force on the inside of the lid. Clark Kent would have struggled in her position.

Lucy went back into the living room, retrieved the handbag from the floor next to where Dawn had been sitting only five minutes earlier, and returned to the freezer room. Pouring the contents of the bag on to the lid of the freezer she quickly picked out the map she'd drawn earlier that morning.

Dawn was one of the old school. She didn't have a mobile phone but she did carry a diary and an address book. They were her lifelines. The address book had her son's new address and telephone numbers and even his personal e-mail address. She may well have loathed him and asked him to find his own place when she discovered who he really was, but like every mother on the planet, she just couldn't break off all means of communication. Lucy had been relying on that. She was now closer to Keith Waterson than she'd ever been before.

Nice touch, Lucy; eye for eye, tooth for tooth, mother for mother.

My mother died at the hands of a man, it seemed like the only fair thing to do; it felt appropriate. I don't think he's going to miss his mum like I miss mine, but like you said, why waste the opportunity?

Just then a groan could be heard from inside the freezer, Dawn was coming round. It was the cruel hand of fate that had allowed her to regain consciousness in such a hopeless situation. Maybe this had been her destiny all along. Whether it was or it wasn't it didn't bother Lucy, she leaned over and flicked the switch onto quick freeze, in an hour or so Dawn Waterson would be frozen solid.

Vengeance is sweet, and sometimes very cold.

Twenty-Seven

Three days is all it took. Three days for the police to come knocking on his door. Three days for the finger of suspicion to point in his direction. Three days for the police to realise whose mother it was that hadn't turned up for work those past three days. Three days for his misery to start all over again.

She was another missing person to add to a growing list of missing people. This one was different though. This one was a fifty-four year old woman. This one was the mother of Keith Waterson, and the police knew all about Keith Waterson. This one was worth the effort, even after only three days.

The main problem the police had in solving this crime, if a crime had indeed been committed, was their inability to see beyond the result that they wanted. They were more than willing to look at the relationship Dawn Waterson had with her son. They were thrilled when they found a genuine breakdown in that particular mother and son relationship.

Working on the principal that murder victims generally know the person who commits the murder he was the obvious choice. That is, assuming she had been killed in the first place. There were some sick officers of the law who were actually praying that she would turn up one day soon, dead, and with enough evidence to get the hooligan put away for a very long time.

The tabloids and broadsheets picked up the next chapter in Keith Waterson's story with relish. Of course, he was completely innocent of any wrongdoing, yet he was a very lucky man that the law stated that he was innocent until proven guilty.

The British newspapers are excellent at causing a hue and cry where none should exist. But then, the British public love a good story and are willing to rise to the bait when it's so eloquently presented. Had the case ever come to court a good defence lawyer would have had it thrown out on prejudice alone, never mind the fact that he would be innocent of all charges.

The only thing the police could have possibly charged him with in this case would be that of 'upsetting a parent or parents over a previous action or actions unspecified'. As of yet that is still not a criminal offence under British law. But if it were ever to become part of British law then the streets would surely be a much quieter place of an evening. They would be desolate, as all parents can attest to.

The case against Keith Waterson for the murder of his mother would, of course, never come to court. Dawn Waterson would remain on the list of missing persons until some evidence of her whereabouts came to light, good or bad. There was little chance of this happening. But you could at least say all evidence was being preserved, at a regulated minus fifteen degrees centigrade.

Lucy couldn't do anything against Keith Waterson until the police were well out of his life. But she could wait. She enjoyed following the story, she even made it into the story in some newspapers. This just served as a reminder to her of why she was pursuing him. Each time she was mentioned it was in relation to the crash, and each time the crash was mentioned so was Jayne, and her part in the accident.

She could wait. She had plenty of work lined up, if anything her celebrity was still growing. To the outside observer she was getting on with her life, not exactly what you'd call moving on, that would be wrong, but people believed she was coping. It was what people wanted to believe, and it was true, she really was coping, in her own way.

Her dreams were happy dreams, when she encountered Jayne in her dreams it was as if nothing had changed. She still had the flowing red hair and pretty face. She still had that wonderful pale complexion and hazel eyes. She still had a head that was fully connected to her neck.

Twenty-Eight

Christmas was never a good time for Lucy. If it wasn't for Rosie at Christmas she didn't know what she'd do. Become insane probably, that was what she thought might happen. But then again, Sally-Anne was always there watching out for her.

On the twenty-fourth of December 2012 Jayne stopped visiting Lucy in her dreams. For the past six months it had seemed that Jayne was always in her dreams, always happy. This had happened before though, she knew the next time she'd dream about Jayne in a happy way would be after some retribution. Lucy placed two red roses of remembrance that day, one on Steve Summer's body and one on Dawn Waterson's body. She retrieved Dawn's address book and diary in the hope of finding a chink in Keith Waterson's armour.

There were only two male names in Dawn Waterson's address book, that of her son and that of Mark Howard. She certainly didn't have many male friends, not according to her address book anyway.

This Mark Howard Lucy, he might be her brother or a cousin, some relative. He might even be her lover.

    Why are you so interested in him, Sally-Anne?
Opportunity?
Opportunity for what?
Revenge.

How would that be revenge, other than the fact that he's male? Revenge I can live with, senseless killing I struggle with. Steve Summer was my revenge on the men at large, been there done that. The person I want revenge on is Keith Waterson. That is what Jayne would want. We've got his mother's body next door in cold storage, remember?

I haven't forgotten that, Lucy. Whose suggestion was it that put her there in the first place?

It was your suggestion of course.

Lucy, ask yourself this question. How did Rosie feel when Jayne died?

She was too young to understand what really happened, she was sad, but probably because she was surrounded by sadness at the time. She was only two years old when Jayne died, Sally-Anne.

And the teddy bears; each one named Jayne. Is that not her own personal shrine Maybe? You say she doesn't understand?

She's four years old, Sally-Anne. She doesn't even understand what dying means, how could she?

But we swore revenge for Rosie or don't you remember that now? Are you going soft again?

Keith Waterson is going to be revenge for Rosie. He caused the pain.

She lost her Auntie though Lucy. Wound for wound, remember?

Yes I remember. He's lost his mother already though, and he doesn't seem too upset by that. Denial is all he's given us so far, no expression of love towards her, no expression of possible grief.

That's right, so we haven't caused him the same wound. He hasn't suffered the same loss. As far as he knows his mother just upped and left and is living the life of Reilly somewhere. Even if he knew she was dead would he grieve any longer than he needs to for a public show? Come on, Lucy; answer me that one.

No, you're right, I don't think he would. But then he probably doesn't care that much for anyone apart from himself.

Wound for wound, Lucy.

Okay I agree you're correct again, Sally-Anne; wound for wound. I don't know how to make him feel that pain, how to wound him in that way. He's such a callous bastard; he doesn't love anybody the way that people loved Jayne. What can we do to him that's going to make him wish he'd never been born?

We'll think of something, don't worry. Just trust me, Lucy, if that's what you want, we'll think of something.

Mark Howard was fortunate. Keith Waterson didn't even know him. He was just a plumber his mother had used a couple of times in the recent past. He was of no use to Lucy and Sally-Anne. He'd come so close, but he would never know that he was being thought of in the terms of an opportunity for revenge. He really was a fortunate plumber.

Lucy now understood that to just kill Keith Waterson would be to let him off lightly. Sally-Anne had been right, before she could put him out of his useless existence she had to cause him some more misery, make him pay what he rightfully owed her. But not only her, there were others who had a claim on his life.

She had killed his mother not to get back at him. That had been purely to do with Lucy's own mother's death. She now realised that any mother would have fulfilled that fantasy, it hadn't needed to be her. Dawn Waterson had just handed her the opportunity on a plate, the only thing that Lucy had done was to take it, with both hands and a fourteen-ounce hammer. It had felt so right, kismet really.

Wound for wound.

...

It appeared, from the outside looking in, that Keith Waterson was untouchable. He had either stopped supporting his beloved Chelsea, or he'd become invisible on match days. The police never saw him there, as hard as they were looking for him. He paid his council taxes on time, and his road tax, he even submitted his income tax returns on time. He was squeaky clean; he could even be seen polishing his car every Sunday morning, seemingly a pillar of respectability.

He wasn't back in the city earning six figure bonuses but he was doing okay. He earned his money playing the markets from home. He'd made a lot of people rich doing it before, and he had a big enough starting point to make it worthwhile. If he could just build up his portfolio over the next few years he would probably be able to leave his 'beloved' Britain behind him by the time he reached forty, move on to pastures new, leave any stigma in his wake.

He only drew a subsistence wage from his portfolio at this stage, and it was only a matter of a short time before he'd be able to get his hands on his mothers frozen assets. She would soon be declared dead in the absence of any sign of her still being alive. As of yet there had been no signs of that and Keith was no longer under any suspicion regarding her death.

Keith moved back home, 'to look after the place until his mother showed up'. He didn't want the house to fall into the hands of squatters; it was his inheritance after all. Dawn hadn't changed her will in the past six years, but then she hadn't counted on dying just yet.

Owning a property in London was becoming the domain of the wealthy, he was sitting pretty. The old bat didn't have a bank full of money, but at least the house would bolster his portfolio. Sell up and move North, Newcastle maybe, or possibly Glasgow, that was his plan. He could practically buy a whole street of houses in Newcastle for what he'd get for his mother's house. The football team weren't too bad either. It didn't really matter to him where he went, away from London and some place he could set up his computer and have Internet access; that was all he needed.

The house; that was it! The same house that Lucy realised she had a full set of keys for. The same house that Lucy could enter more or less at will. Front door, back door, garage, and window locks, she had everything she needed, why had it taken her so long to realise it? What she needed had been in cold storage all this time.

She'd been too busy, she'd lost her focus. Maybe Sally-Anne was right. Maybe she really was going soft. She decided then that she had been working too hard. She was going to be choosier in future about what she would and wouldn't do workwise.

Lucy needed to think, and she needed Sally-Anne's expertise. If she was going to do this she would need a plan, but at least she had the seed of an idea forming in her head from which a full-blown plan could emerge, given time. A little careful thought and the right conditions and the plan would be ready.

Twenty-Nine

Sunday 18 May 2013 was when Lucy and Sally-Anne were happy enough with their plan to put it into action. This was going to be pay back time, it felt so right.

The next day Lucy announced to the agencies that she was taking an extended holiday. At the age of just twenty-one, and with only five years in the industry, she was rich enough to leave the modelling world behind and embark on a different career if she so wished. She could even retire from modelling altogether if she wanted to, she had been approached by several television companies, and she was even being talked about within the film industry as a future Bond girl. There wasn't much the agencies could do to persuade her to change her mind; they were just praying that when she was ready she'd come back to them.

That evening Lucy was, once again, grateful for the impersonality of shopping on the web. Just place an order and wait for delivery, whatever it is, next day, if you want, for a small additional fee. Theatrical costumes, make-up and wigs, a laptop computer, business cards and a three-year-old, bottom of the range, Ford Transit van in dark blue, that would do for a start.

Lucy needed to make it her business to find out what Keith Waterson's habits were, both clean and dirty. She wasn't going to be able to pull it off looking like herself; driving a white soft-top Mercedes, and sticking out like the proverbial sore thumb. So she made sure she didn't.

Looking in the mirror she was pleased with her efforts. She was wearing a black shoulder length wig and a body suit that mimicked perfectly the body of some poor soul who found herself in the seventh month of a long hard pregnancy. A maternity dress, sunglasses and 'sensible' training shoes made her look like any other young mother to be. She didn't look her best but then she didn't want to.

My god, just look at you! That is not a good look, Lucy. But it's one hell of a disguise.

Thanks. Who do I look like?

I don't know exactly, but I think we can rest safe in the knowledge that you're not going to make it onto the cover of Vogue looking like that.

That's the whole point, Sally-Anne. People won't give me a second glance, especially the men. They won't bother looking at what they can't have. As far as they're concerned I'm shop soiled, damaged goods, practically invisible.

For a whole week Lucy stayed in a small hotel around the corner from his house, pregnancy suit and all; complete with French accent just for good measure. For a whole week she parked her van on his street at half past eight in the morning until half past six at night, watching from the comfort of an armchair in the back, unseen, noting down his every move. The van could have been one of thousands of tradesman's vans parked on the streets of every city in the UK any day of the week. It was nothing to attract suspicion.

She didn't mind any discomfort she might feel while she was sat there, hour after hour, just watching. She had a plan, no, they had a plan, and knowing where they were headed was worth any discomfort she felt on the way to getting there.

Where he lived was a quiet street, one of those where eighty five percent of the houses were empty during the day. These were houses where both partners went off to work in the morning, and the kids off to school. Not too many kids in this street though, not much of anything going on really, perfect.

After three days Lucy had noted what a lazy bastard he was, not once had he gone out on foot. She quickly picked up on the fact that he went out for his lunch every day at twelve noon, probably to a local pub. This took between an hour and one hour fifteen minutes. His only other daytime jaunt was to do a shop at the local supermarket on Friday afternoon, again in the car. At no time during the whole week did he have any visitors, male or female.

She'd had enough, he was a creature of habit, lunchtime it would be.

The following Monday she parked her van sixty yards from his house at ten minutes to twelve and sat there with her back to his house, waiting for his car. He didn't disappoint, just after twelve o'clock a flash of blue 4x4 raced past her right on cue. She watched it turn left at the crossroads, just as expected, then climbed out of the van slinging the laptop computer bag over her shoulder of her maternity dress.

Making sure there was nobody on the road she went up his driveway and rang the bell. Thirty seconds and still no answer. She went around the back of the semi-detached property, pulled on her latex gloves and took the bunch of keys out of her bag. Seven keys in total, some obviously keys from work, she found the right one at the second attempt. She turned the key and opened the door. A buzzer immediately sounded; a pre-warning of an imminent alarm. That very same buzzer that says, 'turn me off or run like hell, come on do it now sucker!'

She had thought of this, and she knew she had only one chance. She raced through the house to the front door and found the alarm panel conveniently situated, flashing at her to hurry up. One chance only, she keyed in the numbers six, eight, zero, four. The buzzer went silent, Sally-Anne had been right the four digit number written on the back inside cover of the address book had been the alarm code.

Thank you, Sally-Anne.

No problem, it was either the alarm or the PIN number for her bankcard. We had a fifty-fifty chance at worst.

And at best?

It depends how you look at it. Synchronicity Lucy, can't you feel it? This was meant to happen. Anyway, you have to take a risk at times, especially when the prize is so good. Come on let's not waste any more time.

Had that four-digit number, innocuously written at the time, been anything other than the alarm code Lucy would now be walking away from the house. Just slow enough so as not to raise too much suspicion, her plans, their plans in tatters.

As it was, Lucy ran upstairs, found the study where Keith pored over his personal finances seven hours a day, five days a week, and opened her computer bag.

Look at this place, the guy's a pig, but walk into the study and it's like walking into a show home. Be careful not to leave any trace of our visit.

I wasn't planning on doing, Sally-Anne!
Okay, okay, keep your hair on.
Very funny!

The first thing to come out of the bag was two A4 sized pieces of printing paper, bog standard, nothing fancy; the same generic type of paper currently residing in ninety five percent of the U.K's home printers. These she placed into the printer carefully, making sure she didn't disturb anything.

One down.

The second one was going to take a little longer. The computer that Keith used daily was still switched on. He was as lazy as she'd expected him to be.

Come on, come on, hurry up Lucy said to herself.
Calm down, we've only been here five minutes, everything's okay.
Another five minutes and Lucy had registered Dawn Waterson with a Hotmail e-mail address, via Keith Waterson's, own computer registering her address as the one her son Keith now owned, or very nearly owned.

Two down.

She took an old lipstick out of the pocket of the laptop bag's external pocket. The laptop she hadn't needed because Keith had been so lazy. It was Dawn Waterson's old lipstick.

Find her bedroom, Lucy. It shouldn't take too long, only two to choose from.

The bedroom she wanted was at the rear of the house. It was neat, definitely a woman's touch, but in need of a good dust and polish. She sidestepped the bed and closed the curtains, switching on the bedside lamp to see by and was finished shortly afterwards.

Three down. The Key Lucy, lock the door on your way out. That's going to confuse him.

Looking at her watch she could see the whole escapade had lasted no longer than twenty minutes. They decided to have a last look in the study to make sure nothing was out of place then a quick glance in each of the other rooms, a sort of recce just in case they needed to come back at a later date.

At twenty-eight minutes past twelve she reset the alarm. Sneaking out of the back door she relocked it, removed the gloves, and walked around the side of the house as bold as brass, down the road, and into the van. If anybody saw her they wouldn't have dreamed that a heavily pregnant woman could be up to no good. She gave nothing away with her body language; she could walk confidently with the best of them. It was, after all, what she'd been trained to do. And didn't everyone always tell her she'd been born to do it? She was a natural.

See? It was easy.
That should give the little shit something to chew over.

They stayed parked on his street, in the van, just to check on his regularity. At ten past one the 4x4 came past and shortly afterwards swung into the driveway.

Give it another five minutes. Let's just see if he gives any sign of having noticed anything wrong.

When five minutes had passed she switched on the ignition and drove away. Nobody had noticed anything to cause them any concern, not even Keith Waterson. By that time Keith was back in his study, computer still booted up; ready to play the markets oblivious to what had happened while Lucy drove away.

The markets were slow that afternoon, the FTSE had barely moved all morning. Keith had what he called his bankers, the shares that would make money over a twelve-month period compared to the rest of the market, generally the blue chip companies. These were the ones that he knew he needed to stop himself from being in too high a loss at any one time. What he really liked though was to get the short-term gains that can be had by buying just at the right time and selling shortly afterwards. A bank raid was how he thought of these investments, quickly in, take the cash, and then run. It didn't always work, sometimes he got it wrong, but his experience was paying dividends. He knew what to look for in the company reports, he was adept at being able to read between the lines and pick the winners.

That afternoon the markets were flat and so was he, too much lunch maybe, his mind just wasn't on it. He spent time looking at the local papers. The estate agents in particular were what interested him that afternoon, which one to choose when it came to selling his inheritance. In the end he rang two agents and arranged for valuations later that week. He wanted to get an idea of where the property market stood. He'd only sell at the best time; he was good at that. And after all, the house was only part of his portfolio, it wasn't a home, it never had been as far as he was concerned.

The first thing he noticed was when he went to bed later that night. He hadn't noticed anything earlier when it was daylight but he couldn't fail to notice the faint strip of light coming from beneath his mother's bedroom door in the darkness. He wasn't too scared by this, he was a pragmatist, there had to be a reasonable explanation. Lights just don't switch themselves on he knew that much for sure.

He hadn't been in his mother's bedroom since the day he'd moved back in. There had been no point; he just closed the door on that part of his previous home life, literally.

He was curious, no more than that really to see what was making the light come through the bedroom door. Maybe a neighbour had installed some floodlight system to the rear of their house and it was just shining through the window, it was always dark at night back there. Or maybe it was a particularly strong full moon that night. Whatever the cause he thought he'd have a look.

It was only when he tried the door and couldn't get in that he started to question his pragmatism. He'd never locked the door; in fact he couldn't remember any door ever being locked in this house. It had been his mother's idea to keep the original keys in all the doors; she'd said it was a quaintly Victorian thing to do, dating back to the times when people had been more modest than in these modern times. The doors were an original feature of the house, the keys stayed.

Okay, he thought, the door has swelled somehow and become stuck, no problem. He then decided to take a look outside, see if he was right about the lighting or the moon, just to satisfy his curiosity more than anything. It was only when he got outside in the dark that he realised the moon was behind clouds and the rear of the house was no more lit by extra lighting than it had ever been.

Strange, he thought. It was only when he looked up at the window and saw the curtains closed and faintly lit from within that his heart skipped a beat. Fuck, he thought, someone's been in. But that made no sense whatsoever, he hadn't noticed anything missing. If anybody were to go to the trouble of breaking in surely they would steal something, the television, his computer, anything. But nothing had been taken, nothing of value anyway. The only thing he was certain of was that someone had been in his mother's bedroom.

The question of calling the police at this point never even entered his head. He'd had his fill of the boys in blue. The last people he was going to invite into his house willingly were the police. Before he re-entered the house he opened up the garage and retrieved a hammer and a bolster chisel. He was going to get into that bedroom one way or another, and if he weren't alone then at least he'd have a weapon. He could feel his heart pumping; it was what Saturday afternoons had been like on match day, he was beginning to relish the thought of an interloper in his house. He actually wanted to confront someone and defend his property, maybe give that person a good kicking like the good old days. He was well up for it by now.

He rushed back indoors and locked the front and back doors. If there was somebody there they weren't just going to run out of the house and escape from him that easily. He ran up the stairs, his mission well fixed in his mind, his resolve as firm as it had been for a couple of years.

He tried the door again just in case he'd been wrong. Putting his shoulder into it this time it still didn't budge. Taking the hammer and chisel he gave a warning, "Whoever you are, be afraid, I'm coming in." It took him six blows with the hammer and chisel before the lock gave way and the door swung open on its hinges. Keith was in there immediately with the hammer poised. What he saw when the red mist had settled was far worse than he'd expected. The light source had been his mother's bedside lamp. That wasn't what shocked him though. On his mother's dressing table mirror somebody had written a message for him in lipstick.

I'm back, Keith. Back from the grave. Don't think you can get rid of me that easily.

Your ever-loving mother!

He dropped the hammer to the floor in his surprise.

No body had ever been found. She wasn't necessarily dead. She could still be alive after all this time. He spotted a key on the floor and picked it up, now he was even more confused. Whoever had locked the door had locked it from the inside, but how? He thought. There was no one but him there. The duvet and the pillow had an indentation, as if somebody had lain down for a rest, but where were they now?

The key had been Sally-Anne's idea, it wasn't the bedroom door key but the key to the gift shop storeroom, the same gift shop that had once been managed by Keith's 'ever-loving mother'. Keith wasn't to know that though, it looked like the same type of key as in each of the others in the house, but it had been one of the seven keys on the key ring in Dawn's handbag.

Keith was totally confused; what had just happened? What did it all mean?

Was his mother still alive? Well if she was back, as she'd put it, she certainly wasn't here now.

And why did she leave the message? Don't think you can get rid of me that easily. What did that mean?

Keith had been as convinced as everyone that his mother had died. How she'd died he didn't have the faintest idea. The only thing he'd known for certain was that it hadn't been anything to do with him.

How do you lock a door from the inside and escape? That was his next thought. Ladders maybe, he just couldn't see his mother climbing out of an upstairs window in order to confuse him. He opened the curtains and looked for evidence of escape, there wasn't any. The window ledge was covered in dust, which had obviously never been disturbed. Nobody had been through the window, he even tried to open it and it was locked; now that would have been a good trick, he thought.

The idea that his mother's spirit had come back to haunt him was a preposterous one at best and just plain ridiculous. He didn't believe in all that spiritualism crap, as far as he was concerned when you died it was the end of the story, no epilogue.

What to do next though? If he'd had thousands of pounds worth of goods stolen he would have to call the police for insurance purposes. Nothing had been taken as far as he could see. The last thing he wanted would be for the police to be reading the message written in lipstick on his mother's dressing table mirror. He could just imagine them rubbing their hands together with glee.

'Don't think you can get rid of me that easily', and what exactly do you suggest your mother means by that Mr Waterson?"

No, he didn't want to go there again. He wiped the message off the mirror, getting rid of any trace of the fact that it had ever existed. He put the lipstick in the bedside cabinet and promised himself that he'd replace the lock on the door prior to any future viewing by a potential buyer.

He closed his mother's bedroom door and went to bed. He didn't sleep very well that night; he couldn't get his mother out of his head. When he did eventually drop off into a restless slumber he had a dream about his mother. He couldn't quite remember the details when he woke; he thought it might well have been a nightmare judging by the sweat covering his body and the state of his bed linen.

After taking a shower he looked in to see what a mess his mother's bedroom was in after the previous night. The door lock was broken but otherwise the room was pretty much how it should have been. There were no more messages on the mirror, no more indentations in the bedclothes. He made his mind up there and then that he'd sort out the bedroom door lock, and he'd have the front and rear door locks changed all at the same time. It wouldn't be cheap, but then he didn't want another night like last night in a hurry. While he was at it he'd find the manual for the alarm system and change the code for that too. If somebody had broken in yesterday, and he was now preying that had been the case, then the sick bastards wouldn't find it so easy in future.

He wasn't sure what had happened the previous evening. He'd only been out for his lunch, an hour at the most, and when he came home everything had seemed normal enough. There had been no forced entry, no alarm trip registered on the panel, nothing. It was as if...He didn't want to even consider the possibility.

Lucy waited. She was going to give him a week or so before reinforcing the fact that he wasn't alone any more. He was about to do it all by himself though. His problem would be one of not knowing who was paying him all the attention, his dead mother, or his living mother. Try as he might he could never believe that his mother would 'abscond', without a word, only to return nearly a year later, dead or alive. But return was a strong word, he hadn't seen her, he hadn't even heard her. If she was still alive why didn't she just come home? He was quite willing to move out again, start afresh elsewhere, it just meant his inheritance had flown south but so what. The other alternative, the one where his mother was dead was unthinkable. If that was true, he thought, his mother's ghost was now haunting him.

On the Thursday of that week, with the markets looking flat at best, Keith decided to print off some research. He had been tracking a couple of small companies for the past two weeks with a view to investing, so he printed off the latest copy of each company financial reports to read at his leisure. He was fairly certain he was on to a couple of winners; he just wanted to check the reports again before committing himself.

As the printer churned out the reports he sat back and put his feet up. He hadn't seen any evidence of his mother's existence, alive or dead, since Monday. He'd had the locks changed on Tuesday and that had seemed to put an end to the matter. He wasn't exactly overcome with joy at the fact that it had happened in the first place, but at least it hadn't happened again.

When the printer went silent he reached for the two reports and sorted them into order. It was the last two sheets that caught his eye, caught his eye and squeezed his heart. His whole world stopped for a moment while he took in exactly what he was seeing in his hands. Just the minute before he'd been thinking he was rid of the problem when up it popped, raising its ugly head yet again.

It appeared that whoever, or whatever, was doing this to him was happy to allow him to become comfortable with life once more before firing another shot. It was as if his mother had gotten into his head and was reading his thoughts. Printed at the top of the first two sheets was a message for him, from his mother. It was not like he could miss it either, printed in large bold black lettering.

Hello again son!
I know what you are
I know what's in your head
I know who caused my <u>death</u>

That was the message printed on top of page one.

You <u>will</u> pay the price.
I <u>will</u> have my revenge.
Your ever-loving feckless mother!

This one appeared on top of page two.

It looked like it had been printed on top of the financial report, it stood out so clear. It hadn't of course; it had been printed five days earlier on Lucy's printer. He wasn't to know that though, he couldn't even think straight, let alone try to reason the situation through sensibly.

As far as Keith was concerned everything pointed towards his mother being an avenging spirit; a spirit intent on taking out her death on him, the reason for which he didn't know. The truth of the situation was that Dawn Waterson would still be alive today were it not for her son, so he had been the cause of her death, that was a fact. He didn't know that though, how could he? He didn't even know she was really dead. He'd wished for it on occasions over the past six Months, maybe, but he was truly beginning to believe she was dead now.

'Take it to the police', now there was a thought, a thought that barely registered. How could he take this to the police? He felt isolated.

'I know who caused my death.' Now then, what exactly do you think 'your ever-loving feckless mother' meant by that Mr Waterson? It sounds a bit like murder to me. 'You will pay the price, I will have my revenge.' It's all kind of pointing in your direction isn't it Mr Waterson? What do you say? The police would say.

Maybe he'd take it to the police, when hell froze over, but certainly not before.

Early the following Monday saw Lucy don her disguise yet again. This time, however, she took her every day car. She had a long journey to make so the van definitely wasn't her preferred mode of transport. She was going to Manchester, she wanted to pay her respects to her mother, and then she would cut across to Wigan, she was ready. She had never been able to pay a visit to Jayne's final resting place before now. But now she wanted to explain to Jayne her plan for revenge, on Jayne's behalf. And somewhere on her return journey she planned to call in at an Internet café, keep in touch with Keith, so to speak, much later that evening.

When it came to visiting her Mother's grave she couldn't do it. It wasn't that she'd been overcome with grief and couldn't face it. The fact was that she knew that when she'd look at her mother's name on the headstone her father's name would be just one above it. That fact alone meant she didn't even get past the entrance to the cemetery. The thought of even reading his name repulsed her.

When she reached the small cemetery on the outskirts of Wigan however, the story was a very different one. Having been unable to attend Jayne's funeral because she was in a coma; and having grieved over the fact ever since, she was not to be rushed. The sun was shining and she had a lot to say.

Back in London Keith was having a problem concentrating. His mind was definitely elsewhere; it had been since the previous Thursday. He was just waiting for his mother to contact him again. In his mind it was inevitable. He couldn't believe it, in the space of a week he had gone from what he thought of as, sensible Joe average, into a jumping at shadows, every-day Joe haunted.

His main problem was that he had nobody he could turn to, nobody with whom he could discuss what was happening to him. In short, Keith Waterson had no friends; he didn't even have his mother to turn to now, or so it seemed.

Keith wouldn't be able to play the markets in his state of mind. He thought of it like gambling on horses, if he didn't concentrate on studying form, and place his bets based on performance he would end up losing his stake. In this frame of mind he might as well use a pin to pick his winners. Keith needed to minimise his risks, to do this he needed to be fully switched on. At that moment he wasn't but he was willing to try anything.

He went upstairs to his mother's bedroom. Standing outside he fumbled in his pocket for the key, the new key, to unlock the door. His heart was racing now, he wasn't sure what he was going to be confronted with when he opened the door, but he was going in.

He calmed down when he saw that the room had been left untouched, by anyone or anything, since the locksmith's visit.

If his mother was going to 'speak' to him from beyond the grave he was sure as hell going to have his say too. He picked up the lipstick and went to the dressing table mirror.

I did not kill you.
Leave me alone
Spiteful bitch.

Your never loving son!

He slammed the door on his way out and locked it once again. If his mother was really haunting him she would have no need for a key. If it was somebody other than his mother, somebody playing tricks on him, they would never be able to reply to the message. 'Come on then Mother', Keith thought, 'let's see what you make of that'.

Lucy's time in Keith's house had been spent well; he was unknowingly being sucked in to her game, and his own imagination was Lucy's strongest ally.

He left the house that afternoon, he needed to get away, drown his sorrows and forget. When a taxi dropped him off later that night his mind was anaesthetised to anything much other than sleep. He took a bottle of scotch to bed and ten minutes later was sleeping like a baby.

He wasn't to know that an e-mail awaited him when he next logged-on. It was probably better that he slept, for now.

Thirty

Tuesday was a fine day, and Keith woke from his stupor a much happier man. He'd slept well, the best he'd slept in days. Maybe today was going to be a good day; strong markets would be a good start.

After a long shower, more to fully wake him up than clean himself, he felt good. By eight o'clock he was booting up his computer and then logging on to his e-mail address. Whilst he was waiting he decided to look in his mother's room to convince himself that nothing had happened. When he opened the door and looked in it was relief that he saw everything just as he'd left it. His message hadn't been replaced by a more sinister one from his mother.

Now he felt good, he locked his mother's bedroom and went to work, second door on the left, past the bathroom. When he sat down at his desk he could see the message 'you have mail' flashing. He went directly to his inbox and what he saw ruined his day. Ten minutes past eight in the morning and he already knew his day had flipped over. He was sure it was going to be his mind next.

He had seventeen e-mails that morning, nothing too unusual in that. Most of them were spam. He had e-mail from his brokers. He worked with three different brokers, two of them nearly every day. E-mail was a good method of communicating business. The name Dawn Waterson in the 'from' column, however, meant his life was getting stranger by the minute.

There was an un-nerving inevitability to the manner in which he accepted an e-mail from his dead mother. 'Why not', he thought 'the old bitch is just going to keep on wearing me down, just open it and look at what it says'.

He double clicked on the e-mail.

Keith,
You might not have killed me but now I am dead.
I would still have every reason to live but for you.
I would still be living today but for you.
You have never loved anybody but yourself.
You are an empty vessel Keith, a shell.
You have nothing now, and you never will have.
We need to talk; you need to know the truth.
When I am at rest you will also be able to rest.
Allow me to rest, if not for me do it for yourself.
<u>Please</u>.

The fourth line of text jumped off the page and smacked him in the face.

'You have never loved anybody but yourself'.

He printed the e-mail off and ran to his mother's bedroom. He fumbled with the key needing two attempts to locate it he was shaking so much. When he did manage to unlock the door he looked at the message he had written the night before. Again the fourth line jumped off the mirror and slapped him in the face.

You have never loved anybody but yourself

And what he'd written on the mirror

Your never loving son!

He couldn't believe it; he'd written it on the mirror to provoke a response. Well that wasn't true, he'd written it so he could dismiss the whole episode when no response was forthcoming. But here it was in his hands. Proof, somebody or something was fucking with his brain.
He was struggling to breathe now; he had to get out of the house. He picked up his car keys and his jacket and practically flew

out of the front door, barely turning round to make sure the door was locked behind him. He jumped into his car and drove. He wasn't bothered where to, he just wanted to get away from that house.

Keith didn't notice the dark blue transit van parked opposite his mother's house. Why would he? Lucy was fairly sure though from what she'd seen that Keith had opened up his e-mail that morning. Judging by the look on his face It was either that or he had something more sinister happening in his life than being haunted by his dead mother. She doubted that, not even he could be so unlucky.

She waited a minute, jumped out of the van and made her way down the drive of 14 Smethwick Road. She wasn't going in today though, she just posted an envelope through the letterbox and left. An hour later the postman posted his mail through the same letterbox. There was no sign of the Land Cruiser parked in the driveway, like there was on every other day he delivered the mail to Keith, and there was no sign of a dark blue Transit van on the road. Lucy was back home by then, her new mobile phone switched on and waiting.

Of course, the new phone wasn't in Lucy's name. She had bought a pay-as-you-go phone for cash and registered it in the name of Pippa D Manning. This was the name of one of her old classmates from Manchester. When she had registered the phone she gave the address three houses down from where she had lived in Aldershot. Mr and Mrs Jordan, who now lived at that address, would receive the letter welcoming Pippa D Manning as a new customer to the Orange network, they would think that the sender had mistaken the road name and place it back in the post-box marked 'addressee not known at this address'. The letter would disappear into the black hole that is the mail system; only to be given the same priority a dog gives to local government policy regarding fouling of public areas.

When Keith returned home later that day he was once again the worse for drink. That didn't stop him driving home though; he was one of those who believed lightning never struck twice. He had already had his fair share of bad luck in a car, and at this particular time he couldn't give a shit what happened to him anyway.

Picking up the mail on his way in, he carried it through to the lounge where he sat down and promptly fell asleep. Sticking to the speed limits and concentrating on his driving had obviously taken its toll on him, that and the seven pints of lager currently dimming all his senses.

It was twenty past three when he woke, his neck stiff from the position he'd been sleeping in for the past three hours. He still had the mail on his lap when he stood up to go to the bathroom. It was soon on the floor and he was stumbling to find the light switch before he wet himself. When he reached the downstairs toilet he relieved himself quickly, the ecstasy of this simple act bringing a smile to his face for the first time since the previous morning.

He'd forgotten exactly why he'd gone out until then. Why he'd spent the day in London's seediest districts trying to distract his mind with something more pleasurable. Why he'd then spent time in the pubs around Chelsea Football Club, his old stomping ground. Now he remembered exactly why.

Just at that moment in time he would have loved to feel the softness of his bed and the comfort of being wrapped up in his duvet. He found the thought of climbing the stairs to his bedroom too much though. He would see his mother's bedroom; even with the door locked it was now a fear-provoking place. He also knew that his mother was contacting him through his computer, an essential tool for him to track his investments, now also a fearsome part of his everyday life. He needed to get a grip, and soon, before he lost it completely.

He went back into the lounge and lay on the settee. He'd decided that getting a grip could wait another day at least. Besides which, he was still woozy from the alcohol in his system, he knew he couldn't guarantee any of his actions in the state he was in.

He woke the next morning just before seven, his head banging out a steady rhythm he just couldn't quite place. He was just about to go for a shower when he decided it could wait; the shower was upstairs and he wasn't ready for that yet. He decided on a cup of tea instead. He would come round fully then take on the world, and its mother.

He took the mail from the previous day with him into the kitchen, determined to keep his mind from wandering too far so early in the day. Two companies offering loans, both addressed to his mother, one asking the addressee to sign up to their pay per view network, a gas bill, and a letter addressed to him. If he had taken the time to look he would have noticed there was no postmark on the stamp. This was because Lucy wanted to guarantee delivery the day after sending the e-mail.

He quickly disposed of the junk mail, put the bill to one side and opened the letter. It was a handwritten note with a business card attached. The business card was in the name Pippa D Manning. The card had on it the name, a telephone number and the single word 'Medium' printed in gothic script. Lucy thought the gothic script added just the right touch of mystery. That along with the high quality of the card, she hoped, would be enough to convince him that this was no hoax. His mind was so revved up at that particular moment though that she probably could have written it in crayon, on the back of a cigarette packet, and he would still have been in a mind to believe. The note attached was simple enough.

Dear Mr Waterson

Please forgive me for writing to you in this manner. I can assure you that it is not something I would consider doing under normal circumstances. These circumstances though, are far from normal.

As you can see from my card, I am a medium by profession. This means I can contact the spirits of people who have passed away, usually for the comfort of a grieving friend or relative. Under normal circumstances the contact would happen at my behest. As I wrote earlier though, these are not normal circumstances.

I understand the prejudices that people have against things they don't yet understand. Please read on Mr Waterson, don't condemn this to your rubbish bin just yet, for your own sake.

I have recently had a spirit contact me, asking for my help. I believe this spirit to be the spirit of your recently passed mother. She desperately wants to talk to you. She told me your name and the address I could contact you at. Obviously I felt in the circumstances that the best means for me to contact you *initially would be by mail. Some people need a while to take these things in, alone, rather than being confronted face to face.*

Your mother is not yet at peace and says that she needs your help to find it. She has set out on a journey that we all must make eventually. Some spirits need to resolve some issues they had in their previous life before they can move on. This is nothing to be afraid of.

As you can see this is not the type of letter I am in the habit of writing every day. I apologise if I have upset you in any way but I do believe your mother needs you at this point in time. Please contact me Mr Waterson, I feel it will be to your benefit to do so; a restless spirit is a difficult thing to have to live with.

On your Mother's behalf,

Pippa D Manning.

Keith read through the letter three times in disbelief. He reread the card, one name, one telephone number and one other word, 'medium'. The telephone number was a mobile number but that didn't seem unreasonable, surely mediums have to be mobile in business too, Keith thought.

The last line was one he could sympathise with, 'a restless spirit is a difficult thing to have to live with'. No shit, thought Keith. Nothing to lose was the next thought that came to him. He was clutching at straws but until now his only friend in all this had been a pint of lager or a bottle of whiskey. The only spirit he wanted at the moment with which to numb his senses.

At eight o'clock, with two strong cups of coffee inside him, he picked up the telephone and called Pippa D Manning.

"Hello, you've reached the answer phone of Pippa D Manning. I'm currently in communication elsewhere. Please leave your message after the tone and I'll get back to you."

Keith just put the phone down, he needed to speak to her direct, not leave a message. This was hard enough without talking to a machine. The next time Lucy switched on her mobile phone though, on the hour every hour, she'd know she had him. Three missed calls– Keith Waterson. From then on she would leave her phone switched on constantly. She knew he'd ring back; he had every reason to.

Hook, line and sinker, what a sucker.

We're not there yet Sally-Anne, but I think we're very close. Let's see how keen he is.

Keith Wateson proved to be very keen indeed. The second call came ten minutes after switching on the phone. She answered it on the fourth ring.
"Hello, this is Pippa Manning." said Lucy cheerfully.
"Thank God, I was beginning to think you'd never answer." replied Keith. "I'm Keith, Keith Waterson, you sent me a letter."
"Oh yes, she's your mother, Dawn, Dawn Waterson. I know who you are. From the fact that you've called I take it you're willing to help your mother?"
"Will she leave me alone, if I help?"
"You mean she's been trying to contact you too?"
"In a manner." said Keith, "Yes she has. You have to help me."
"It's your mother that needs my help just now," replied Lucy, "that's why she's been channelling through me. As for helping you, well I think that you're the only person who can do that. But I can put you in touch with your mother, only after that has happened can you both feel peace."
"Then put me in touch with my mother, please."
"Okay, it's what her spirit wants. I can put you in touch, but I can't guarantee what the outcome will be, that depends on you. Do you understand?"
"Yes, okay, it's me she wants to speak to. You can only put us in touch. Is that right?" asked Keith.

"That's exactly right. I think we'll get along just fine, the three of us. You just need to put your trust in me. If you can trust me Keith everything will be okay."

With that Lucy then went on to arrange a 'sitting' that evening at her place, where her 'power is by far the strongest'. Keith was okay with this; he just wanted it over and done with. She told him where to come, giving him directions, and saying she looked forward to meeting him as she felt she knew him already.

At six thirty that evening, when Stein studios was empty, Lucy changed the simple brass number plate at street level for one that she'd had made weeks ago. The number was the same but etched beneath the number was the name Pippa D Manning. It was just in case he needed a little extra reassurance when he arrived, that little extra push to go ahead and ring the bell.
At seven thirty that same evening he did ring the bell.

Come all you sinners
Come one come all
Like lambs to the slaughter
Come live in my thrall

"Hello, Keith; come in and just keep climbing until you can't go any further, the door will be open." Lucy's voice came through the intercom.
When Keith reached the top floor the door was open. He walked in, fearful of what the evening had to offer. That unfortunately was as much as he would remember for the next seventy minutes. He had been quite correct in his trepidation. A baseball bat to the back of the head, however, can remove any feelings of trepidation immediately. In fact a well-placed blow from a baseball bat to the back of the head can remove any feelings at all, not just trepidation. That is until you regain consciousness.

When Keith woke up his head was banging, but that appeared to be the least of his worries. He was naked apart from a tight fitting, full head leather mask. The only holes in the mask were for his eyes, his ears, his nostrils and one just big enough to fit a straw through in front of his mouth. His legs were chained together and his wrists shackled above his head. He was on his tiptoes, the chain connecting his wrists together hung on a hook that looked like it had come straight out of a slaughterhouse. He was alone in what looked like some sort of medieval torture chamber come bedroom.

Twenty minutes later his captor walked through the door carrying a brass number plate and a screwdriver.

"We won't need that again," said Lucy to nobody in particular. Turning round to look at her catch, she moved in closer.

"Good to see you awake again, for a minute back there I thought I'd spoiled everything before we'd even begun. But I can see everything is fine now. Sorry about the bump on the head though, it couldn't be helped."

Keith couldn't believe what he was seeing. Lucy Kirkpatrick. His heart rate jumped at the thought of how much Lucy Kirkpatrick must hate him. He knew in her shoes he would feel the same.

"Oh don't try to talk, Keith. You won't be able to anyway, the mask is a nice tight fit. I think a grunt is probably the best you can manage just now."

Keith's mind was racing. It was as if reality had stopped and something else had taken over, maybe this was what madness feels like, he thought.

"Oh. How rude of me, Keith. Where are my manners?" said Lucy, "Allow me to introduce myself I'm Lucy, Lucy Kirkpatrick, but you know that already don't you? We bumped into each other a little while back, remember? I'm also Pippa Manning. I bet you didn't know that, did you? Not to worry, I've stopped being Pippa now. I'm Lucy again from now on."

Of course he knew who Lucy Kirkpatrick was. Every man in Britain knew who she was, thought Keith? That and the fact that he'd been driving the car that had killed her lover, of course he knew who she was, why wouldn't he?

"Oh, Keith, your mother still wants to say hello." said Lucy. "Silly me forgetting that!"

With that Lucy swung Keith around on his chain to face the opposite direction. Keith gasped; he couldn't believe what he was seeing. Less than two feet away chained and suspended from another meat hook was his mothers frozen body, slowly defrosting. He tried to scream but couldn't, the leather was holding his jaw in place.

"Now you two get reacquainted while I sort a few things out. Before I forget Keith I need your alarm code; I take it you've changed it since I was there last."

Everything came to Keith then in a rush. How stupid could he have been? Taken in by circumstance he'd let his mind fill in all the spaces. His mind had been only too willing to accept that his mother was dead, it had suited him. He'd been taken in by an offer of help, an offer to rid him of his problems. Pippa Manning had offered to put him in contact with his dead mother. She hadn't been lying when she said that; there she was in front of him.

"Your alarm code Keith. Come on concentrate." With that Lucy held up some cards in one hand and a drill in the other.

"I'm going to hold these cards up one by one, when we get to the first number just nod. Okay? Then we'll do the other numbers in order. If you refuse to do it or give me a wrong number I'll drill holes in your feet. Now take a good look at your mother. Do you understand?" said Lucy.

Keith nodded. Self-preservation had always been one of his specialities.

"Good."

Within twenty minutes Lucy was driving Keith's Toyota four-wheel drive monster back to his house. His keys were in her handbag and the new alarm code in her head. The disguise was having its last outing, then that too could go back into storage, just like Dawn Waterson would later that evening. But for now she was going to let her hang around for a while. After all Keith hadn't seen his mother in such a long time, it seemed cruel to spoil their reunion too soon.

She parked his car on the drive and went in. He'd given her the correct alarm code; she didn't have to drill holes in his feet, not yet anyway. She found the letter she'd sent along with the business card and checked the rest of the house.

While she was there she took all the perishables out of his kitchen, things like bread and milk, things that the police would look for straight away when they got involved later on. No perishables usually mean a person has just gone away without telling anybody, a premeditated event. She left no trace of her visit and was happy when she left that nothing would point in her direction when people eventually got round to looking.

When she eventually made it back home she got changed into jeans and a T-shirt, disposing of her disguise in a cupboard. There was nothing unusual in a model like Lucy possessing the odd disguise, it came with the territory. It was how you carried it off that made it successful or not, and Lucy was good, very good, she seemed able to change character at will.

Back in the 'guest room' Lucy lowered Keith's mother to the floor and unshackled her.

"Have you had fun, Keith? Caught up on old times?" asked Lucy.

Keith could only grunt a reply, which sounded faintly like "bitch." When she returned from putting Dawn back in her coffin she gave him five sharp blows with the baseball bat to his body, just in case the word had indeed been bitch.

"Now we don't like that sort of attitude, Keith," said Lucy after the fifth blow, "carry on like that and you won't even make it to Friday." Turning the light off and leaving him dangling all that he heard as she shut the door was, "goodnight, Keith. We'll see each other again tomorrow; we're going to have such fun together. I just know it."

It was as much as Keith could do to weep, and even this was painful. Looking up in the dark to see if an escape was possible he saw his cause was hopeless. Within the hour his legs and stomach were cramping up, she was torturing him and she wasn't even there. He didn't even want to contemplate what tomorrow might bring. While Keith wept Lucy slept the sleep of the righteous and looked forward to the next day with great anticipation.

The sun was shining when she eventually woke the following day; summer had come early for once. As far as Lucy was concerned having Keith Waterson under her control was like having all her Christmases come at once. She was like a child who didn't know which present to open first. Maybe first she'd open up his chest, see how much pain that would cause, or maybe just a leg, for starters. She'd read that a really good torturer could keep a victim alive for weeks. Knowing just when to stop, that was where the real skill lay; to bring your victim so close to death that you could smell it, then backing off. That was the pain she wanted him to feel. That was the pain he'd made her feel, anything less would be a failure on her part.

Okay, Lucy; let's go and enjoy ourselves, for Jayne's sake.

Yes, for Jayne.

It wasn't until she got close to him that she sensed something was wrong. It could have been his colour; it could have been the way his head lay against his chest. It didn't really matter, what she'd set out to do was no longer possible. She couldn't cause him any more pain if he was already dead. She wanted him alive; Sally-Anne had wanted him alive.

"No, no, no, you bastard; you can't be dead, not yet, not for a long time yet!" Lucy said to the corpse that until three o'clock that morning had been Keith Waterson, as he lived and breathed. He would have still been living and breathing had it not been for the last hit with the baseball bat. She'd only meant to soften him up but she'd broken a rib. When the cramps came and he'd been writhing in agony the rib had punctured a lung and he'd drowned in his own blood. It wasn't a nice way to go but at least he would have chosen it over what Lucy had planned for him. In a sense he was a very fortunate man to have suffered so little, looking at him hanging there, naked and grey but for a blood encrusted leather facemask.

This wasn't supposed to happen, Sally-Anne; not like this.
No Lucy, it wasn't.
For Jayne, for me, for you, for Rosie, it wasn't meant to be like this.

No Lucy, not like this.

Thirty-One

Lucy's sense of vengeance, her need for retaliation would never now be satisfied. It had been something Sally-Anne had built up carefully. A little nudge here, a quiet word at an appropriate moment there.

Only one man could have satisfied that desire for retribution, but now she would never be able to settle that score. Don't be mistaken, she'd killed him, there was no doubting that, there never would be, even in Lucy's feeble mind. But Lucy had wanted so much more from him than just his death. Now he could never give her what she'd wanted, really wanted, more than anything else. She would never be at peace. Lucy knew it, Sally-Anne knew it. She did still have Rosie though, a glimmer of hope on the horizon maybe?

To get revenge is one thing. To have revenge in your heart, waiting to be had, is yet another. To have that revenge snatched away before it's had; well that's something completely different. She'd had a need, now she was an empty shell.

She didn't even bother taking his body down. It would have given her no pleasure. She had planned on keeping him alive as long as possible; she had even planned the final act to be on Jayne's birthday, 24 June. That was still two weeks away. Two weeks of pain, two weeks to make him feel years of pain. She'd had it all planned out; it really was going to be fun.

There was nothing Sally-Anne could say to console her. Sally-Anne was quite prepared to mark it down to experience and move on. There are plenty of other men in the world. That had been Sally-Anne's argument; it had always been Sally-Anne's argument.

Come on, Lucy. It's only the end of his world, not yours. There are plenty more fish in the sea. Okay, you might not find that perfect specimen again, but that doesn't mean you stop fishing. You just go out and buy yourself a bigger boat.

For Jayne?

No, for us, Jayne's gone now Lucy. We had our chance, we blew it.

I blew it.

Trust me, Lucy. Everything is going to be okay. You do trust me don't you?

Silence…

…

Lucy went to bed with a heavy heart that evening. She felt empty, alone, unloved, and unable to love. It took some time before she could sleep; her mind was awash with memories. She had difficulty recalling the good times she'd had with Jayne. She even struggled to remember her voice, whenever she spoke she sounded like Sally-Anne.

It had been Sally-Anne after all who had first spotted Jayne. It had been Sally-Anne who had made the first move on Jayne. Had it been Sally-Anne whom Jayne had loved all along? Lucy couldn't get the thought out of her head that she had been played, like a pawn in a game of chess, ever since that day, years ago, outside of school in Manchester.

At two thirty that same night Sally-Anne put Lucy's mind into the padded cell next to hers. She took the straight jacket hanging from the rusty nail and made sure it was a tight fit. When she left and shut the door behind her she locked it using the big fuck off padlock that Lucy didn't know existed. Sally-Anne had an idea; she thought she knew what would make Lucy smile again.

Lucy was dreaming again, floating on air, rising above the clouds with a presence close by. She couldn't see who it was; she just knew there was somebody with her, guiding her, an angel, a guardian angel helping her, pointing her in the right direction. It felt so right.

Within minutes she was at her destination. She had a choice to make, her guardian angel said. She would have to choose a door through which she could enter one of two rooms. Before making that choice though she would be able to see inside the rooms, in order to make the right choice. She was told she had only one choice. There was no changing her mind once she'd made her decision.

Moving to the window next to the door on the left she saw a waiting room. In the waiting room were people she knew. Her dad was the first person she saw. He obviously couldn't see her though. Lucy thought it must be a two-way mirror she was looking through because the next person she saw was Patrick Stein, combing his hair looking directly at her from the other side of the room. Sat together to the left of Stein were Terence Sandford and Georgie Dunston, playing cards. To the left of them was Steve Summer making notes in a book.

It would have been a strange choice for Lucy to pick this door, a room full of people she despised or who had let her down. Just then she noticed another door in the room. The door opened and in walked Keith Waterson with his mother. They were hand in hand, like mother and son often are before small boys become big boys.

She hoped the second room was a better choice than the first. It was. As she approached the room she could see only two people, both sat down. Just before she reached the window though both people stood up, they could both see her. On the other side of this glass stood Jayne and Lucy's mum. Both began to cry tears of joy as they began to run toward the window, hands outstretched. Lucy couldn't hear what they were saying, she didn't need to, here were two people she loved and who loved her back. Jayne was just as she remembered her, she longed for her touch again, wanted to hear her voice again. She was so close to something she had thought she would never happen again.

Two doors, one choice, the decision was hardly a tough one. Do I go with the people I love, or the people I hate and despise? Not very difficult...

Lucy pushed open the right hand door in her eagerness to enter. She ran in with both hands outstretched, a big smile on her face, desperate for the reunion to follow. She was in the left hand room. Looking back at her were six pairs of eyes she'd never wanted to see again. She rushed out of the room slamming the door behind her.

The left hand door opened just as easily as the other. Again there were six pairs of eyes looking back at her. The same six pairs of eyes she'd seen only seconds before. She rushed out of the room again, once again slamming the door behind her. Rushing to the window she could see Jayne and her mum looking back. This time they were crying. Opening the door a second time she saw six pairs of eyes once again.

Back outside the two rooms she realised that her dream had become a nightmare. She felt a hand on her shoulder. Looking round she saw a woman smiling.

"Come on now, Lucy. You've made your choice; in fact, you made it a long time ago. Do you understand?"

"No, what's happening? What do you mean?"

"Oh come on, you made your choice when you were thirteen. You're mine now. You've been mine ever since you were thirteen. Trust me; I know what I'm talking about. You trusted Sally-Anne, now you'll just have to trust me. You don't really have much choice in the matter from now on, you're mine. Join me in hell."

"You do trust me don't you, Lucy?"

A dream turning into a nightmare isn't much of a problem. The nightmare turning into reality, now that's a problem.

Her body wasn't discovered for three days. John hadn't been able to stop Rosie following him into Lucy's apartment. When he turned round to throw up she was there behind him, looking up in amazement at the scene in front of her. He was sure she'd not been there long, staring at Lucy's body strung up from the ceiling, a leather whip wrapped round her neck, her tongue hanging out and her face looking in more pain than a person should ever endure. She was hanging there right next to the body of Keith Waterson. A knife was stuck into her stomach up to the hilt, pushed there by Sally-Anne, her final act of Lucy's short life.

Both bodies were found in a fairly bad state. Three days hanging around with nowhere to go in a warm early summer can do that to you. It was four days in the case of Keith, but they weren't to know that yet. In fact, by the time the police had finished in Lucy's apartment they knew much more about Lucy than they had ever known before. They still didn't know about Sally-Anne though.

The scandal was huge. A major celebrity, one of Britain's most favoured daughters was a murderer; not only a murderer, a serial killer. The press had a field day. More pages were written following Lucy's death than had been written about a death since the death of Diana. Her celebrity grew to ridiculous heights.

People wanted even more of her now that she was dead. By the end of July there was already talk of a book and a film. Actresses were clamouring to play Lucy, just for the kudos it could bring to their careers. None of them would be able to do the role any justice however; there were no plans to cast anybody in the role of Sally-Anne. However hard they tried to bring Lucy back to life on the big screen they would always be missing one of the main characters. They could only ever show half of the story…

Thirty-Two

It was twelve months before Lucy's body was released to John. He'd grown tired of his sister following the first month of her death. The stories, the revelations, the thought that he never really knew his own sister, it all became too much.

John, Steph and Rosie moved to France before the end of January 2014. John relocated his studio to Paris, he was still one of the best in his trade and his business had a worldwide market. They went to escape the vultures. And they did escape them, mostly. A few of the vultures followed them but even they soon got tired. The British as a nation likes to be as close to any scandal as possible. It soon tires of reading about things happening in France. After all, France is still seen as a country far, far away by most Brits, and that's how they want to keep it, thank you very much.

John, Steph and Rosie did visit Steph's family on occasion, but mostly it was them who came to France, it was just easier. On 8 September 2014 the three of them did travel to Manchester. The furore associated with Lucy's life was passing, but even so they would land in Manchester late in the morning and be back in the air by three o'clock. The arrangements had been made with the same undertaker he'd used for his mother and father. No service was required, just open up the family grave and lay her to rest. At rest only, not at peace, he didn't think she would ever be at peace.

Everything was ready when they arrived. There were no reporters, no photographers; everything had been done very quietly. The last thing they wanted was for a circus to hit town. If it had been left to John the three of them wouldn't even be there. It was a family decision though; they took a vote on it. It was Rosie who gave the casting vote to make the trip. That's what comes of allowing a six-year-old child to vote. Children of that age are prone to wearing rose coloured spectacles whenever possible.

It was just as she was getting into the limousine that would take them back to the airport that it happened…

Hello, Rosie; can I be your new friend? Don't be scared, my name's Sally-Anne. I won't hurt you. See, I even know your name. You can trust me, Rosie. You do trust me don't you? ...

Sally-Anne introduced herself to Rosie on a cold windy day in Manchester. The parallels were too good to ignore for Sally-Anne. She'd seen potential in Lucy one day in Manchester, now she saw potential in Rosie too. She was practically overflowing with it.

Epilogue

Ask me no questions, I'll tell you no lies.

So ask yourself...
Can apparently good people let an evil force invade their lives, their very being, to such an extent as Sally-Anne invaded Lucy?

Or do you think a person's destiny in life is set as they leave the womb?

In other words, was Lucy incapable of resisting Sally-Anne because whatever was going to happen had been decided on 10 December 1991?

Could you resist such an evil force if it drew you into its trust, a force so manipulative and powerful?

Or does evil just trawl through the airwaves searching out vulnerability? And when it's found a particular chink in a person's armour, exploit it to the full? Picking carefully, choosing the people with greatest potential for harm?

In reality, who's to know?

And what of Rosie Kirkpatrick...Born into an evil world. Now aged six, and with Sally-Anne having taken up residence in her head, manipulative and powerful in every sense. Will she fair any better in life than her Aunt Lucy? Is it possible she has any Irish blood running through her veins? Could she really be that lucky?

What do you think...?

Rosie posie, pudding and pie,
Kissed the boys and made them cry,
If those boys knew Rosie well,
They'd poke her eye and run like hell.

If those boys turn into men,
She wont be kissing them again,
And if those men are stupid or brave,
She'll cut off their heads and dance on their graves.

Rosie posie, pudding and pie,
She'll hate all men and make them die.
Sally-Anne ensures they die,
She won't let Rosie live a lie!

For all the men I've yet to meet,
Please don't think your life's so sweet,
I know all men so very well,
You see,
The devil is a woman and I'm her messenger from hell...

See you soon boys
Sally-
Anne xxx

…You didn't really think it was going to be any other way did you?

...

<u>Springtime 2042</u> (Somewhere in Brussels)

The secure videophone rang just as Rosie was about to make a call herself. No problem, it was Jack Sulltz on the line, President of the United States of America, the same Jack Sulltz she had been just about to call herself.
"Rosie, good to see you." Jack said.
"Likewise, Jack. So, tell me what the President of the USA could possibly want from the President of the United Nations of Europe, and only two minutes after leaving a three hour long meeting with his joint chiefs of staff."

"Good one, Rosie. Goddamned security stinks; this place is about as leaky as Bill Clinton's pecker at a lap dancing joint."

"Nothing ever changes, Jack. As hard as you try, we're still two steps ahead of your donkeys in security."

"So you should know what I want already?"

"You want UNE backing over a full scale war with China. The first war since twenty-three, it's a big ask Jack, you're going to owe me big."

"We can't go after the little bastards without Europe, Rosie; you know that."

"I think I can get you what you want, they're all like puppy dogs over here when I start to talk. You know you can depend on my backing Jack. Whatever you need, you only need to ask, nicely. Will I see you again this weekend?"

"I can't wait, Rosie."

"And, Mr. President; make sure the champagne is on ice this time."

"I will do, Mademoiselle President."

Goddamn Yankee asshole!

He's really not that bad, Sally-Anne; and anyway, we've got him right where we want him.

In our bed is not where we want him, Rosie.

One last time, Sally-Anne; then his day is done, it will all be over for him. One way or another Jack Sulltz is next week's history; he just doesn't know it yet. That is the way you want it isn't it, Sally-Anne?

One brain, two minds, one big red button, BOOM

...

Come all you sinners,
Come one come all,
Like lambs to the slaughter,
Come live in my thrall.

...

The world's hospitals; criminally secure and not so secure, are home to many people who truly believe they hear voices in their heads. These are the schizophrenics thought to be too dangerous to be allowed out in public. There are many others that aren't in hospital, and never will be, because the voices are a secret...

But what if they're right and the voices are for real? After all, can you actually get inside someone's head and hear what he or she is hearing, prove or disprove what he or she says to be the truth about what they hear?

Peter Sutcliffe, AKA the Yorkshire Ripper, was convicted of thirteen murders and seven attempted murders in 1981. All of these crimes were committed against women. He was sentenced to twenty life sentences; his destiny for six years of his life was to murder or attempt to murder women until his evil reign was brought to a close and his celebrity fixed forever. He has since been declared clinically insane, a paranoid schizophrenic, although remarkably it took some time for the authorities to reach that diagnosis.

And from the day he was captured, what reason has he consistently given for committing those terrible crimes?

The voices in his head told him to do it...

Peter Sutcliffe believed that he was told to commit those crimes in messages from god. But could the messages have come from the devil?

After all...

...Angels are thought, by some, to be immortal spiritual beings acting as intermediaries between God and humanity. In other words messengers from God. Some people believe they exist, others believe they don't...

If you believe that God exists, isn't it implicit that you also believe in the existence of the devil?

If God has messengers in the form of angels, surely the devil could have them too.

Isn't the devil after all a fallen angel?

And if you weren't so sure one way or the other, could you take it on trust?

Maybe we should talk; after all, you can trust me.

...

You do trust me don't you?

...

I'll tell you no lies!

Three score and ten an expectant life,
Too quickly how it passes,

A warning here from me to you,
Learn from these meagre classes,

The Devil walks this earth today,
An army she amasses,

Trust is all that she requires,
A power so vast my pretty young lasses,

But remember girls!

Should you decide to try that power,
Assured of it you must be,
For come judgement day you'll be in hell,
And then the Devil owns your asses.

...

The End

Norman Wills

Thanks

To everyone who gave me encouragement, advice and help when I needed it

Especially Emma, Joanne and Sandra

Printed in Great Britain
by Amazon